KENTUCKY DREAMIN'

∼Against All Cults∼

BY RON STAUFFER

Outskirts Press, Inc.
Denver, Colorado

This is a work of fiction. The events and characters described here are imaginary and are not intended to refer to specific places or living persons.

Kentucky Dreamin'
Against All Cults
All Rights Reserved
Copyright © 2004 Ron Stauffer

Outskirts Press
http://www.outskirtspress.com

ISBN: 1-932672-20-6

Printed in the United States of America

KENTUCKY DREAMIN'

A novel of romance and suspense, steeped in philosophy

BY RON STAUFFER

PROLOGUE

"Did you hear that?"

"Yeah, somethin' in the laurel . . . where's the light?"

Sheila groped beside the sleeping bag and found one of their flashlights. "Here," she said, switching it on.

Daryl rose from his kneeling position and advanced toward the edge of their campsite, shining the light toward the noise. "Probably a raccoon or . . ." He heard a muffled shriek behind him. Feeling a sudden chill the length of his spine, he turned to see Sheila, naked from their love making, being dragged away. He dove into the tent for his .38 revolver when he heard a hard voice.

"Won't do ya no good . . . we got ya surrounded! An' we got your sweet black-eyed pea fer hostage."

"Wh . . . who *are* you?" Daryl asked as he saw his weekend companion squirming against the grasp of a bearded giant of a man. He had one hand over her mouth, and the other tightly gripping her left breast.

"These darkies sure are sassy," the bearded man said to someone – someone whom Daryl had yet to see. "Git 'is gun afore he has an accident," he said again.

Daryl pivoted, only to be met with a rock to his temple, which dropped him cold.

When he awoke, he was aware of his hands and feet being tightly bound by some kind of thin line that was cutting into his flesh with the smallest amount of movement. 'Fishing line!' he realized. At the time of the intrusion, he and Sheila had been basking in each others' arms after a particularly intense session of lovemaking. It had been his idea to hike this portion of the Appalachian Trail near Front Royal, knowing that Sheila liked camping as an escape from the confines of the District of Columbia. He had thought it safe, hiking in the pristine wilderness – away from the madness of the world.

"We saw ya's cuddling up close together at the fillin' station this mornin', an' thought maybe you should be wized up some about you messin' with someone other than your own race," the bearded man said as he casually looked about inside the tent.

"Nice gear you have – you city slickers got the best of everthang, don't they Furrel?

"Yer right 'bout *that*, Nolan," the bearded man's sidekick answered.

Daryl saw Sheila, bound and gagged and tied to a sapling on the other side of the campsite – the light of the rekindled fire dancing eerily on her naked bronze flesh. He tried not to think of their vulnerability in their unprotected condition. He, too, was naked, and the bearded man was eyeing his privates from time to time as he expounded on virtue and small talk.

"Wut's yer name, lover boy? It ain't po-lite fer us not to make yer acquain'ence before we shows you a lesson or two. This here's Furrel, and I'm Japheth . . . you can call me Nolan, like all mah friends do." Nolan's eyes blazed with the reflection of the campfire.

Daryl remained silent, knowing it didn't matter. He heard himself mutter, realizing it would be to no avail: "Let her go . . . do what you want with me, but let her go!"

"Sure, we will . . . but first, wut's yer name?" he asked again in a subdued, almost consoling voice.

"Sez here on his license, Daryl Mac . . . somethin' or other." Furrel stated before Daryl could answer.

"Alright then, Daryl . . . pleased to make yer

acquain'ence." And he stuck out his hand.

His mentioning of a handshake brought a stabbing, cutting sensation to his bound wrists.

"Oh, I'm sorry! Yer bound hand an' foot an' can't shake. Sorry 'bout that." He smiled mischievously. "So wut's your sweet pea's name?"

Resigned, he muttered her name.

"I'm sorry, I cain't hear ya . . . speak up!" he threatened. "Furrel, help him speak up . . . with that faggot you got poked in the farr."

"Sheila!" he fairly screamed as the sparkling ember was thrust into his side.

"Ah, now that we knows each other, I believe it's time fer a Sunday school lesson. Is it Sunday yet?" he asked Furrel. "I left mah watch in the Explorer."

"Yesir, indeedy . . . it's 'bout twelve fifteen by mah watch."

"Well then, let's git started." With a serious countenance, he stared at his prisoner. "You familiar with the Old Testament, Daryl?"

Daryl nodded his head.

"How 'bout sweet pea, over there . . . you know the Old Testament? Daryl . . . wut's she tryin' ta say? Daryl, you better answer me or I'll get Furrel to remind ya ta speak up with that burnin' stick 'es holdin."

"I . . .I think she's tryin' to say yes." Daryl, on his knees with his head hanging low could hardly speak because of his blubbering.

"Next time I ax you a question, you better pipe up so's I can hear you . . . or we're gonna trim back her finger nails an' I'm not talkin' just to the cuticle." Nolan strutted over to Sheila and looked menacingly at her bound hands. "How many times did he put it to ya today, darlin'?" he asked looking into her tear-filled eyes. "Daryl, yer gonna have to help . . . can't ya see she's got her mouth full? Furrel, help him remember"

"Twice . . . three times."

"Don't ya know that a nigger ain't human? Wut's a white man like you doin' fuckin' a nigger beast, anyway? You know it's unholy!"

Daryl couldn't hold back his sobbing.

"You know, to go agin God's law is to suffer death. Numbers 25:6 through 8 is quite distink 'bout sleepin' with one that ain't yur own feather. Zimri, the Israelite took Cozbi, a Midianite, to bed fer you-know-what, and God moved Phineas to slay them both as they lay together. And God saw that it was good and made it so that Phineas would be granted a covenant that all his male descendants would be of the priesthood." Nolan then let loose a stream of tobacco juice that hissed when it hit the fire.

The sobbing of both prisoners was uncontrollable.

"It's a good thing we went fishin' this weekend, Furrel. We we're favored to see this iniquity and the chance to make it right in the *eyes of God*," and Nolan looked up at the moon. Then, looking at Daryl's privates whose penis was barely visible within the scant protection of its scrotum, he said: "Here, Furrel, loop this 'round his balls." And he handed his sidekick some fishing line with a loop already started.

As Furrel approached, Daryl rolled to the side to escape the very personal intrusion, but was stomped on by Nolan. "*NO!*" he cried out as he writhed free of the boot – only to be stepped on again. "WHAT DO YOU WANT? TAKE MY MONEY FOR GOD'S SAKE!"

"Oh, we will do that . . . all in good time! But now you must also atone fer takin' the Lord's name in vain just now."

Furrel finally succeeded in cinching the squirming man's

balls, and handed the end of the line to Nolan.

"I don't think you'll be fuckin' that nigger ever agin . . . or anyone else fer that matter." And wrapping the line several times around his gloved hand, tightened the cinch with increasing pressure to see that it was secure in its purchase.

Daryl cried out in agony, knowing full well his fate the immediate future offered.

Nolan let loose some slack on the line, then suddenly spiraled to his right, ripping the line with a sweeping motion, garroting the man's nuts. *"Damn"* he exclaimed as the fishing line broke. "Shoulda known better ta use hunnert-pound steel leader!"

Daryl's screaming ceased as he passed into unconsciousness.

"Yer sure 'bout bein' sure there ain't no other campers aroun'?"

"No one 'round fer a quarter mile. They sure picked a good spot off the trail to be alone."

"We gotta tidy the place up a bit. Furrel, machete that saplin' she's tied to so she falls backward – looks like she fainted, too. Yeah, that's it . . . now help me get 'im atop her." And they struggled with their grisly task as blood gushed from Daryl's wound.

With that effort complete, Nolan smiles and says: "We gotta finish 'em off jus' like Phineas did . . . with one thrust of his spear."

"We ain't got no spear, Nolan."

"We got ourselves this machete . . . it'll do. Do you want the honor or you want me ta do it?"

"You been playin' *priest* all night, Nolan; I think *you* should do it."

Nolan looked high again, up at the moon, and grabbed the machete in both hands. Raising the machete to full height, he suddenly yelled: "THY LORD'S WILL . . . SHALL BE DONE!" Then he plunged the small sword downward into the faintly stirring torsos with all his strength, again and again, until he penetrated the two bodies.

* * *

Erin ran her fingers through her cropped red hair as she eyed her open suitcase. Her assignment to the War College in Carlisle had been handed down at the last minute – or so it seemed to her. She needed to organize her thoughts – and her clothes – as soon as possible.

The easy part was done. Her dry cleaned uniforms were zipped up in a garment bag, hanging from the hook in her car. One of the advantages of military life was that you never had to wonder what to wear the next day. When Erin wasn't in uniform, she preferred jeans or sweatpants. She grabbed a few of her favorite T's, including the recently acquired *"Well behaved women rarely make history"* shirt she'd ordered from evolvefish.com. She liked to provoke comment and hopefully make people ponder their cherished illusions.

"Hi, Pepper," she said to the gray tabby who had joined her in her inspection of the luggage. "I'm really going to miss you. I want you to be a good boy for Aunt Wendy! No trying to convince her that you are allowed outside. You know you have absolutely no street smarts!"

Pepper purred his agreement as Erin ran her fingers through his lush fur. Anything Erin said was just fine with him. After all, she had saved him from a terrible fate when she adopted him at the local animal shelter two years ago. Even when duty called (as she liked to say) and she was forced to leave him behind, she always made sure that he was happily installed at the home of her sister. 'Aunt' Wendy doted on Pepper. She bought him catnip and even planted a container of grass for his salads!

Erin tucked panties and socks along the sides of the suitcase. Thank goodness she was small breasted and could dispense with bras! She enjoyed her minimalist approach to underwear. Grabbing her bag of toiletries, she thanked her youth and her genes that she also needed to use very little makeup. Usually, a touch of lipstick was sufficient. On those rare occasions when she dressed up she might use a dab of blush and some eyeliner.

It had been more than six months since her last date. What a fiasco that had been! She and Andy had gone to movies, dinners together locally, even a day trip to the Inner Harbor in Baltimore. But on all of those occasions, the subject of religion had never raised its ugly head…until that last night. When Andy asked Erin what church she attended, she responded forthrightly that she was an atheist. At first, Andy laughed – thinking it was a joke. When he realized that her answer was serious, he began to bombard her with questions (the answers to which he did not appreciate). The evening disintegrated quickly. When they parted, Andy acted as if she had suddenly developed leprosy.

Erin sighed at the memory. Maybe it would not be possible to find a fellow freethinker with whom to share her life. She noticed that the PA Nonbelievers meetings, which she attended, seemed to be comprised mostly of middle aged and elderly men and women. Erin was determined to avoid what she considered the worst kind of mixed marriage: that between an atheist and a religious person -- especially a Christian.

Turning back to the task at hand, she tossed in that bosom-ripper paperback she'd bought three months ago and had yet to open. Maybe she would have some free time at her digs in Carlisle.

Just then, the phone rang. It was her friend, Tina, calling to wish her well in her new assignment.

"I wish we could have had lunch before you go, Erin! It seems like ages since we actually sat down and caught up on each other's news."

"I know, Tina. Life is so hectic anymore! Let's plan to get together over the Christmas break, okay?"

"Fantastic! Meanwhile, take care of yourself – and have some *fun*, girl! Maybe you'll meet Mr. Right at the War College!"

Erin laughed. "Mr. Right-Winger would be more like it! You have no idea what a bunch of conservative tight-asses these guys are. Besides, I'm not looking. I enjoy being on my own."

"We've been down this road before, Erin. I know you are a committed career woman, but I still expect a white knight to sweep you off your feet one of these days," said the irrepressible Tina.

They spoke for a few more minutes, promising once again to meet over the holidays. Erin felt a touch of sadness when she hung up. Tina had been her best friend since fifth grade, yet her constant carping about Erin's lack of romance was tiresome. Why couldn't Tina just accept the life she had chosen?

Erin made a final inspection of her small apartment. The bed was made. All lights were turned off and air conditioner disengaged. The garbage had been taken to the Dumpster. Mr. Mills, the building's manager, had been informed of her pending absence and would be keeping an eye on things for her. Mail would be forwarded, starting today. As she counted these items off on her fingers, Pepper rubbed her leg and butted it with his head.

"Okay, pal. Time to get in the old carrier!" Pepper was so accustomed to travel that he made no objections. Once inside the car, he curled up facing Erin and promptly fell asleep. He was a true military cat; he made his home wherever he found himself!

An hour later, Erin gave Wendy a big hug and promised to call once a week.

"You are such a mother hen . . . I couldn't possibly get assigned to a safer place than the War College!" she reassured her older sister.

She turned the car toward the turnpike, and Carlisle. "Let's see what the future holds," she murmured to herself.

I

Carl

"So you didn't agree with Reverend Pleasantforce's sermon?"

"No; I must say not."

"So . . . what *do* you believe?"

"Well . . ." Paul hesitated in thought, "seems to me we got a right to make out our own understanding of what it's all about -- right?" Without waiting for a reply, Paul went on: "We didn't ask to be born -- least I didn't. So where does some mealy-mouthed preacher get the right to try to make me feel so low?"

Carl looked at him askew. "That's what he's trained to do. He's trained to point out to us how we are all sinners . . . in a terrible, sinful world."

"And you believe that you're a sinner? Why, you have hard enough time swattin' a bee."

"I have sinful thoughts all the time." Carl hung his head.

"Oh?" Paul pried. "Gimme a f'rinstance."

"Well, Just like President Carter did . . . I lust . . . I lust to get into Cindy's panties all the time."

"Cinderbox! I didn't know you had the hots for her!"

"Well . . . now you know" Carl said, coloring a bit.

"Oh, I get it. You evangelicals think every natural urge is a sin. Do you feel the same way about taking a crap or blowin' your nose?

"'Bout sexual things, *Paul*" Carl mustered. "Sex is for makin' children, and not to be enjoyed too much."

"Wow, where do you get that idea?"

"It's in the Bible, *Paul*."

"Where?"

"The Bible . . . Luvicurous, or somewheres."

Carl and Paul have been friends since Early childhood, growing up on the west slope of the Appalachian Mountains in southeast Kentucky. Paul was back home visiting, on leave from the Army where he was a young Lieutenant. He had studied and acquired a degree in the field of geology, and had been in the State University's Reserve Officer Training Corps program. While in college, he had rubbed elbows with students of different backgrounds—one was even an atheist. For hours he had debated the independent thinker as to why such an amiable fellow was so sure there was no God. He always came away from their conversation a little less certain of what his parents -- his cultural heritage -- had imparted to him regarding religion. By the time he finished his studies and graduated, he was a full-blown skeptic.

"Don't you want to go to Heaven?" Carl countered.

"Sure! But I don't think there is such a place."

"Then you're goin' to Hell, for sure."

"*Carl,* that really hurts!"

"Better mend your ways and get with the program, buddy."

Paul realized now that going to their old church together had not been a good idea. He was reluctant to attend but accepted Carl's invitation because he was curious as to how the old spiritual surroundings might affect him. It was the first time he had heard the Reverend Pleasantforce, who was a young preacher taking the place of the retired and feeble, Harry Harkinrode. The sermon was classic fire and brimstone, summoning the powers of God to trample the atheistic judiciary that seemed to always side with the gay and lesbian movement.   It was the usual assault on the wall separating church and state that *he* felt should remain inviolate, even as the judiciary had given ground in school vouchers and faith-based initiatives. "We are having your Hell right here on Earth, My friend!" Paul muttered in a vicious undertone.

"Say again," Carl snapped.

"Don't you see--we are upsetting the very political philosophy that this country has been steered by since its founding!   We are replacing government neutrality with fuzzy, feel-good ideas of salvation."

"And wut's the matter with that?"

"'Cause we need to focus on what's *real* – problems that are real!"

"And God don't help us any? Prayers don't help us any?"

"I don't know. I don't think so."

"So you learned to hate God in College—right? You're too smart for us folks back home now that you been to college—you think you got all the answers, don't you?"

"I'll tell you somethin' *Carl*: maybe college has taught me to realize how much I *don't* know. It seems the more I learned, I realized the less I knew about most other things."

"So how come all of a sudden you know so much more about religion . . . that you can say it's a bunch of hooey?"

Paul looked at his good friend sympathetically knowing what he was going to explain might hurt his feelings: "Because I think it is an extension of superstition – similar to the way we laughed at the Indians' religion, and all those superstitious African tribes we saw in the movies."

"So, what *do* you believe in, if not God?"

"I didn't say I don't believe in God, Carl. I just don't think we'll ever know him or her personally like Pleasantforce says we should. I s'pose I'm a Deist, if I had to

3

make a claim."

"You gotta have faith, *man*!"

"Yeah, I heard that. And maybe I would *see* it that way 'cept . . . *which Faith*?"

"Whad'ya mean?"

"Well, take Gulf War II, or any war for that matter—we asked God to bless our troops – right?"

Carl nodded in the affirmative.

"And those rag heads over there asked for Allah's blessing – right?"

Carl nodded again.

"Don't you *see? Which* way is the truth . . . the true faith -- theirs or ours?"

"Why, we're right of course. Theirs is some kind of false religion the Bible's always warnin' us about"

"You wouldn't stay alive for very long if you said that over there. Those people will kill or be ready to be killed to defend their faith in Allah."

"They're sick . . . deluded."

"And, maybe . . . so are we – deluded in *our* religions too."

Carl shifted his stance, putting his hands on his hips. "You didn't go and become a bleedin' heart liberal, did ya? Them liberal college professors got to ya, didn't they?   I warned ya 'bout 'em before you went away. Wut's a deist, anyway – some hippie on drugs?   You college boys are somethin' else!" Carl continued, not waiting for an answer.

"Calm down, man. Whad'ya say we get a burger and some pop?" Paul suggested. "Then I'll tell ya what a Deist is."

The two young men sauntered into their favorite eatery and ordered their usual greasy staple and a couple of Nehi's. After exchanging pleasantries with some of the local acquaintances, Carl stared across the table at Paul and blurted, "So whut's an all-fired deist?"

"Why're you so interested in other religions all of a sudden? You thinkin' of bolting Pleasantforce's church?"

"Whut's it to ya, you liberal commie lovin' college boy . . . c'mon, hit me with this deist crap!"

"It's not really like a religion at all . . . it's more like an intellectual respect toward a possible deity. You don't have to pray. . ."

"Don't have to pray?" Carl asked incredulously. "Whad'ya mean by that?"

"Well, there was a time in Europe -- before our revolution against England -- when a group of scientists and philosophers became disgusted with the single-mindedness and contempt of the various religions, and came to the conclusion that God was indifferent to the bickering factions."

"You sure have learned a lot of big words!"

"Jefferson and Madison and other bright men of the time subscribed to the possibility of such a God and called themselves Deists for their belief that a Creator had initiated everything and then left the creation to run in accordance with His or Her natural law. Their Creator was indifferent and detached from the plight of man . . . prayer was of no effect. We had to learn to be responsible and solve our own problems, mainly because we were the cause of the problems in the first place."

"What about Heaven and Hell, man?"

"I don't believe they thought there such a place, Carl."

"You know, Paul . . ." Carl lit up a cigarette, "Almost everyone in this town would say you are full of shit!"

"You're probably right."

"Isn't it kinda lonely being the only guy in the hollow thinking such weird thoughts?"

"What's weird about what I just said?" Paul queried. "It makes sense to me! It satisfies my psyche! As far as I know, I think this country will still allow me to believe in what eases my conscience."

"Yeah, and Jeffrey Dahmer's conscience said eat 'em, eat 'em . . . then bury the bones."

"Christ, Carl, you think like that priest who once said that an open mind is like a garbage can without a lid – you can put anything into it!"

"That's rich . . . that's really good!" Carl smiled mischievously.

"It's about *freedom*, Carl. It's the nature of Americans to exercise their freedom . . . this is one of them."

"Wut about *freewill* that the preachers are always talkin' about? God gave us freewill – to do good, or to be lustful and greedy and do bad. We kinda make our own bed of goodness or evil."

"Well, that's a simple explanation. Preachers are always cutting to the simplest of explanations – it's easier for the flock to understand." Paul took another sip from his orange pop. "The creation in six days; the beginning of evil and death in the Garden of Eden – it's all very simple explanations of how we got here, what we are . . . those stories have been around forever – long before Reason and the development of science."

"You *are* going to Hell, man!"

"Don't you see! The religionists stress the peoples' lowliness – sinfulness – so that they are easier to manipulate and control. A controlled population is easier to lead and govern, which is generally good for the whole. Look at you! You *fear* Hell and are convinced in the safety you have within your church's flock. They got you believin' that if you don't think their way, you are going to go to Hell . . . going to Hell even if you were a good person but just didn't believe Jesus is salvation – now that smells fishy to me!"

"But that's the way I was brought up . . . how could I think that it's all wrong?"

"Carl, has prayer and religion ended all the misery and warfare on this planet?"

"No."

"Have you ever noticed that some our most enduring wars are kinda differences of opinion as to which religion is true?"

"Yeah," Carl sensed that his friend was suckering him into a trap, through logical examination. "You ain't leadin' me into a bullshit proof like the one where you showed that 2 + 2 = 3, are ya?"

"That was a trick that really isn't allowable in mathematics, Carl."

"Then, why waste my time tryin' to unseat me from my beliefs."

"We're having a conversation, Carl . . . Does that make you uncomfortable?"

"They say it's impolite to talk about religion and politics."

"Hey, you were the one who asked me if I agreed with that Bible thumper's sermon . . . and besides, I find it interesting to talk about it. It *needs* to be talked about!"

"Didn't you have to swear an oath to God and Country when you became an Army officer?"

"You'd think so the way this country is goin' . . . but no, Carl; the oath I took was that I promise to protect the Constitution of the United States of America."

"Why do all the presidents end their swearin' in oaths with "*so help me God*?""

"It's a tradition that really isn't required by the

Constitution – I looked it up! I'm tellin ya, Carl, we've adopted some traditions that smack of breaching the wall separating government from religion!"

"Reverend Pleasantforce says the wall is only to keep the nose of gov'ment out of religion – no holds 'bout religion helping gov'ment!"

"Well," Paul sniffed, "I read Madison's *Memorial and Remonstrance* and I think Madison points out that the wall is to keep each of their noses out of the other's business. Who the hell ever heard of a wall that keeps one side out and not the other? I thought homefolk like you had more common sense."

Carl squirmed a little at the affront – quietly, he nodded his head, not knowing how to come back.

"Want to hear what my version of heaven would be, *if* there is one?"

Carl deferred to his old childhood buddy: "I guess you're gonna tell me."

II

The Deist's Heaven

*(In the tradition of Mark Twain's **Extract from Captain Stormfield's Visit to Heaven**)*

My death was soon to be expected, and before I knew it, it was over. I could see the few of those concerned for me as I drifted away, unable to tell them goodbye. I was pulled by some unknown but irresistible force, first this way, then that way – I think up . . . no, *down*! It was worrisome that my present direction was down as I pondered my vacillation in believing in any kind of afterlife at all. Those nimrod clergymen were right after-all – I'm going to Hell, to burn for eternity – oh shit!

Just then I was pulled sideways and into a wind – a seemingly cool wind that took me laterally over an ocean. Yes, it was the Atlantic Ocean 'cause I could see the New York harbor with Miss Liberty standing in its guard. Now a tug down . . . no, a tug up. Why, what a sensation being pulled this way and that –and it didn't hurt any 'cause I guess spirits don't have any nerve endings, bein' all spirit and no material.

Now I was hurtling upward at a stupendous rate, just missing – no, going through – the wing of a jetliner. Uh oh, the upward pace fell off and soon I was in free fall down into the ocean threading through schools of fish and a submarine. I could see the bottom raising up at a prodigious rate, and I began serious worry. I know what you're thinkin' out there:

that if this were a story about Heaven, why in tarnation would I be heading toward Hell?

Your misgivings were my misgivings . . . but wait! The brakes were applied and I started to rise again as my spiritual low point just missed the bottom of the sea. This time I floated upward at a nice easy velocity, as if the fates or whatever had finally made up their mind(s). I broke free into sunshine just aft of a super tanker out of Monrovia.

The upward drift was pleasant enough and I wish I had a smoke. Wait! What made me think of smoking – I hadn't smoked for many, many years. But there appeared in front of me a lit cigarette . . . and I could smell its aroma! Who said wishes don't come true? I realized then that *I* had said, "wishes don't come true," many times. Oh, how I realized how wrong I was, and I began to worry about another free fall from altitude. As I began my worry, my ascent slowed and I began to fall – talk about setting a course by the cobwebs in your mind. I was falling fast now when suddenly I realized maybe another wish was in order . . . a positive wish *this* time – by all means! "I wish I were up, I wish I was going up," and, lo, my descent decelerated and I only got a little wet this time as I hit my perigee in the Sargasso Sea.

Ugh! That seaweed is unpleasant stuff, and filled with ungodly, smelly little critters all looking for their spot in the sun. Leaving that unsightly sea swamp, I, again, was drifting upward at a pleasant enough rate of climb trying to accentuate the positive in my mind. It seems that I could steer by the way I wished to go, and I realized that my life had pretty well gone in the direction that I had unconsciously wished it to go. No! I had *consciously worked* toward achieving certain goals – not wishing, but working toward my ends. Hey! Maybe that's the way it is in the afterlife – 'cept, instead of working, you only had to wish! I began to feel real good about this after death thing . . . 'specially free of the aches and pains of that wore out body.

Could it be that heaven is what you wish . . . havin' *worked* toward achieving peace of mind while on Earth? I s'pose I was going to get that question answered PDQ now that I was unmoored from my home planet. I reflected that I had achieved peaceful co-existence with myself 'bout the age of twenty-five, and life had been a hoot ever since. 'Course I had dropped the religion thing, it seems, to get to that state of unadulterated freedom, and then experienced a wonderfully intimate, loving relationship with my wife. We really believed we had achieved everything a man and woman could want by our later years, as my wife and I often reflected, lying in bed together in amazin' embrace: "We had *earned* each other . . . and our state of bliss." She had come from no bed of roses early on, either.

"Paul," I then said to myself, "keep thinkin' positive, as before, and maybe I'll keep my fanny from bein' scorched in a place everybody called Hell." It was now clearly evident to me that Hell is possible *everywhere*. Well, that had been my theory while on planet Earth; it seemed that some people went way out of their path to find ugliness. And they found it, sometimes even makin' it up! Now, I'm not goin' to go negative and mention names and professions seein' that I am in a very precarious position 'tween Heaven and Hell right now. I floated along conjurin' up all kinds of peaceful thoughts, an' that wasn't too difficult.

I wished again for that cigarette and, presto, there it was . . . with that wonderful aroma I remembered from long ago. I never disdained the second hand smoke that so many railed about -- unless it got into my eyes. 'Course, if I stopped at a roadhouse for a coupla beers, I usually came out smellin' of stale tobacco, which wasn't good. But I did enjoy the aroma of a cigarette now and again. I understand that smoking has been banned in all restaurants and roadhouses in California; I never thought that would ever happen in *that* State!

Beer! I had to mention beer, of all negative things! But I never really considered beer a bad thing, so long as I didn't let it get the better of me. Two or three beers from time to time helped the appetite, thirst and disposition . . . at least *my* disposition. There are those about, like the Irish and the Native American, who seem to be poisoned some by beer. I have seen *Hell* in roadhouses where they were allowed to trade. Henry, my brother-in-law 'til recent, who was of Irish descent, used to joke that whiskey was invented by God to keep Irishmen from rulin' the world! They could become good priests and cops, but they weren't allowed to rule the world.

I slipped a little in altitude and I thought I better start thinkin' less about disparaging things as carpin' on the Indians and Irish. I was bein' judge-mental, and obviously that wasn't good. I started to fall faster. Not to panic, I started humming a Stephen Foster tune 'bout my old Kentucky home. My descent slowed a bit, and leveled off as I thought of bein' in Alabama, freezin' to death. That did it – turned me around again – thinkin' cool thoughts. I had always found humming a Stephen Foster tune comforting, and it was a great antidote to ridding some dog-gone tune that got stuck in my head. I was floatin' upward again . . . I couldn't imagine Stephen Foster *not* bein' in heaven – even though he *was* a Yankee! Oops, my up-take leveled off and I started to drop again, but I had everything under control. You see, that was a test 'cause I don't really dislike Yankees – only some of them who like to cause hell . . . but people who like to cause hell were *everywhere*, from everywhere. I leveled off again in flight as I thought it interesting that a

Pennsylvanian would want to write so many songs of the South. And, I remembered my befuddlement when I found out that Camptown was a village just south of the New York line, and the horse race was by a bunch of Yankees to a river.

I decided that testing my current traverse might meet with consternation, so I quit!

I thought back to the good times that I had experienced, even before I had found earthly Nirvana.

I had traveled a lot, and enjoyed seein' the sights of the world in the Army, and my work as a geologist. It was an education in itself, opening my eyes to the customs of the world. It helped me understand that there were a lot of differences and that all people didn't think like us Americans. They even worshipped different Gods, or the same God in diff'rent ways. Contrary to the order some think, education ain't all that bad; it helped get me to the attitude and place I am today. Eatin' that apple like Eve did, and findin' knowledge: I still think was a lot of bunk . . . whoa, another unplanned test -- and my direction didn't change! But, I must stop doing *that*!

I was drifting into the stratosphere now, which seemed cooler – but not cold. I thought that maybe my visual perception was controlling my apparent lack of senses. But *vision* is a sense too, I recollected. How was I able to see? I realized now that the appearance of the cigarette only brought back my recollection of its aroma – maybe ten times in intensity. I surmised that it was in wishing so, either consciously or subconsciously, that I could see about in a need for guidance. "Oh well," I thought to myself, "mustn't think too much about details or I might wind up gettin' fried."

Now, I was like driftin' in a junkyard – space artifacts that hadn't come down or burnt up yet. Not near the amount of garbage on earth, though. Well, give 'em time! (I shouldn't of said that negative inference 'cause after drifting above a cylindrical hulk, I soon found I was again below it. A few bars of *Old Susanna* put me right back up again.)

Before long I was above it all . . . or to the other side anyway. It seemed like Earth wasn't down anymore, just kind of lateral to me now – like the Moon was, only in another direction. It seemed now the pull was becoming stronger as planetary gravity diminished . . . or was *it* another sort of gravity?

Now, there had probably been thousands of deaths on the day mine occurred, but I saw not one unlimbered soul – at least not 'til I got to what I surmised to be the gate of Heaven. Then, I didn't see anyone else either – must have been some sort of privacy protection thing. But, to my surprise, was who was minding entry to that splendid place of regard. It was Tom Jefferson himself! And when I approached for what amounted to an interview, he smiled in a disarming, knowing sort of way.

"Paul, how does it feel to be summoned to the place you always hoped might exist?" He said in an easy east-slope Virginia charm.

I said -- carefully minding my manners to speak with absolute respect to the one American I most cherished: "Sir, it is my humble pleasure to be in the presence of someone so eminent. But I must confess I doubted the concept of an afterlife that so many of humanity was brought up with, in their theistic ways."

"Yes Paul, you were one of the few to disdain what amounts to self-serving, preserving, mindless delusion. You are here this moment because of your untiring and tenacious efforts to maintain what *messeigneurs* Madison, Penn and Roger Williams believed to be a better, more effective form of governing. They too, as you well know, labored in the face of the status quo and mediocrity to *progress* humanity's tolerance of others' thinking." He shrugged his wide shoulders and continued his welcome of me: "Contrary to what the clerics allow, you had an inalienable right to *doubt* what could not be tested! It is so intellectually obvious that given any number of circumstances, most would rebel at the thought of chicanery, except in the most insidious circumstance: that of religious indoctrination from birth. We found it to be the grand proof of our consciousness."

"You mean you haven't seen a god up here . . . if I may respectfully ask?" Paul blurted in befuddlement. "I sort of thought *you* were God's right hand angel."

"Me? Heavens no! I am just taking a turn at welcoming new comers, relieving Mr. Arouet, who had the duty for quite sometime now. Arouet, you know him probably as Voltaire."

"Well, I read a lot but didn't know that!"

"Yes, Francois-Marie Arouet – like our own Samuel Clemens who took the pseudonym of Mark Twain.

"He is here, yes?"

"Most certainly! His writings always skirted the established norms of his day, ruffling feathers of all kinds with his wit and satire. So many enjoyed his writing, but little of his lessons were able to penetrate the lacquer veneer of the ever-so-sweet mind-set of those who hold dearly to their cradle-to-grave security blanket."

Timidly, Paul ventured another question. "Sir, is that to say there are other places for the souls in denial?"

"Regarding *eternity*, you ask?" Not waiting for my nod, the tall Virginian, with drawn eyebrows, continued: "No, Paul, the ignorant and arrogant wretches have lived out their misery. The fact that some have been responsible for others experiencing misery leads them to suffer knowledge of what could have been. As I understand it -- and I do not like to dwell on negativity -- their period of suffering is a lengthy mental anguish that eventually fades with time into nothingness, I think, as the universe more and more expands."

I stood quietly upon hearing all this, fearful to say a word that I might step on my tongue. I was nervous as to what to expect next, hardly confident that this was not all a dream.

"No doubt you would like to meet some others who have *earned* their privileges?"

"YES SIR!" I blurted again, not feeling this way since I received my diploma from the University. I touched my mustache thinking it might have dropped off after hearing of such intoxicating possibilities.

"Mr. Madison is busy presently in the Tenth Sector but will be returning soon for a welcoming convocation that he and Mr. Clemens will host for American arrivals. But now you are tired so I'll have Terrence escort you to the Central Library."

"Library, sir?"

"Yes Paul, where your mind can relax among the collective works of humanity. You don't find that strange, do you? I must tell you that the appreciation of reading is one of the pre-requisites of being here."

"Absolutely . . . do . . . enjoy it, sir." I said, hardly holding back tears of joy.

"You'll even find the complete collection from Hypatia's library at Alexandria."

'But I don't know Greek or Latin,' Paul thought to himself . . . 'but I guess I'll have time enough to learn.'

III

Politics and Carrolyn

"Paul, you are so *full* of it. Where do you get off describin' Heaven like that . . . being the unbeliever that you are?"

"Okay, so what's your take on the big pie in the sky?"

Carl furrowed his eyebrows for nearly a minute before offering his reply. "Fust of all, it's not pie in the sky'" he said, buying time. "I think it's more like whut Pleasantforce says it is, as it's spelled out in *Revelations*."

"You're sure Heaven's not more like some wonderful wished for place in each person's mind, and that their church has more or less rubber stampcd a confirmation of same to keep the unsuspecting sheep within their influence."

"Paul, *that's* blasphemy . . . and you know it."

"I'm tired of being polite, Carl. The fundamentalists don't give a hoot about fair play, or logical arguments based on science and history. They demand their preaching and graven images in our public buildings, oblivious of the abundance of their own tax sheltered temples of worship. They aren't courteous either, being that they are always so inclined to scowl at a person, tellin' them that they're going to burn in hell, forever. I could go on and . . ."

Carl interrupted him, "But whut about all the good things they do – the programs to help the poor, the sick?"

"The government and secular groups would do more of these things if *they* didn't. And they won't allow atheists to undertake any care giving, because we are too despicable in our apostasy to do good works."

"Really?" Carl asked, sincerely.

"Think about it. We can't adopt a child or be a foster parent."

"Why?"

"Questionnaires, Carl -- questionnaires that always ask you your religion . . . under the auspices of matching the parties. What chance does an atheist, agnostic or freethinker have when the child was whitewashed with religion at birth and now has to be stroked?"

"Yur pretty damn in-courteous yourself." Carl criticized.

"*And it's so much fun!*"

"See how arrogant you are!"

"Since it seems I can't change anything through polite conversation with any of these jay birds, I might as well have a little fun with them – poke them a little with a few barbs and zingers of my own," Paul said with a diabolical smile.

"Yur lible ta git smacked."

"Nah . . .they're afraid that we apostates have devilish powers—they really believe that—so we can damn near say anything we want . . . except to zealots."

"Why not zealots?"

"'cause they are the defenders of the faith and they *will* react with a vengeance . . . try to drive a stake through your heart – that sort of thing."

"Here in Kentucky?"

"Yep, my friend. The religious afflicted here in good ol' K - Y aren't much different than the Taliban in Afghanistan."

Carl pondered Paul's verbiage, and for a few moments remained silent. When he did speak, he changed the subject: "So when're ya leavin' to go back to the dark side of the planet?"

"Wednesday, a week, if I don't get orders to go to school"

"You told me how nice it was over there."

"Carl, it's a *toilet bowl*!"

"Yeah . . . Bush really got us into a mess."

"And he was too proud to backtrack and ask for help from the U.N. or NATO – that was his biggest sin . . . with the exception of declarin' war in the first place."

"I remember you sayin' it was a bad mistake to go in, but I thought it a good idea to replace Seldom Sane – the evil dictator he was."

"Well, we all know now that Bush's research and diplomacy – not to mention his intelligence – was woefully lacking in preparation for such a lunatic adventure."

Carl, who had supported the preemptive strike, apologetically defended George W's failed reasoning: "It was s'posed to be a cakewalk to Baghdad – the walk his daddy should've took when *he* had the chance."

"I know . . . and he had to listen to Rove, Wolfowitz and Cheney instead of Laura, the Pope and his own church's leadership."

"See," Carl jumped in, "there you go with a Freudian slip 'bout somethin' good religious folk can do."

"Well – *duh* – they're *supposed* to do good. And the president is supposed to listen to *all* council and do good, too."

"Just thought I'd mention . . ." Carl bantered. "You know . . . a lot'a people 'round these parts thought he did good by attackin' Iraq like he did."

"And Afghanistan?"

"Absolutely!"

"The problem was . . . President Bush's primary goal in Afghanistan was to get Osama bin Laden! And his primary goal in Iraq was to get Saddam Hussein. He failed on both counts, but should have stayed focused on bin Laden."

"But they finally did get the Ace of spades." Carl added.

"Yeah, after the dictator had gone totally loony," Paul dissed. The ensuing quiet was discomforting. "Did I tell ya 'bout the letter I wrote to our Senators right after 9 – 11 happened?"

"I saw it in the paper . . . your letter to the editor; *that* was a good idea you had!"

"Theirs was an highly innovative attack, and needed to be responded to likewise in some innovative way . . . at least I thought."

"Dumpin' garbage on them 'til they turned bin Laden over to us – out of pride, more or less – was an innovative idea . . . if not for the messiness."

"Messiness, Carl?" Paul recoiled. "How many Afghans and our people would've been saved in that war if we had dropped just garbage and not ordnance?" Not waiting for an answer, he went on: "Look at all the crap we could've got rid of – without worryin' about EPA permits; *and* the money we would've saved in outfitting an army and blasting a desert wasteland into a pock-marked desert wasteland. I mean . . . cover the place with dog shit, sewage sludge, old refrigerators and tires until they cried uncle Osama bin Laden. Theyd'a handed him over to us on a platter! The one thing A-rabs can't stand is to be offended . . . dumping garbage is offensive!"

"Did you send a copy to the President?"

"I didn't . . . I didn't think he'd ever read it considerin' all the shit that crosses his desk.

I thought maybe he and his advisers might listen to one or both our senators. Now this country is in deep doo-doo with his everlastin' war – the war that he thought would get him re-elected."

"Kinda like Nixon's campaign to get re-elected, you

think?"

"Smelled that way to everyone . . . and he got his ass canned from office in last year's election –even his God wouldn't come to his rescue – lost every state, including Texas."

"Yeah, too much cronyism, demagoguery and arrogance." Carl offered.

"Sure he had the courage of his convictions and appeared to be a tough leader, but so did Hitler. Hitler was smarter though – and loonier."

"You think that was best . . . for the country to dump him like that?"

"The moral majority finally came to their senses when they saw all his cronies chipping in vast amounts of re-election money to keep their own well greased juggernauts rollin'; our soldiers bein' killed every day by the chaotic populace of that unchained religious hell-hole. And Bush blindly attributing those attacks to a few of Saddam's henchmen – what about the suicide bombers? *That's* religious zealotry, out and out!" Paul took a deep breath before continuing his tirade, "But, nooooo, 'this wasn't about religion, 9 – 11 wasn't about religion, The attacks on everyone who worked with Christians were not about religion – they were all terrorists!' Tell me, Carl, how does a terrorist, if not religious, advance his self-interest by terminating his life?"

Carl blinked, choosing not to answer.

"You commit suicide – Jihad against the infidel – to get to a better place, in the eyes of Allah! It's a *religious* experience . . . you don't have to be a neurosurgeon to figure *that* out!"

Knowing he could say nothing else to bring his old friend to a better frame of mind, Carl begged dismissal, citing some errands that he needed to attend to.

"Yeah . . . sorry – guess I got kinda carried away."

"You've been over there – you know about things better'n I do." Carl got up from their table began shuffling toward the door. "Gimme a call before you go back . . . maybe watch a game or somethin'. Kentucky plays Tennessee Saturday . . . I might have a chance at some tickets."

"That's a thought, Carl . . . I'll give you a call." Paul watched his friend Carl disappear into an autumn scurry of leaves, then returned to his own reverie. Life had been good to him his last few years in college -- until that fateful day when his fiancé was killed in an automobile accident on the way to work. He was at OCS then, and life had been opening up to him in a kaleidoscope of opportunity. Its brilliance matched his childhood memories of the gaiety of the blue, red and green hues of the Christmas tree lights that he used to stare at for long periods of time. His six month romance with Carrolyn had transcended even *his* expectations as to what happiness could be experienced in life. They had found love in its deepest, consummating mist, and luxuriated in its endless, magical embrace. Then came the accident -- which devastated him. He remembered how he had cried for nearly a week, oblivious to how he would be able to go on in life without her. She was so vibrant, so intelligent, so supplemental to his being. Her beauty was inside, though she was not unattractive looking. She filled out a shift or jeans in a way that set him afire, and between their lovemaking they would talk endlessly about most anything – like one would to a best buddy, even more so than with Carl whose growth seemed to have stopped with high school graduation.

He thought it odd that Carl hadn't mentioned Carrolyn this day, but then Carl had been witness only too well to his despair in the wake of the tragedy. But he hadn't even asked if there might be someone on the horizon! Probably thought that it was still too early for speculating on the future, especially since how his parents were constantly riding *him* to find someone nice to tie the knot with. What were the chances of finding another soul-mate like Carrolyn? How many find even one truly intimate love in their lifetime? How many even *try*? To too many people, it seems, the wonderful fairy tales and romance stories are only fantastic dreams and are not really possible for themselves. 'Only money purchases happiness, purchases a sex mate or fuck-buddy' as some of his colleagues would say. He only knew he wasn't ready to search just yet, still basking in the warm memory of her loving touch, their early morning embraces when he returned her home from their lengthy evenings together. Time will tell, he kept saying to himself cognizant of the fact he had his military service to keep him occupied and then a career in geological exploration and theory to lose himself in. Even in the futility of the war in Iraq, he was growing out of the melancholy of his loss, the luster of life was still there; he was still young and optimistic. He had always been optimistic – hope for a better way always in the forefront; each step an adventure -- even if some of those steps were backwards.

His personal (and professional) life was going forward in fits and starts. True, he had only a rare date now and then, always at the instigation of others, and the war was finally coming to some coherency through the leadership of the new administration, and the United Nations. He had too much respect for his life to give up, even in the dark days following his loss of Carrolyn – it was just too much of a gift to disdain – to *blame*. Funny how the religious refer to life as a gift but, unlike him, they, in another breath, disdain this life for all its wickedness, and ungratefully state that there is yet another, better place – talk about blasphemy! They thank God for this wonderful existence, and then *beg* forever that they will be delivered from this evil life to live for eternity in an infinitely better place.   Kind of makes their life rather moot, and certainly unproductive in this one, he thought, recalling how Lynn Jessup had thrown down her M–16 so that she could pray as her captors closed in. Jessup wasn't in his unit, but he remembered how the Bush administration tried to paint her as a hero at a time they were grasping at straws to put a smiley face on that tragic theatre.

He got up from the table and left the restaurant after paying for the refreshments.

IV

Mom

The radio came on at 7:30. It was Monday morning and the world news was infiltrating his troubled dream. At first it augmented the dream as the list of casualties were itemized from over there -- then Paul stirred with the incongruity of a cereal commercial. The off-white ceiling plaster came into focus as the news broadcast continued:

". . . and at this hour, the foreign ministers of Germany, Russia and France are meeting in Bonn." The familiar dialect of the BBC correspondent droned on with little excitement of what really amounted to a world event news flash: "It is strongly suspected that this impromptu meeting of the three continental European powers is all about forming an intimate military alliance in order to match the strength of the United States as another, and competing, world presence."

'Wow,' Paul thought, '. . . and even after our present government had reached out to those countries to mend the insults of George Bush's administration.' He listened attentively as the broadcast continued:

"This event is thought by many to answer a growing threat of having only one super power on the globe. With all the negative attributes of the late Cold War, a certain balance was achieved between what many considered a tug of good versus evil. Of course, it has been said that nature abhors a vacuum and in this case it does seem that a power vacuum exists between the U.S. and the rest of the world. As democracies have seen, two or more strong parties are required to make the system work, and that may have to be the way with world leadership until the United Nations can design otherwise."

He arose and went about his morning routine, upstairs in his parents' house, so wonderfully removed from his sand choked quarters in the Green Zone of Baghdad. The radio continued with the local news and weather before he turned it off thinking he would catch the whole story unfolding in Germany, later on CNN. 'I was wonderin' when those guys would get together and become a formidable front, especially to the retrograde and dismal policies of the Bush White House.' He was especially infuriated by Bush's remark "Bring 'em on" challenging those prayer rug nuts to test our resolve, and the naïve imposition of *his* values upon their foreign culture.

While dressing, his eyes wandered to the portrait photo of his late sweetheart. The familiar emptiness and despair momentarily overwhelmed him, bringing tears to his eyes. He allowed himself to drift back to their caresses . . . and the kissing – how his lips got so chapped from their endless enjoyment of each other. 'Nah, it can't happen to me again,' he muttered to himself as a tear rolled down his cheek. 'Better to have loved and lost, than to have never loved at all,' he added, giving thanks to the fates that at least he had been lucky to have that experience.

He perfunctorily bussed his mother's cheek before sitting down to a hot stack of flapjacks.

"How's Carl doin', honey?" she asked.

"Oh, 'bout the same as he's always been, I guess." Paul evaded telling her of their disappointing get-together the previous day.

"You and him were such good playmates when you were children."

"Yeah, but he's so stifled now."

"It's what happens when you git tied down with a mill job." She rationalized. "I'm so proud you got the gumption to git'a education and make som'thin of yourself."

"It's just that . . . you only go around once in life, so you should make the best you can of it!" He enjoyed reiterating his outlook on life.

"Jus' like it says in the Bible, it's a sin not to use your talents."

"That's what you always taught me, Ma." He said, hoping she wouldn't start about the religion thing.

"It was nice that you and Carl went to church last Sunday." She doted. "I worry that you don't go more off'en."

"Do you think I'm doin' a lot of wrong – sinning?"

"We're *all* sinners, son."

"Well, *I think* it's just an excuse for a lot of so-called Christians to do wrong . . . that it's inevitable, they say, so why not give in to temptation . . . and repent later."

"But aren't you concerned about your soul . . . and where you'll spend eternity?"

It just never ends, he thought – the fear provoked proselytizing. "Ma, it just doesn't make sense to me any more. If you'd tell me why you feel the way you do about all the Catholics, the Jews and the Muslims, then you might understand why I feel the way I do about our religion."

"But they're all *false*, Paul."

"Think about it, Ma." How many times had they gone around like this? It was similar to a cat chasing its tail -- a true Catch 22 dilemma. "What makes Baptists so special in objective comparison to the other religions of the world? It's a 'My God is better than your God' mentality, which is now threatening to consume this planet in cultural conflict."

"Reverend Pleasantforce *does* talk a lot about the Cultural

War . . ."

"What he talks about – Cultural War – and what I'm talkin' about are not the same thing," he cut her off.

"You think you're so smart, with your college education." She was hurt, now. "We should've sent you to the seminary instead of the University."

"I'm sorry, Ma, but I gotta live my own life . . . it's a matter of conscience with *me* too."

"But you're turning your back on your heritage . . . *tradition*."

"If you mean that the white wash I received from birth is peelin' away, yes, and I welcome the freedom of the warm light of day . . . that . . . that knowledge has shown me there really is nothing to fear."

"I'm afraid for you, dear."

"As a mother should be . . ." He got up from the table and kissed her again. "Just let me find out on my own what my path in life should be. Have I brought disgrace or dishonor to you?"

"No." she happily said. "Just keep a look out for all the false prophets out there, ready to lead you into iniquity."

"I'll certainly do *that*!" he assured her. And then he grabbed his coat and rushed out the door.

V

Dad

That evening he watched the CBS news with his father and grandfather. The segment covering the meeting at Bonn Germany lasted just over ten minutes. Paul had caught bits and pieces of the event on CNN during the day; now the summing up would be ladled out when all news sources had been digested – its contents regurgitated at 6:30 P.M.

"That would be a rather unholy alliance," said the old man, remembering the intrigue between Russia and Nazi Germany during World War II. "History's goin' to repeat itself – mark my words!"

"I thought that kind of intrigue had been laid to rest, durin' and after the Cold War." Paul's father remarked.

Paul had been weighing the day's developments, and added to the conversation: "I guess this is pay-back for Bush's unilateral actions."

"Pay-back?" His father barked, "Why, he did the world a mighty big favor by ridding that country of one demented dictator."

"But Dad, his actions smacked of illegitimacy; we went in there under phony pretense – not just one, but several. *We* started a war! The first time ever our country made a pre-emptive strike, against a country that had done *us* no wrong!"

"Served Hussein right." His father huffed. "Terrorists have to be dealt with."

"The terrorists were the Taliban and the Saudi nationals that piloted the planes of 9-11, not Saddam Hussein's Iraq,

Dad! Innocent people have been killed because of the dumb thing Bush did."

"Don't you feel safer . . . now that Hussein is in custody?"

"We might have bought some degree of safety . . . but the price we paid will set a precedent – a precedent of jumping to paranoid conclusions . . . out of fear!"

The old man cleared his throat. "Paul has a point. Roosevelt, Truman and Ike would have weighed the consequences of this war far more fully before committing our forces to fight a sandstorm. Hussein was a two-bit thug – hardly a threat to us. Now we feel obligated to re-build his country 'cause we knocked it apart."

Deferring to the old man, Paul's dad added, "True, Bush ran for office stating that there would be no 'nation buildin'on *his* watch." Paul's grandfather, whom he called 'Granpap,' was a pillar of good old common sense. Though registered as a Republican, he had voted the other party too often to count. It was *him* that he identified with and asked for advice in matters that were important. Perhaps it was because he was a man of few words – words that were carefully thought out before allowed. "But he did the right thing, goin' in there to punish those rag-heads"

"Don't you see?" Paul objected, expanding his question: "It was a knee-jerk reaction . . . in slow motion, deciding beforehand what he was going to do, then arguing his points at the UN"

"Somethin' had to be done," his dad insisted, ". . . to let the world know that we won't be pushed around by a bunch of fanatics."

"You absolutely hit the nail square on the head," Paul agreed. "Trouble is, how do you define and identify the fanatics?" He hesitated in thought, "And how do you deal with them after you know who they are?"

"They're al-Qaeda for God's sake . . . we *know* who they are!"

"Yeah, but dad, Bush and a lot of Christians are in denial that al-Qaeda is about religion.

Bush said they were terrorists, plane and simple, with no agenda other than denying their people and the people of the world their freedoms. He didn't talk about this being a religious war, but what else could it be . . . with the suicide bombings and all?"

"What diff'rence does it make?"

"Well, for one thing you don't go agitatin' a bee's nest, randomly pokin' a stick at it. It's a good way to get stung!"

"So he went after the terrorists that were harbored in Iraq . . . the weapons of mass destruction that Saddam would have eventually sold 'em."

The old man leaned forward to follow the give and take.

"There was no proof that he was harboring either terrorists or weapons of mass destruction."

"Then you think Bush, Rumsfeld and Powell lied to the people?"

"And to the world . . . it sure looks that way to me and quite a lot of other people. Why else did Bush get turned out of office?"

"Then you think it's a war about religion?"

"*I* think so." Paul emphasized. "And if it is, we should be addressing those sensitivities before the world community."

"You mean the United Nations?"

"Exactly."

"What a bunch of mealy-mouthed do-nothings!"

"That's because they haven't defined the problem either . . . and they are only trying to treat the symptoms." Paul leaned forward in his seat. "The differences between Bush and the United Nations were how to treat the symptoms of a malady no one had the stomach to define."

"And you know how to describe the problem?"

"Dad, they're *all* in denial. It's a religious war – plain and simple!"

"Well, Sherlock smarty-pants, when're you goin' to let all these dumb-bunnies know?"

"I have written our two senators."

"You and your letters – your mother and I are embarrassed by all the neighbors' questions whereabouts you get your ideas. Why are you always trying to upset the apple cart?"

"Because the apples are beginning to rot."

The old man's gravelly voice butted in, "Now son, don't be so hard on your boy. He has a right to his opinion too – they say this is a free country."

"Dad, your grandson is an *atheist*, for chrisake!"

The old man reclined in his chair and muttered: "Maybe he learned somethin' in college we all should have been taught."

"You mean you agree with the hogwash comin' out of his mouth?"

"I sort of agree that this conflict might be more religious in nature than anyone has cared to admit. You know, son, the old adage, 'don't talk about religion or politics in polite conversation'"

"Because of religion, the world is terrorized?"

"Or about to *explode*!" Paul interrupted. "The explosions are like frictional earthquakes on the outer edges of a tectonic plate; the plates themselves must merge if true world peace is to be experienced."

"And which religion will your so-called merged plates resemble?"

"*None of the above!*"

"Wow, you are a howl, Paul."

"I admit that I'm the consummate optimist, dad."

The old man roared with laughter.

"I'll tell you what you are: you're loony – you are out of your gourd! Do away with religion? *Impossible.*" Paul's Dad blurted.

"I don't mean outlaw religion, but religion has to be relegated to the personal level only, and not mixed with national policy."

"We already have separation of church and state."

"In this country, yes – and in most western democracies. That is why we are so prosperous and religion flourishes. But the Arab world lacks the separation of religion from politics . . . therein lies the rub."

"Oh, I see. We'll just send all the Arab countries a polite little note explaining they should remove Allah from their government offices – and, suggest that turning to atheism would be a nice touch."

"It doesn't seem plausible, does it?

"Plausible, my ass. The messenger would be decapitated, disemboweled and dragged through the filthy streets of their towns – that is what would happen."

"Then the world will explode."

"Explode? His dad smirked in away he had never seen before. "Why can't we just go on with this terrorism thing for awhile and maybe they'll tire of, or run out of human bombs."

Paul knew he had earned his father's sarcasm. And it would be mild compared to criticism he would meet from political scientists, not to mention orthodox clergy. "Their birth rate is the highest on the planet. Their average age is considerably younger than any of the western nations save Latin America; they'll continue to recruit the naïve and ignorant youth with promises of heavenly reward if they dedicate themselves to Holy Jihad."

His dad, a pacifist, half joked to his grandfather, "I guess we should nuke them . . . melt Mecca and Medina into glass."

"That's part of the explosion package, Dad!"

His mother interrupted to announce that coffee and dessert was on the table.

VI

Dream Recurs

Thoughts of the day mingled with visions of Carrolyn, as he fell into a deep slumber. . . .

The library was huge, but it didn't seem to have outward walls – only pillars of considerable dimension. It was adorned in the old style with no visible computers. Terrence left him in the lounge area after explaining the various divisions of knowledge and a leisurely tour of all in the vicinity. Paul thanked him and sank into the softest but firmest easy chair he had ever known. He was tired and would have dropped off to sleep except for the excitement of the place swirling around him. It was total relaxation without the bothersome feature of losing consciousness. He stared at the overhead, which was obviously supported by the pillars, but noted that the pillars were few and far between. Must be a different type of gravity here, he thought noting that the extensive tour of the heaven-like complex was traversed with little effort – in fact, he didn't remember physically walking.

In time (or outside of it) he noticed that this was all he would have ever dreamed in any hopes that there be a heaven. As a non-believer of any earth-bound religion, he had disdained *all* of the heavens they promised – because of the fear-invoking conditions that were always attached. But he was hopeful that there might be some kind of reward, if he followed the dictates of *his* conscience: to be truthful in all endeavors; to struggle against unreasonable claims and conditions; To give fair value in trade with others while suppressing thoughts of avarice; to enjoy life without taking the enjoyment of life from others; to question and understand rather than criticize nature's laws; and not to spoil the environment. In short, to live by the law of reciprocity which is commonly referred to by the Christians as the Golden Rule. He knew of some who grappled with atheism -- reluctant to leave their childhood faith – but entertained the hope that their *transgressors* would get *their* just desserts, just as his friends expected to be rewarded for staying their righteous course. He didn't like to dwell on such negativity. And, if Mr. Jefferson was right, such negative personages would fade away in the hell they made for themselves.

But he had not *expected* a reward – satisfying his *conscience* was reward enough, being happy and content that he had done his best to sully the world as little as possible. He could sleep at night. He wouldn't *beg* for something better than the heaven he had already made for himself on Earth. His existence, along side his fellow humans, represented the ultimate achievement of Mother Nature, therefore conferring on him certain responsibilities: to enjoy the gift of life, and attempt to put back at least an equivalent of what he extracted from it.

Too many others failed to appreciate the wonderful possibilities of intelligent life, and let its essence slip away as they accepted their mundane station as unchangeable. Existence was a bore to many – to those who could not or would not search for the few possible routes to happiness. Hardships were accentuated over the positive allowing pessimism to rule their lives – so the preacher's heaven became more of a focal point, a goal that would allow escape from the trials and tribulations of the world. But their questionable comfort would come at a price. They would trade their intellect for a nebulous notion of security. They would subscribe to a pious transcendence that would promise them eternal life as opposed to burning forever in some hell – and, unbelievably, unquestioningly, they *convinced* themselves to accept just that. They would not be guilty of that sin of 'thinking too much.' Too much knowledge was a dangerous thing – wasn't that flap in the Garden of Eden -- Eve eating the apple of knowledge of good and evil, all about?

Paul continued his reflection in the soft comfort of his new surroundings: . . . The authors of Genesis were a morbid, disallowing lot. In one fell swoop, they put down intellectuals and women (whom they should have remembered were the ones who gave them birth). And in doing so, gave cognizance and definition to the commencement of evil. Such defeatism! Such melancholy reduction of our existence! 'Our Lady of Perpetual Sorrow,' reeks with such numbing negativism, that it is difficult for any subscribers of *that* faith to raise themselves out of the morass of self-loathing. But when the few that do escape to the light of day, their exuberance knows no bounds as they run away in freedom.

Evil is only a tool to the ignorant, and to the lascivious profane whose greed is unquenchable. It lurks behind its inventors and users who hold shields bearing crosses and crescents to in-distinguish them from the pure of heart. Priests using children as sexual play-things; preachers behind pulpits spewing fog to obscure any notion toward social progress; rabbis wailing continually about ethnic discrimination and imams calling for holy war against the infidel – which just happens to include all the others – are manifestations of the evil humanity has inadvertently developed. He chuckled to himself as he remembered Mark Twain's comical lecture statement about how generations and generations of those poor innocent Sandwich Islanders had gone through life and died, having no idea that there was a Hell.

Maybe he would meet Mr. Clemens soon. And he was looking forward to shaking Mr. Madison's hand. They were very much the inspiration of his philosophy of life. Twain cut through the blubber right to the bone with his self-deprecating analysis of the buffoons around him. He included *himself* in the critique of his contemporaries, and he brought out the poignancy of the ill-educated as they struggled with life and ethics. But, excepting Jefferson, his favorite was the engine of constitutional and political reason, James Madison. He reflected that Madison's intellect was truly global – universal in its scope. His studies, like Jefferson's, had been obtained through religious and non-religious tutors and institutions, and he saw early on religion's efforts to expand its policies as far in any direction that vacuum would permit. He was aware, early on, of the differences arising among the various sects, as did Jefferson become aware of clerical impropriety at William and Mary – indeed that discovered impropriety persuaded his father to send the young Madison to the University of New Jersey (now Princeton).

Madison had disdained a notion to study for the clergy in order to pursue a liberal education, the law, and ultimately, politics. The clergy's loss was America's gain as he struggled in the face of uncharted national identity. At the sometime enthusiastic wishes of his constituency, he spread his efforts between the Constitutional Congress and Virginia's House of Burgesses. In either place he would be rebuffed by personages no less than the Quakers, John Adams and Patrick Henry. Yet his youthful idealism and vitality carried the day on the most important issues, his efforts being consummated over the carcasses of earlier defeats. He, with

Jefferson, turned the world on its ear with their success at winning the debate on religious freedom – enabling Jefferson's long pending bill against assessment that would have supported the State's teaching of religion. And then at Philadelphia, with Jefferson in France sending him some 200 books on history of ancient and present-day confederacies, he literally directed the writing of the United State's new Constitution – all of that from a frail young seminarian of questionable health who found immediate and total rejuvenation in the world of ideas!

This was soooo relaxing, he thought, sitting here day dreaming, knowing that he had been somewhat right in his life's course all along. There was *no* heaven – religious, that is. But there *was a heaven*, really, of ones own making! He had conjured up proofs of there being no God on several occasions, but he couldn't bring himself to deny the *total* impossibility of some prime mover in the cosmos. But it was probably more likely that there were no god or gods than the likelihood that they existed. He remembered Carl Sagan's assessment of that conundrum by announcing that if there were a God, how then did *He* come into existence? The clergy preferred to answer: 'God is the *uncaused* cause of creation.' It was no longer of any consequence – obviously you could believe or disbelieve and still wind up in this place so long as one's attitude was *positive, hopeful* and *productive*. Mr. Jefferson inferred that he had not seen God, or, for that matter, the Manager of this realm. It was run by mature, like-minded former citizens of the world, in a way that seemed a continuance of their fruitful, humane efforts on Earth. It was an intellectual plateau that apparently transcended death, topping even the most possibly fulfilled dream.

VII

Kentucky vs. Tennessee

The day was very bright, without a cloud in the sky. The rolling hills, partially framing bluish-gray mountains in the distance, revealed their array of autumn colors in typical southern football tradition. It seemed all the traffic heading south on I – 75 were sporting in some fashion or another, either 'Wildcat' blue or 'Volunteer' orange. Carl and Paul's friend, Jenkin Wood, offered the two young men tickets to the Kentucky – Tennessee game after he heard Paul was home on leave. As a season ticket holder, he had been devastated that his business required him to be on the West Coast that Saturday of the big game. "What's our chances this year?" Paul asked, breaking the quiet viewing of the changing panorama. "Like always, they're favored by one or two touchdowns I think."

"But it's great to visit Vol Stadium . . . those Tennessee fans really get into the game – and their colors, so consistent with this time of the year."

"Yeah," Carl replied as he guided his yellow compact down the expressway. "But we knock 'em off once'd in a while – like last year."

"They are to us in football like we are to them to them in basketball."

"S'pose we do git our licks in . . . on the courts."

The traffic was thickening now, as they approached downtown Knoxville.

"Guess there's nuthin' like this overseas." Carl observed,

commenting on all the snazzy cars now bumper to bumper.

"This is what's missin' in the Middle East." Paul replied. With tongue-in-cheek, he added: "No sports, no intramural rivalries for the masses to vent their frustrations – that's what's missin'!"

"You may be onto somethin' there, Paul."

"Compound that with outlawin' pig meat and certain sexual acts, and you got some very unhappy, confused people."

"Freedom seems to be a problem for them."

"Yeah, they sure as hell can't handle *that*! But then, there's a lot of people in this country who can't handle it either."

"What d'ya mean by that?"

"Well, you got all those real religious nuts out there who can name all the sins that can be committed." Paul continued in an acerbic tone. "They're not satisfied to practice their restraint alone but must make damn sure that no one else is tempted to do what *they* consider bad behavior."

"You mean . . . like the Mormons and the underwear thing?"

"It never ends! They should take the time to think that they can *never* be too pious . . . have enough *faith*. Carl, some people spend most of their day praying for deliverance from evil."

"They're some sickos out there for sure."

"Hey, I'm talkin' about people who are normal otherwise . . . you know, make a living at some job. And remember the Clarks who wouldn't get medical attention for their children and two of 'em died of simple childhood ailments?" Paul went on, "They were normal folk other than they went to that holy-roller church up Brown's Hollow. We got 'em here in Kentucky, too, my friend."

"So, I guess there'll always be weirdos around; whut else can be done?"

The lines of traffic began to fan out into the stadium's parking area.

"Well, for one thing, don't let them fundamentalists get the upper hand."

"There you go criticizin' my congregation ag'in."

"I'm sorry, Carl . . . it's just that . . ."

"*Drop it!*" Carl demanded.

He knew he had hurt his buddy. Why did he push him so? Did he want to lose him as a friend? Wasn't there anything else they could talk about? *It's just that every turn in the conversation brings up another rub*, he guiltily thought. *Must be more considerate.*

The game opened with Tennessee returning the opening kickoff 85 yards for a touchdown. "It's goin' to be one of *those* games," Carl muttered as the crowd went wild, stamping its approval.

"Yeah." Replied Paul, thinking to himself how quiet it was going to be on the long ride home.

The final score was a dismal 42 points to Kentucky's two field goals. Tennessee scored touchdowns in every quarter, humbling the Wildcats in all categories. They left early to beat the traffic, but many others had the same idea and it was difficult getting out of town.

"Maybe next year," came the in-unison utterance of the defeated fans, as they headed north toward the state line.

"Tennessee's always tough," Paul tried at the small talk.

"We'll get 'em this winter." Carl offered coldly.

"Well, it didn't cost us anything. And it was a nice drive through the mountains."

"You know what'd be nicer?" Carl brightened. "Let's take ol' Route 25. I'm sick of the Interstate."

"That's the best thing you said all day."

"Be less traffic, too."

"And we got the time." Paul added, thinking about all the twist and turns the older federal highway entailed.

"Yeah, we could stop at Nolan's roadhouse up past Jericho, for a brew and the post game scores."

"Sounds good to me, ol' buddy!" Paul added, thinking that at least his friend wasn't averse to having a beer now and then. "That place still in existence?"

The seedy tavern was just as crummy as ever. It seems bars and roadhouses just get more run down and tackier every year until they burn to the ground and maybe get rebuilt, spanking new, under different ownership. Nolan's was no exception. Built in the Early 20th century into the foot of a cliff overhanging the highway, it was just wide enough in its narrowest dimension to house a bar early the length of the place. Restrooms and a small kitchen occupied remaining space at opposite ends.

The young men mounted stools among a string of pedestals not yet decapitated. "Jeez, Carl, this place is a *dump*!"

"Brings back memories, don't it?"

"I'm surprised some boulder hadn't crashed down on the place by now."

"You're the geologist, why hadn't that happened?"

"One thing's for sure about these old hills: they're stable! We're not anywhere near the edge of a tectonic plate," Paul said, while ordering a couple of drafts. "These hills are ancient mountains that were once as tall if not taller than the Rockies."

"It'd take a long time for them to wear down to the size they are now."

"Exactly."

"'Bout how long would you say?"

"Hundreds of millions of years, if I remember my studies correctly."

Carl was quiet and Paul sensed the reason, remembering his flare-up when he mentioned the fundamentalists. The barkeep brought the beers and then asked them if they were coming from the game. Then, at their request, he changed the channel of the TV that hung out from the wall of the restroom. They watched the post game scores in silence, Carl seemingly deep in reflection and Paul hardly inspired by what used to be a necessary scoreboard pilgrimage.

The fact that Alabama lost to Auburn made no impression on Carl's blank stare. "What's the matter, bud?"

"I dunno . . . thinkin' too much I s'pose."

Paul hated that simple expression. "Why . . . what are you thinkin' about?"

"Nuthin'."

"Whad'ya mean, you just said you were thinkin' too much!"

"Let's not go there."

"Go where?"

"So, you're returnin' to Iraq, Wednesday?" He forced a change of subject.

Sensing that Carl's preoccupation might have something to do with geologic-age conflicts with the Biblical creation timetable, he welcomed his old buddy's question.

"Nah, I got orders to report to the Army War College at Carlisle, Pennsylvania."

"Wow, so there's a chance you might survive this war!"

"Yeah, lucky break."

"How'd you swing that?"

"Put in for it . . . I'm just naturally curious about the political aspect of war."

"Yeah, you sure are curious."

"Well, I got this idea . . . and I don't know where to start. Thought maybe I'd try to learn the *system*, seein' that I'm an officer and all that – maybe earn some *establishment* credentials."

"So, whutr'ya getting' at?"

"It's just that I got this idea about the electoral process."

"You mean, electin' candidates to office?"

"Yep."

"What's the military got to do with electin' candidates to office?"

"I dunno yet . . . but I got to start somewhere, and the Army's payin' for me to educate myself." Paul took a sip of his beer. "Letters to the editor and to congressmen just don't cut it – 'specially when one proposes limits on them getting into office. I gotta learn the ropes."

"Wutd'ya mean, *limits on them getting into office*?"

"You know how dumb some of these politicians that get elected are?"

"They're all dumb if ya ask me!"

"You know why?"

"'Cause the smart ones stay on at their day job. . . and don' get mixed up in thankless, back-stabbing politics."

"Exactly, but it leaves the field wide open for those who like the prestige. Who would dare to be king . . . like in that movie with Sean Connery and Michael Caine."

"Uh, yeah, I remember it . . . Afghanistan, I think.

"Yeah, the Khyber Pass."

"Sean Connery wasn't so smart after all, in that there."

"No."

"So how do ya propose 'limitin' the dumbness factor?"

"Examinations!" Paul wistfully continued. "Candidates will have to pass an examination for the particular office they are striking for."

"Scuse me?" Carl gave him a lowbrow look.

"Remember Dubya's 'No child left behind' education program?"

"Vaguely."

"Well, it was a system that was funded only if secondary education requirements were successfully fulfilled in the classroom. Standardized examinations were used to establish the results."

"Okay." There was that same low stare. "Children in school districts not passing the grade were what – left behind?"

"No, silly, they were supposed to be given vouchers to attend better schools, but . . . that's another story."

"What's this got to do with smarter elections."

"Don't you see? Candidates for office who can't pass simple examinations testing them on the fundamentals of the office they're seeking will be barred! Dummya would have been barred! Your 'favorite' state senator would have been barred from office because he knew very little about the state's judicial system."

"Why you always pickin' on George Bush? You sure he'd be eliminated when he ran for office back in 1999 like that?"

"Because he was dumb . . . probably the dumbest president we ever had! I like to think of my president as bein' smarter than I am – way smarter!"

"That's why presidents have advisors."

"Yeah, having one hand in the treasury, while speakin' nice, fuzzy soundin' homilies out of their mouths to please the simple-minded."

"Your 'simple-minded' folk just happens to be in the majority!"

"Scary, isn't it?" Paul blew some foam off his second draft. "Do you want one of the 'good- ol'-boys' to run your country, Carl?"

"He had a good touch for the common man."

"But he was unprepared to go into Iraq the way he did – diplomatically, historically, politically!"

"We trusted him . . . he meant to do good – and protect us from terrorists."

Paul realised it was time to desist. He had heard it before how his pal had insisted that God had controverted the presidential election of 2000 by virtue of the Supreme Court's 5 to 4 opinion, although the nation's popular vote had gone against Bush. "All-right already. But I can't take back the fact that the Supreme Court justices voted along strict party lines."

"It was God's doin'! He put this country into the hands of the *one* candidate who had the balls to protect us."

"Carl, that doesn't make sense! You mean to tell me that God knew nine-one-one was going to happen within a year of Bush takin' office?"

Carl thought a minute before answering. "Lots'a people think that way . . . and that's what Rev'rend Pleasantforce assured us. He said that we can't know why God allows some of the things that happen, like earthquakes and floods. But it may be because, like Jerry Falwell said, we're bein' punished 'cause we've taken God out of so many things."

"If that were the case, then Allah must be the true God, to allow the Muslim fanatics to do what they did."

"There you go ag'in, readin' things into that event that just ain't true."

"Why ain't, er, isn't that true, Carl?" Paul countered, trying to maintain his learned vernacular.

"Why, Allah is a false prophet! They worship a false god

Ron Stauffer

over there!"

"You are one loony puppy dog. You have puke all over your brain!" Paul shook his head, remembering, now the discussion they had after church the week before.

"It's in Scrip'ure."

Some of what Carl said was true, he thought to himself. A lot of people – mostly fundamentalists – actually believed what Falwell had blurted out on Robertson's '700 Club' show several days after those two airline jets crashed into the twin towers of the World Trade Center. The Cultural War had taken its toll in America, where freedom of the people all began. We had been the envy of the world as we flourished and grew into the greatest nation on Earth. Other nations soon mimicked our Constitution in re-writing theirs. Most all of Europe, Japan and the Americas followed suit in establishing Philadelphia Freedom. Our founding fathers had established a wall separating religion from government.

His love of reading history and biographies had augmented his formal education, but there were few in his class, or, indeed, in the engineering school that agreed with his growing liberal view of things in general. As Ayn Rand had put it '. . . to some degree, *everyone* is an intellectual.' He now recognized her meaning, though he felt very far from being a C. P. Snow or a Bertrand Russell. But too many considered mind improvement to be silly. What was necessary was a good paying job, and the ability to go anywhere and do anything one wanted. Too few found books exciting like he did; the rapture of following the adventure of another life in another time period was lost on the many who preferred mind numbing television. But it was the non-readers, the anti-intellectuals that railed most about the way things were. It was, to them, a travesty, that only the nation's judicial system seemed out of step with the majority's

48

sentiments. Of the three branches of government, the Judicial was aloof to the outcry of the country against minorities that seemed always to get their way.

The American Civil Liberties Union (ACLU) was particularly vilified because of it's constant stand against the violations of the Constitution's Bill of Rights. One Pennsylvania congressman went so far as to announce before a crowd of several thousand that had gathered to support a petition to renounce Michael Newdow's complaint about the words 'under God' being unconstitutionally added to the *Pledge of Allegiance*: '. . . we are against the tyranny of the Minority!' That congressman was a fitted shoe replacement of his father in a Republican District that had never voted Democratic, even during Franklin Roosevelt's four term progressive and protective era.

The executive and legislative branches of the government were vulnerable to populism and demagoguery, and the smoothest talking, best looking, sacred-cow protecting candidate always won. He remembered what H. L. Mencken once said: 'The men the American people admire most extravagantly are the most daring liars; the men they detest most violently are those who try to tell them the truth.' Woe to the candidate who advocates sincere support for the needy and for education, or taxation of church property—he would be just too sensible, or progressive, endangering the status quo. These same conservatives, in their next breath, extol the virtues of the founding fathers, not cognizant of the fact that they were, indeed, progressives. They will not admit that it required much *progressive* action to unseat a mother country like Great Britain. And the Constitutional Congress of 1787 was about as progressive as the political world would ever get, with the conception of the United States' new Constitution. Yet, upon asking any conservative whether the

Constitution should be altered to allow less protection for minorities, there is an overwhelming chorus of 'No, our Constitution has been ordained and blessed by God.' It is next to Biblical Scripture in reverence by *all* of its citizenry. He enjoyed John Stuart Mill's observation concerning conservatives: *'Though it is not true that all conservatives are stupid, it IS true that most stupid people are conservative.'* That quote was not well received when he called in to the local conservative talk show.

"Other than the Bush bashing, what d'ya think of my idea?"

"Gimme some time ta think about it." Carl downed the remainder of his mug. "We better hit the pike if we're to get back ta Corbin safe."

VIII

Orientation

Paul was in awe during his first day of Army post-graduate school at Carlisle. His class of 24 mostly junior grade officers was 70% – 30 % male majority. He was struck by the comeliness of some of the women. That first day of orientation was an eye-opener concerning educational opportunity and the scope of the curriculums. However, his orders required him to take the special course on Cultural Politics in War Theaters. He would not be eligible to take other electives in U. S Government Operation. He did reflect though, that fate had been kind to him in winning *this* twelve week special billet, which materialized to fill a need for understanding other cultures. And if he performed at a B average or better, he might qualify for another twelve weeks of advanced work there – at the outskirts of a small, sleepy city 20 miles west of Harrisburg, Pennsylvania's capital.

To him, Carlisle was a metropolis compared to his hometown. There was adequate transportation to Harrisburg—both civilian and military. The local citizens were proud of their historic town being the location of one of the World's finest post-graduate military schools. And, though Harrisburg resembled Lexington / Frankfort in population and seat of government, it was much closer than his boyhood home had been to the latter – plus the fact it had excellent commuter rail connections to Philadelphia, and New York.

He noticed that there was quite a cross section of officers

from the Navy, as well as the Army, including a Marine Warrant Officer. In front of him sat a woman Army Lieutenant with striking red hair. He was a push over for redheaded women, and her hair was not much different than that of Carrolyn's.

Pen and note pad had been placed on each of 24 desk tops, and he started writing on his as the instructor kept voicing dos and don'ts of the complex . . . what time the mess would be serving, and the "O" Club hours. He had checked into the BOQ the afternoon before, and found his room comfortable. It was austere, containing a single twin bed and a latrine that was shared with the adjoining room. That intervening space also contained a vanity with sink for each room in order to lessen Early morning wash-up traffic. Smoking was allowed outdoors only, but since he only smoked on occasion, was not bothered by the inconvenience. He considered himself very lucky that he could easily regulate his smoking and drinking, as opposed to many other men who seemed to be, too much, under the control of those substances. And he didn't really mind second hand smoke as long as it didn't offend his eyes.

At coffee break, he surveyed his colleagues and found them a typical blend of the Officer Corps. There were several that had rugged, chiseled features – the Warrant Officer especially -- and there were the office-pinky types, balding with the start of a paunch. The lady who sat at the desk in front of him was even more striking as she leaned forward to draw some coffee from the silver- plated urn. He wanted to introduce himself but found he had been pre-empted by one of the office-pinky types. 'There's plenty of time' he thought – and anyway he was still awash with memories of Carrolyn. Indeed, he had dreamed of her overnight that, in a way, obviously stimulated his interest in the opposite sex. *That* was one drive he found difficult to control, especially after his steamy relationship with his first intimate love.

Classes broke up at 16:00 hours and it seemed all the men, Paul included, headed for the Officers Club. That oasis like attachment to any military complex was an on-base escape from rather mundane classroom lectures and confining protocol. It was perhaps the one true place where an officer could speak his mind and mask his latent intent with the excuse he was 'under the influence.' Still, he found it wise not to abuse that privilege on a regular basis, lest he be branded a pariah. And he found it difficult to steer "O" Club bull sessions from the talk of sports or NASCAR races – except around election time when his colleagues' politics surfaced somewhat.

He sat alone at a corner table observing classmates and faculty as they rolled dice for drinks at the bar. Several who were previously acquainted shared a table here and there, but he knew none of the participants in this place. None of the women were present, which didn't surprise him; tradition unofficially required women to be escorted into such a den of iniquity.

But he *wasn't* alone. His memories of Carrolyn always drifted to the fore when he had the time to luxuriate in them. The bottle of Heineken assisted his reverie, and he caught himself smiling -- and then feeling sad -- as the parade of their time together unfolded again amid his relaxed, imbibing trance. Though he was sitting by himself, he felt comfortable in his significance – in his personal mission that he viewed so plainly as a goal -- he would be a vociferous member of a *growing* minority of really independent thinkers.

If changing the election mores of American politics was his adopted mission, what would be the opposition – if any? There was always the conservative status quo that accepted change as if their thumbnails were being extracted. They superficially played by the rules, but their mistakes and gross improprieties underscored their vulnerability. Their constituency was large and subject to believing anything said by the leadership against liberals as gospel. Mysteriously, they were much influenced by defrocked firebrands like Ollie North, Pat Robertson, Colson Jones, G. Gordon Liddy and Rush Limbaugh – radio commentators all, who preached. sermonettes about '*Do as I say, not as I did..*' They were a confused bunch, not prone to action – complaining minions who often had difficulty keeping their tongues out from underfoot.

The real hard-line opposition, he thought, might be the extreme orthodox of militant churches like the fundamentalist evangelicals, Catholics, and, to a lesser, disjointed degree, the Mormons, not to mention the forces of Jihad. Fundamentalists preferred to be called *Evangelicals* so as not to be confused with the Taliban or Shi'ites from '*over there.*' His thoughts wandered to the more arcane conservative Catholic groups like *Opus Dei* and the *Jesuits* who he suspected as being the preservers of the faith – possibly, by *any* means. Religion was a very personal possession, but these entities scoffed at the notion of state and religion separation, and worked continually and shamelessly to its dissolution. Professional politicians found them to be a convenient ally, oblivious to the violation of the Constitution's original intent.

Too often, it seemed, religion became the common denominator in his thoughts. Was he *obsessed* with ecclesiastical excesses and interference? Of course maintenance of the *status quo* would be his enemy, and what was more representative of the status quo than religion? However, religion would probably not interfere with any constructive modification of candidate selection.

But he disliked religion; did not trust religion; despised its fluffy promises that really *anyone* could make and not be held accountable. He identified very much with the statement Professor Massimo Pigliucci, Professor of evolutionary biology at Tennessee, once said: *'Why is it that we cannot face the simple truth? Religion is at best unsubstantiated superstition.'* Or what Clarence Darrow of Scopes Monkey Trial fame said: *'The modern world is the child of doubt and inquiry, as the ancient world was the child of fear and faith.'*

But what raised the hairs on the back of his neck the most were the insidious, not-so-subtle actions of a phantom group called the *Phineas Priests*. They were vigilantes of the 'nth order, which glorified in continuing the violence associated with the Old Testament. They interpreted the messages of that tome in a very narrow way, exacting what they deemed as justice, in accordance to Scripture. He suspected that the Reverend Fred Phelps of Wichita was a member, the way he vilified homosexuals, protest marching at their funerals when they died of AIDS or were murdered. An attorney, turned preacher, knew how far he could ratchet-up fear without violating the law.

And *fear i*s what it is all about! Learning from the ubiquitous clergy, fear had become an available tool in the hands of the politicians. It wasn't so much what they knew about the office they were running for, but how to corner and cow the opponent whose intentions in many cases were more honorable. A good example is the proposed Constitutional amendment to outlaw the burning of the Flag. The conservative fear-mongers have the less committed libertarians on the run for their political lives, trying to explain that they were just as patriotic, which only detracted from the fact that if the amendment was approved, it would be a lost freedom of expression. But patriotism plays in Peoria when you *defend* the flag -- the populace not understanding that a harmless burning of a piece of cloth is preferable to more violent forms of protests.

The same was true with Dr. Michael Newdow's petition to have '*under God*' removed from the Pledge of Allegiance. When the Ninth Circuit Court found in his favor, upholding the First Amendment's establishment clause, every member of Congress gathered on the Capitol's steps the very next day, to recite the Pledge in its uncut entirety. Woe to the politician who would ignore God by not showing up! Those members of Congress stuck in traffic called on their cell phones that they would be at the recital as soon as possible -- most would rather miss their child's recital than this one. It was demagoguery in its finest hour!

Somehow, honor had to be restored to that branch of government, as well as to the Executive. His thoughts on establishing an examination intent on weeding out the whining populists might not pass Constitutional muster, though – the electorate had the right to vote for glossy dumbness! The politician was becoming the last of the 'confidence men,' or was it a new trend toward national nihilism? Polls indicated that politicians were now at the bottom of the heap in the category of trustworthiness, next to used car salesmen and lawyers. Gone forever it seemed, were '*Profiles in Courage.*' The consummate politician *traded* on the fear of the unknown, fear of terrorists, fear of liberals that would supposedly expose our flanks, fear of laws that would upset what '*good*' things we have now. Slowly vanishing was the national acclaim of '. . . *home of the brave and the land of the free.*' The country was becoming what many abroad often thought: a nation of spoiled, fearful whiners instead of intrepid, can-do Americans.

IX

The Party (1)

With orientation over, and reading assignments issued, formal classes were dismissed for the end of year holidays. His class was strongly advised, however, to research some of their assignments at the Penn State – Dickinson School of Law library, there, in Carlisle, in the interim.

Not wishing to rush home to the inevitable clashes of opinion, and eager to get a head start on learning political science, he opted to stay at the BOQ a few days to do research and study.

12-16-05

The library was intimidating in its strobing blandness. Volume after volume of State and Federal statutes and opinions presented a seeming wall of obfuscation. 'Thank the nerds for computers' he thought, as he honed in on the particulars of his assignments.

During a restroom break, he stopped at the bulletin board in the hallway, noting a colored map. He liked maps, especially the multi-colored geological maps that vividly portrayed rock inclines and anti-clines. But this was a map showing the environs of York, Pennsylvania, which was about thirty miles to the southeast of the school. Various routes were highlighted in different colors as how to reach a certain destination north of that city called Mt. Zion – of all names. At the top of the map it announced PAN SOLSTICE

PARTY Saturday Dec. 17.

'Ah, the Winter Solstice,' he thought. He read on to see that it was sponsored by the Pennsylvania Non-Believers, Inc., a group of freethinkers, agnostics and atheists. That would be tomorrow night, he realized, and began copying directions how to get there. He was excited that there was a group of like-minded people that were actually organized – the first time a group like this had come to his attention. He knew from his reading that atheists and agnostics existed everywhere – it was just that they never advertised their presence. It was not made a big thing because most were quite content with their self-assurance, and it would only invite pity or ridicule from the religious. But he realized that something had to be done to show the mentally deluded that not everyone was ready to cave in on the church / state separation thing. Maybe groups like PAN underwrite such activism.

12-17-05

The party turned out to be a normal social gathering of animated talkers, mostly of middle age. The bar downstairs was well stocked with mind numbing beverages but no one seemed under the influence. The pool table was occupied by some jokers, and the dartboard was vacant. The few teenagers present were banging away at a pinball machine. He took a Yuengling Lager back upstairs where the more animated conversations seemed to be occurring. Earlier, he had been introduced around by Arlee Hartman, who was the gracious host, along with his good looking, charming wife, Natasha.

Now there were new comers he hadn't met; one of them that caught his eye was dressed as an Arab and was handing out gold coins – chocolate wrapped in gold foil, and saying it was a gift from Haliburton. He heard bells and looked to see what might be a gay man crossing the room with sleigh bells on his shoes. There were Doctors (the joking Arab who wore the headdress to cover hair loss), nurses, lawyers, teachers, engineers, clerks, secretaries and military veterans.

Their laid-back demeanor was impressive, saying to him, we are content if not happy, we are serene if not enraptured by the goings-on in the world today. We are *here, in-your-face,* and not going away! He left the kitchen/dining area and entered the living room where one wall was dominated by a new entertainment system, turned on to a bowl game – it was as vivid as being on the fifty-yard line. At the opposite end of the large room, there were three women seated on a luxurious corner settee. They appeared to be deep in conversation, but the one on the right looked familiar. Paul circumnavigated the football game viewers and halved his distance of view. It was *her*! It was Erin – the redhead who sat in front of him in the orientation class at school. He had learned of her name from class roll call.

He rubbed his eyes in total disbelief. A like-minded *looker*! He could not believe his good fortune. Closing the distance in a trance, he tripped over a black cat that was scurrying toward some quiet refuge, and spilled some of his beer on the carpet where he landed. Erin looked up and recognized him.

"I know you," she said, as he looked up sheepishly into her face from the prone position. "Are you all-right?" She didn't know his name.

"Quite . . . okay, I think," he muttered, trying to sound intelligent.

Arlee crossed the room and helped him up. "Paul, I should have warned you about the cats!"

"I wasn't looking where I was goin' . . . I mean walking."
He sounded like an idiot, he thought.

"You're Lieutenant Paul Beck___ . . ."

"Beckwith, ma'am. Paul Beckwith."

"…from the War College, right?"

"Yes'um," he said, forgetting to mask his Kentucky
drawl.

"Ah, you two know each other?" Arlee intervened,
relieved that the young man was unhurt.

"Sorry 'bout the beer."

"Oh, it happens all the time with this motley crowd."
Arlee smiled. "Beer adds luster to the carpet."

"Really?"

"That's what they say." Arlee added with a grin bordering
on the mischievous. "So you're a warrior from Carlisle . . .
like Erin, here?"

"Yeah, though I'm originally from Kentucky."

"I thought I recognized a southern accent." Arlee
continued, "Bill over there is from West Virginia."

"I'll have to talk to 'im." Paul answered, hoping for
another chance to talk with Erin.

"How did you find out about the party?" She piped up.
"Did you see the sign I posted?"

"That was your sign?" He asked in surprise.

"Yeah . . . Arlee sends out these nice maps, and I thought
it would be interesting to post it in the austere surroundings of
that library – if nothing more, to raise eyebrows. I couldn't
do it at the War College."

"Well, it raised my eyebrows, for sure."

"So, you're a free-thinker, or have you come here to spy
on me?"

"Guilty on both counts, your honor." He said with a poker
face. "I was dyin' to meet you . . . ever since orientation

day." He smiled sheepishly, now that it was out.

"Then you are not a spy from the DIA?"

"What must I do to convince you?" he sensed the slightest hint of a challenge.

"Let's see . . ." She furled her brows in straight-faced thought. "Who was the great 19th century atheist activist – who was also a Colonel in the Civil War?"

"Robert Ingersoll!" he answered without a blink.

"You could have been prepped for that question." She teased. "Answer this and I'll buy you a drink, soldier."

"Shoot."

"The name of the children's free-thought summer camp in Alabama . . . it's named for a woman?"

Not familiar with free-thought organizations, he begged more information, hoping that he had twenty questions.

"She headed up a library that was destroyed by religious nuts."

"Would that be . . . Hypatia -- the Library at Alexandria?"

Her light blue eyes brightened as she announced, "You pass muster, soldier. Now what is your poison . . ." she looked down "as it seems you have spilled your drink?"

The Doctor who was dressed like an Arab overheard the banter and chided, "Erin, you're so tough! The poor guy obviously just wants to make time with you."

"A Woman has to be careful these days," she answered demurely.

"Pshaw, this guy is no shill for the Christians . . . he took my bribe of gold coins and *thanked* me. He's too polite to be one of *them*!"

"All-right . . . if you say so."

The slightly inebriated doctor made a flowing motion with his robes, raised his nose and moved on, quite satisfied with his efforts.

Paul was intoxicated himself, marveling at the light humor of the exchange with the complete strangers. They seemed so at ease, and made him feel at ease – so welcome.

"Soldier, just go down those stairs and mention my name to the barkeep . . . and he'll get you anything you want to drink." She left him to get something to eat.

Retreat was in order, he thought. Not a very auspicious beginning he thought again, in his descent to the basement bar. West Virgina Bill had made it to the bar before him and was sipping a Heineken at the end stool.

"I've been told you're from hill country?" Paul introduced himself.

"Yeah, workin' in Maryland, now." Bill answered. "What part of Kentucky, did you say?"

"Corbin . . . Where the Colonel started frying chicken."

"Love that stuff, man!"

"So what brings you down to the flat lands?"

"My woman's from New Jersey, so we kinda compromised, she being a purchasing agent an' all." He was skinny, accentuating his height, and affable; his goatee gave him a devilish look when he smiled. "She's down south just now."

"My first time at an organized heretics meetin'" Paul said.

"Great that you could make it."

"So, how'd you come 'bout your persuasion?"

"You mean the religion thing?" His dark eyes glistened. "Got tar'd of mah dad's preachin'. I was brought up in real backwoods fundamentalist area and . . . it just got the better of me, the hypocrisy an' all. Joined the Navy and saw how the rest of the world was . . . an' I never looked back." He sipped some of his beer, and with bottle in hand added. "I foun' that this world ain't so bad after all . . . it's a really pretty *cool* place!" After another sip, he asked, "And you?"

Paul gladly released his pent-up observations of life – never having been asked to do so before. He ordered another Yuengling and awaited Bill's response. "That's a pretty good tastin' beer!"

"Yeah, it is. It's brewed not too far from here . . . up the river I think. I understand it's America's oldest brewery." The response was a question, "So yur an officer and a gentleman?"

"I try."

"That's *cool,* that's cool!" He continued, "I think our membership includes a gal who's an army officer. . . an' we have an FBI agent."

"Really?"

"Yep. And he's a ball-of-fire of an activist."

"I think Erin, upstairs . . . the gal you mentioned, is at the Carlisle War College, where I'm assigned."

"Yeah, that's right. If I wasn't already involved, I'd be bird-doggin' her."

"Guess that leaves me free to try." Paul smiled. "She from around these parts?"

"Yeah, Wrightsville . . . on the Susquehanna. She's one of the charter members when PAN started up."

"Why'd she join the army?"

"Beats me! You'll have to ask her."

X

The Party (2)

I *will* ask her, he thought. And he thought better about having another bottle of beer if *that* was his intent. After a polite interval of time he excused himself from the conversation, feigning that he was hungry. Upstairs, he immediately noticed two newcomers dressed as a nun and priest. Like the Arab dressed doctor, they were mingling with the crowd handing out what appeared to be religious tracts they carried in little black shopping bags. The nun's bag had a sign on it asking: *WHAT DO ALTAR BOYS HAVE THAT I DON'T HAVE?*

Paul neared the priest who smiled and handed him an orange square of construction paper with gothic lettering on it:

> "There she lusted after
> her lovers,
> whose genitals were like
> those of donkeys
> and whose emission
> was like that of horses."
> *Ezekiel 23:20*

He smiled to himself, thinking these people are having so much fun. Looking around, he finally spotted Erin talking to the hostess. This time no mistakes, he promised himself, as he wandered over in their direction. She was even more striking standing erect; her close cropped red hair accentuated her yellow dress which conversely, hinted of supple breasts. She was looking his way now, and seemed eager to say something.

"I'm glad you saw my map."

"I am too. This is a *great* party!"

"So you're a heretic from the South *and* an officer in this-man's-Army! Wow, you don't see *that* very often."

"Kentucky is a border state." He reminded her.

"Oh, yes . . . I forgot," She smiled. "Please forgive me."

"Sooo, what makes a foxy-lookin' gal like *you* join up?"

"Eager to see the world at government expense, I s'pose . . . and get out of Wrightsville."

"Wut's your field o' study?" he absently blurted in his old drawl.

Recalling Russell Crowe's performance and accent in "*A Beautiful Mind*" she found his native dialect charming. "Library Science and History."

"Really!" he gushed. "I love history."

"And libraries too, I surmise . . . or you would have never seen my map."

" This is quite an idea," he said looking around at the festive group, " . . . of celebrating the Solstice instead of Christmas."

"Why not? Whether they know it or don't, Christians have really adopted one of our cherished phenomena."

"True."

"But they haven't figured out what to do on the Summer Solstice yet," she added.

"You mean . . . you guys party on June twenty-second, too?"

"Absolutely . . . on a Saturday 'round about."

He thought for a moment. "Probably, the Christians

aren't likely to adopt that area of the calendar as the heat might be too close to representing Hell."

She smiled.

They found a couple of chairs and talked about the War College. Erin was interested in cataloguing possible al-Qaeda targets in and around military installations. Like him, she had lobbied for her assignment and placement at Carlisle, seeing the academic need for anticipating the enemy.

"Do you think this is a religious war?" Paul asked.

"Oh, *yeah*!" she emphasized. "Don't you?"

"So many at the top are in denial." He went on, "They haven't a clue! The new administration isn't much better, but at least they're stroking a lot of ruffled feathers."

"The Democrats are really the left wing of the Republican Party. Religion is truly a *sacred cow*, no one wants to touch it . . . bring it up as the great repository of malaise and stagnation that it is."

"The symptoms have been around for centuries . . . millennia. Just look at the social and economics of the countries in Latin America, Italy, and Iberia. The Catholic Church is extracting extortion from the subdued populace in exchange for a dream ticket to heavenly bliss."

"What a racket – it's a confidence game." She agreed. "And all of it is offered to the ignorant and uninformed in such ornate pageantry and piety . . . under the cloak of doing good."

"I believe it is the mysterious pageantry that hooks them . . . kind of like a mental opiate that plays to human's innate desire for conspiratorial possibilities."

"And UFO's, and Loch Ness Monsters, and the Abominable Snowman . . ."

The evangelists for profit were dissected, especially those who had tried to make a comeback -- Franklin Graham's and

Jerry Falwell's vilification of the Muslims.

They talked on about the various cults that strangely appealed to the confused, like Jim Jones's People's Temple, Heaven's gate, the Branch Davidians. "What was the name of those Texas fundamentalists who went to Israel at the turn of the century, to hurry along the Second Coming?"

"I believe they are known as the '*Concerned Christians.*' And they were from Colorado, not Texas. My unit would like to find out more about them."

"You mean, they're still in existence?"

"Yeah, they were arrested and deported from Israel . . . some went to Greece, where they were again deported. It is believed they are in the Philadelphia area now."

"What do you know about the Phineas Priests?" Paul asked. "They *really* scare me."

"As they should . . . scare anyone." Her pretty, wide eyes narrowed in their intensity. "

They're pretty way out," she intoned a declarative phrase like a question, which was increasingly fashionable. "Their actions appear to be uncoordinated in that there appears to be no set leader or definable group. But attacks have been made against interracial couples, homosexuals, and Semites by fanatical fundamentalists calling themselves *Phineas Priests.* They may have taken their cue from white supremacist Richard Kelly's books that appeared about 1990. They could be *anywhere*!"

"And they are driven by a Biblical Message?"

"Numbers, I believe . . . somehow these nuts always finds some passage in the Old Testament that excites their neurons."

His neurons were excited -- excited by the scope of this woman's knowledge. He had always found intelligent, no-nonsense women sexually appealing. Often, the terms 'bitchy' and 'feminist' were used by other men whose machismo seemed threatened by assertive women -- he couldn't understand why. 'Of course they're different – women are *supposed* to be different -- to enhance that lure for the male gender.' He contemplated. But being smart thinkers, smarter than them, was a turn-off for many men.

Their conversation continued well into the evening as other free-thinkers joined in their conversation and then drifted on. The priest and the nun offered them more bits of paper with seldom cited Biblical quotes. Introducing themselves to be from the central part of the state, they talked awhile, then exchanged e-mail addresses with him before they left. The Arab and a few of his disciples spoke in lewd undertones about some of the world's deluded leaders before they drifted away for more pizza.

Arlee came by and, putting his hand on Paul's shoulder, chided him for monopolizing Erin most of the evening. "Had the military had women of Erin's looks when I was younger, I would have joined up! I envy that you two have so much in common," he said with that devilish grin.

Erin, stole a look at her watch.

"Arlee's right, I have buttonholed you too long, so I'm going down to the bar and see what's happenin'"

"I've enjoyed our little talk," she answered sincerely.

"We'll have to get together for coffee or lunch at the school."

"That would be nice," she said before turning to Arlee.

XI

(Recurring Dream)

He felt a buzz when his head hit the pillow, but it wasn't from the few beers he had. His meeting Erin seemed to have been the intoxicating element. But the room's ceiling didn't rotate like it did when he had too much to drink. . .

Hearing Mr. Clemens speak was more entertaining than he anticipated. This was truly a heavenly place he thought as he gleaned every word, every inflection of the sage's Midwestern twang. " . . . and please don't be surprised if an elephant crosses your path – it will not fall from here and take you with it, as that phenomenon of gravity, here, is being studied even as I speak." He took a long puff on his cigar before continuing. "You see, we know so very little of this place – hardly understanding . . . why we are here. Some think it is our due reward for living a tolerably moderate life, being reasonably tolerant of the aberrations that abounded below. But it may be dangerous to arrive at such venal conclusions, seeing that most if not all of us got here by not makin' such venal conclusions."

Another puff, and he slowly strutted stage right. "Now, we're not sure that this is all a dream. Certain characteristics of this place do not fall into the dream category, like. . . we have died but are still in communication with others – here, of course. We have died, sufferin' pain in most cases, but are now experiencing wonderful numbness . . . and the ability to conjure up certain senses. But to answer the question of a few of the lustier of you out there: 'will I regain *all* my *preferred* senses?' I am not at liberty to say, since that is a terribly personal area that I rarely spoke or wrote about in even my better previous days. All I can say is, you're on your own in that category. But, I remind you that continual indiscretion is not what got you here!" the group laughed as he paused for another puff on that cigar.

"Indiscretion – that mighty propensity to brag about this and that, and conquests of the opposite gender, has taken its toll even *here*! Several have dropped from sight, never to be heard from again, because of various indiscretions that affected others' supposed reputation." Returning to stage left, he continued: "But a few of you have been in wonderment about the whereabouts of your loved ones. I can only tell you this: you will see them; you will be with them; but only as you desire. And not everyone of you will be able to conjure them up, if in fact the object of your desire did not achieve this plane. Not to mention names, but a tall, former American president is almost always alone, as he was in the past. Right now, it is too Early in your new situation to feel *that* desire – no more on that, so forget for now what I just explained." There was more laughter.

Was this a dream or some self-deluding trance complete with hypnotism? Was this a state of incongruity that flowed out of the subconscious that with *final effort* reached out to one's desires and aspirations? Was this all a trick of the mind in the early stages of death and decomposition, sort of like the physical death rattle and muscular twitches that often were evident? It is true, he felt no compulsion to be with the opposite sex, but was relieved to hear that that was a possibility.

"Mr. Einstein has corroborated Sir Isaac Newton's study of *this* gravity and they found that it is *not* gravity at all, but somethin' similar that makes us stick somewhat to one place.

Of course, Gallileo, the recalcitrant he has always been, disagrees. So there you have it – how far we've advanced science in this place. The fun seems to be in the findin' out – just like on Earth. Indeed, it seems that we have graduated to a more complex location where the problem solvin' is more challengin'. Those of you who love puzzles will enjoy working at them here." He stopped his pacing and turned to us, his cigar held at a safe distance from his side. "One thing, though, and then I must leave: there is no Internet! The particulars of that concept have not been worked out in this realm of undulatin' ether – that's what I call it much to the consternation of Messgrs Oppenheimer and Einstein who seem just about as perplexed as I. They anticipate the arrival of a certain William Gates and some politician named Al Gore to assist in unravelin' the complexities and promoting what *they* call 'Cyberspace-to-the-2nd power.' So all research, reading and puzzle solving will have to be in tune with your own personal writin' and cypherin' abilities."

Paul followed some of the new arrivals back toward Library Central. He was now thinking about his project on Earth, the one he was working on when he died. Killed? He remembered little of the event now, as he looked back. In fact, the more he tried to replay that terrible time, less of it would retrieve – like a poorly remembered dream. He did recall that he wasn't all that old, and that he was making some headway lobbying influential and honorable legislators across the country to initiate some clearinghouse of elective office seekers – legislator wannabes. Was his demise in relation to that? He couldn't remember. It was all like a dream . . .

XII

Live and Let Live

12-18-05

He awoke with a start. It was that dream about what he remembered explaining to Carl about Deists. 'Wow, what entertainment . . . and validation of my thinkin' Paul muttered to himself. And the party – talking with Erin, excited him; he was in love with life. Never had he felt so vibrant with purpose.

After breakfast, he pored over his course outlines and made a critical path flow chart of efforts he proposed to achieve before classes started again in January. He was determined to make the cut and qualify for the second term, especially since a potential soul mate would be likewise in attendance. 'Damn,' he winced, 'I didn't get her phone number or e-mail address. Oh well, I guess I can get it from Arlee and Natasha, since I got theirs'—if I even need it. With Christmas coming, she'll be busy, occupied with family and friends.

'*Friends*! What if she has a boyfriend! No engagement ring on her finger – and she wasn't with anyone at the party', he remembered, letting out a sigh of relief. 'Maybe I should call her to see if she'd like to go out New Years Eve' he considered. 'Well, maybe Natasha could fill me in a little about her since she seemed real familiar with her.' He stopped daydreaming about his budding social calendar and got back to his outlines.

Classes commenced again on the 2nd of January amidst a Nor'easter snowstorm. He had only to walk to class from the BOQ, which wasn't too bad since the walkways were continually cleared by maintenance. Erin came into his thoughts, remembering how she had politely turned down his request for a date. He didn't know why – she had just said that she already had plans. 'Well, it was short notice' he allowed. 'Competition makes the prize that much more challenging.'

The classroom was filling up when she entered. He thought he caught a demure smile toward him as she turned to sit down. But she took a seat *across* the room, near the door – someone else occupied the desk in front of him. *Damn, no seating assignments were ever made – Chrisake, this isn't high school!* he chided himself.

At break time he approached her at the coffee urn. "How were the holidays?"

"Too long. And you?"

"Made it home for the 24th and 25th -- that was it."

"It's such a drag, family viewing you as a pariah because you no longer accept all that bullshit."

"You too?" He wasn't *really* surprised.

"What profanity!" a Navy Lieutenant standing nearby, declared.

Paul was irked that his attempt at small talk had been overheard – and interrupted.

"Name is Stevens, George Stevens." He announced with an air of complete disregard of amenity. "Hope I'm not interrupting," he said without a visible care of doing just that.

Damn Naval Officers . . . they all consider themselves budding Horatio Hornblowers, Paul thought.

"Erin," and she offered her hand.

"Paul Beckwith," as he followed suit. He stood quietly as

73

Erin tactfully led the superior officer on a circuitous explanation of her overheard expletive.

Later, at lunch, Paul made a concerted effort to be with Erin. She was sitting alone at a small table, and the Naval officer was not yet through the line.

"May I join you, fair heretic?" he asked, approaching her table.

"Please do."

"That was quite a subterfuge you used on that Stevens guy."

"He's not ready for the truth."

"Wow, you're tough!" Paul blurted, unable to conceal his admiration.

"Shhh, there he is."

The tall Naval officer made his way in their direction. Seeing that their table wasn't quite big enough for a third, reconnoitering the situation from a distance, he moved on to where some other junior officers chatted nearby.

"Whew, that was close! He probably ran some tugboat aground on a reef somewhere and, as punishment, has been sent here to annoy us," Paul heard himself joke.

She laughed, smiling at him. "You're a funny guy."

Feeling on confident ground, he bit into his sandwich.

"Oh . . . I forgot to say grace." He looked up at her sheepishly.

She laughed again. "You should be ashamed of yourself."

"It's a wonder they don't broadcast some kind of blessing over the PA system . . . along with the Pledge of Allegiance."

"Not too loud," she invoked. "They just might take up your suggestion."

"You know, it just enervates me to no end how they can justify the addition of 'under God' in the *Pledge,* as non-

74

inclusive as the original Pledge was, in one breath, and then in another breath deny gay and lesbian marriage as not being the original intent of matrimony."

"I *know*!"

"Not that I am of *that* persuasion, mind you. . . I was pretty homophobic myself at one time." He searched for some acceptable escape from hypocritical judgment.

"I know . . . me too." She allowed. "It's a fair conundrum that we must accept, if we, ourselves, live by the dictum 'Live and let live."

"It's a tough world." He went on, subtly realizing that he had acquired her heart. "Why juxtapose anymore severity on an already befuddled world?"

"Have you seen any Broadway Shows?" she asked out of the blue.

"No . . . can't say that I have."

"But . . . it seems that you *have*!" she empathized. "*'Fiddler on the roof', the Man of La Mancha,' Annie',' South Pacific,'* you've never seen any of 'em?"

"Yep, I saw the movie *'South Pacific'* and *'West Side Story.'*

"And what impact did they have on you?"

"Tremendous impact. I think that's where I found the soft spot in my heart for . . . for contrarian views – for alternative opinions on questions that are not so easily answered in conversation."

"They are all stories of social inequity. As the world shrinks, cultures begin to intrude on each other."

He agreed. "Parochialism is right up there, hand-in-hand with xenophobia."

"The world must absorb this culture shock with more empathy than has been shown in the past. Nine-one-one has underscored that necessity!"

"Do you really think so?   Look around at the retreat to fetal piety."

"I suppose you're right.   It seems to have galvanized *everyone's* belief model . . . ours as well as theirs."

There was quiet as they both reflected – and ate their lunch.

Finally, she asks, "So where do you go . . . from here?'

"I guess . . ." he asks, "Can I see you again?"

"Your place, or my place?" She accedes.

XIII

The Rendezvous

1-6-06

Both of their places were bachelor officer quarters – hardly conducive to initiating an intimate get-together. Friday evening found them checking into a secluded motel separated from the remainder of the world by great evergreen and cedar trees. It was more than the young couple could have hoped for: wildlife pastoral scenes adorned the walls while mirrors everywhere, including the ceiling, concealed nothing. Finally left alone by the unassuming Innkeeper, they embraced in total relief.

During the holidays, he had looked around the town for some place like this where he might romance Erin if their relationship evolved as he hoped it would. During their lunch, he had suggested meeting later in the week for Dinner, at a small Mexican restaurant in town. The week passed slowly enough, but he was in the clouds with anticipation of their approaching date. Their chemistry – both biological and intellectual – mingled well in the interim, and here they were in each others' arms. She was delighted when he had presented her with a single red rose.

"Ah, no Early reveille," he sighed, after a long kiss.

"That's enough of the small talk, soldier" she winked. "Now, get out of your uniform."

"But I'm not in uniform!"

"Anything covering your body is a uniform to me, pal."

Without hesitation he submitted to her unexpected demand, peeling clothes off in 'double-time.' "Wow, you're a fast women!" He looked up to see the unveiling of wonderfully pert and ample white breasts.

"You like, soldia' boy?" she teased in mock-oriental accent, while holding the rose between them."

He was struck by her sudden switch from demure discretion to bawdyhouse demeanor.

"You free-thinkin' women are a mind-boggle of surprises."

"Why should men have all the fun of seduction?" She laid the rose down.

"It does eliminate many of the barriers." He said, nuzzling her nose, and then each of her nipples, pausing ever so slightly before engaging each bud for a longer revisit.

They fairly toppled onto the bed, as he tasted the recesses of her fair neck, here and there, as if it were a delicious morsel that might disappear at any moment.

"My, you are quite a hungry . . . and horny guy," she said, taking his protruding organ into her hand. "How long has it *been*?"

Feeling all aglow, he looked into her eyes and reluctantly imparted to her, "Not since my first love . . . she was killed in an accident while I was in college."

"I'm so *sorry*," she said, suddenly experiencing a rare sense of guilt.

"That was a long time ago." He shrugged. "Now, I have you!"

"And I have you!" she smiled as she swayed his schwanz from side to side. "My, you are so slippery wet! I hope he is crying out of happiness."

"Sheer happiness, me lady!" he said, guiding it towards its objective. "May I, or should I put on a condom?"

"It's all right . . . I'm on the pill . . ." she uttered, her eyes nearly closed in rapture.

They laid together in sweet embrace, kissing, and kissing again. On occasion, he visited each of her budded nipples, licking, nibbling and sucking as if at a sumptuously arrayed table.

He was amazed at his self-control as she moved under him, and they subtly wrestled into new and delightful positions. "You sure know how to show a gal a good time." She whispered while sticking her tongue in his ear. "A girl likes her man to have staying-power . . . I'm such a slow comer . . ."

"I surprise even myself . . . but you are so undemanding, so subtle in your movements!"

"As you are too."

Finally, atop him – the movement was too much and he involuntarily erupted in a momentous release.

She smiled at his convulsions of love and whispered, "Maybe next time we'll *come* together . . ."

"I'm sorry . . . it's been such a long time!"

"Don't apologize . . . it just takes me . . . a long time." She added, "It was wonderful . . . you were wonderful . . . all that I could imagine for a first time."

"I'll be alright shortly." Paul said, lamely.

"I certainly hope so." She smiled demurely, almost maternally. "The evening is still young."

They crawled between the sheets and warmly entangled. "I feel so comfortable with you." She purred.

He indicated likewise, and then they talked about classes. He explained his goal of instituting a qualification exam for wannabe candidates.

"Sounds awfully quixotic." She judged, propping her head and looking alternatively at each of his eyes. "You have such nice hazel eyes."

At the sound of her compliment, he felt a significant stirring below. "And you have such beautiful *blue* eyes!"

She could feel his organ growing against her and reached down to feel it. "And what is *this*, if I may ask?"

"It's my alter ego." He gloried in her deft attention to his enlarging detail. "We go back a long ways."

"It's certainly *long* . . . and big around. I can hardly get my fingers around him." Her attention to his now glistening rod only increased its hardness. ". . . and, oh so stiff!"

"Flattery will get you everywhere." He wanted her so much to experience orgasm, but was apprehensive about inviting himself into her again. "Would you allow me to . . ."

"Yeess?" she cooed, encouraging him to finish his sentence.

". . . *eat you*?"

"I thought you'd never ask." She smiled. "But first let me kiss your lifelong friend." And she bent over on him, and he kissed her marvelous hair while she sucked and stroked his member.

"Enough, *enough*." He cried, fearful that he would explode again. "Now it's my turn, you vixen." And he got down between her legs, promptly kissing the inside of her thighs, in their turn.

"Ooohh, that feels nice." She gasped as he closed the distance to her very wet cunt.

He tantalized her with kisses on her reddish mound, still ever so slightly closing the distance to the entrance of heaven. "I particularly like women with red hair," he said in a muffled tone. Now his tongue was brushing ever so lightly beneath her clit – then a little more pressure, and she squealed with delight.

"Oh, do it again," she pleaded. "It feels so good."

Hardly hearing her invitation because his ears were pressed tight by the softness of her thighs, he sensed her pleasure -- the vibration of her being as he stroked her clit again and again with the tip of his tongue. She writhed more and more as he kept licking the inch or so lower approach to her little darling. By this time, the top of her right foot was cradling his balls, and he hoped he could bring her to climax before his tool exploded. Her writhing and squealing grew in intensity and his yard grew harder and harder amidst his jiggled balls, until she arched her legs high, toward the ceiling gasping: "Oh my God! *My God*!" Vibrating and shaking her well shaped legs over his head, she intoned, "Oh Paul, *darling*! That was wonderful. What a wonderful tongue you have!" Seeing his hardness and wanting to please, she reached for his rock hard pecker and, turning her rump toward him, took him inside her, doggie style. "My, are *you* hard."

The coolness of her derriere against his abdomen was very pleasant, as she guided his entrance into her heavenly moist chamber. He knew he had gotten her off, and now he felt free to explore her vagina to his desire and inevitable conclusion. "Go for it, soldier boy." she invited while reaching down to fondle his balls. And he poked and prodded while she squeezed him, eliciting little noises of pleasure from her, until he finally experienced ejaculations of his sperm deep inside her.

"Oh, honey, that was wonderful. What a wonderful lover you are," she chirped. "You seem so *experienced* with your tongue!"

"It was my first time . . . *eating*, that is."

"And *my* first . . . being eaten . . . and tasting, *this*!" She delicately touched his receding charmer.

"I s'pose it comes natural . . . when you feel the way we

do 'bout each other." He didn't want to say *love* just yet. "I never thought I'd be lucky enough to experience intimate romance again." He said, holding back a tear of joy.

"You deserve to . . . and I'm so glad you enjoy me." She added with a glowing smile, "You must tell me about Carrolyn, sometime."

They fell quiet in each other's arms, and were soon asleep.

XIV

The Challenge

Classes were over for the day, and Paul prevailed upon Erin to join him for a drink at the Officer's Club. They were comparing their notes taken in class, when Lt. Stevens asked to join them. Permission, bordering on reluctance, was granted and he sat down "You guys are becoming quite an item."

"Is it *that* obvious?"

"I would say holding hands and kissing before and after class is *obvious*, especially in a military setting."

"Have we violated some code or other?" Paul pressed, ". . . because, if we have, we'll certainly correct our behavior seeing that you are a superior officer and have made *us* your business."

"Beckwith, it's an *unwritten* code of military conduct, like, a military man does not carry an umbrella." Lt. Stevens loved citing tradition – it was obvious from his classroom participation.

"If I said we would be more careful of showing affection in the future, will you go away?"

Not insulted easily, the naval officer continued, glaring at him, "And the other day, in the *mess*, profanity . . . your girlfriend here used an expletive."

Paul could hardly contain his glee when he saw the man had no chaplain's emblem on his collar. "A *sailor. . .* offended by an expletive! That's rich! Isn't that like the pot calling the kettle black?" Erin held back a giggle as some officers at the next table turned their heads.

At that, the straight-laced Lieutenant left them and went to the bar.

An officer at the next table leaned toward them and warned: "Take care . . . he's a real puritan . . . and if he can get you for anything – he'll nail ya."

The couple looked at each other with questioning eyes. Paul finally broke the silence,

"Nothin's easy, is it?"

"It's not too high a price to pay . . . staying out of *his* path." She offered. "We'll have to be more careful . . . I think he just read us the riot act."

"Yeah . . . and guys like him have friends in high places."

"It's best to assume that."

He smiled at her, saying, "But, on the other hand, we have each other . . . I feel I have everything. I s'pose we'll just have to be more discrete about it." He hesitated a moment, and then, looking into her eyes, he whispered, "I love you."

She blushed, and answered, "I love you, too."

Their concentration of course studies obviated the winter weather conditions, as well did their weekends together – holed up in the cozy motel, alternating between making love and studying. They complemented each other both spiritually and intellectually as they saw a future together unfold.

"Let's get married!" he blurted one Saturday.

"We're as good as married now," she answered. "But. It would be nice . . . and it would get us off Stevens' radar screen."

"Monday, I'll look into the availability of marital quarters. We'll make plans from there."

He found that an apartment efficiency was available on base, or they could qualify for a housing allowance off campus. To lock in the apartment, their marriage would have to be effected immediately.

"I guess a big wedding is not practical nor possible considering our alienation of family members." She rationalized.

"And we haven't much time." He added. "Are you sure this is what you want?"

"I'm sure," she snuggled up to him. "I've never been more sure of anything in my life."

"Too bad the Summer Solstice isn't near . . . we could marry then, in front of our friends in York."

2-14-06

Paul and Erin were married in a civil ceremony by a local magistrate in Carlisle on Valentine's Day morning, February, 2006. That same day, they took up residence in the apartment efficiency and missed only one day of classes.

Nosy Lt. Stevens offered them his blessings at lunch break the next day. "Made an honest woman of her, did ya?" he asked, shaking Paul's hand. "You guys hiding something, not opting for the big wedding and all?"

"We're Atheists, if you haven't guessed that by now."

"Why does that not surprise me," he sniffed. "That explains a lot of your off-beat views you always come up with in class."

"Are you familiar with the term *diversity*?"

"Oh, I get it. I'm the bigot, right?"

"You said it – I didn't."

"I didn't know atheists got married."

"There appears to be a lot you don't know."

"Listen, Beckwith, I'm up to here with your insubordination. I could have your ass court- martialed."

"And your unsolicited harassment would be my defense."

"Now, now boys." Erin interrupted. "I think the good Lieutenant really is sincere about offering us congratulations, honey."

"And maybe he'd like to debate me sometime – on the issues of conscience. There are a series of debates required at the end of the course."

Lt. Stevens realized his hand was being called and it was time to put up or shut up. "You're on, dogface. I'll see Major Troutman right away about setting it up."

"Would it be too much trouble if I went along with you to see the Major?"

"No, not at all." Stevens gave a sly smile, "Do you suspect me of pulling rank on you, buddy boy –asking for unfair advantage?"

"Why, Lieutenant, the thought never crossed my mind."

"So what do you boys want to debate?" The bald and pudgy Major asked. "I know you have your differences – you're at each other's throats on almost every topic." He cleared his throat, "Does make for interesting classroom discussion, though," he said with a smile.

"It's a question of morality, Sir," Stevens began.

"You have differing views on morality, is that *it*?"

"Sir, I think the better word would be about *conscience*." Paul contributed.

"I see." The major rubbed his chin with his hand. "Paul, you are a Jeffersonian Republican and I believe Mr. Stevens, here, is a John Adams Federalist – correct me if I am wrong."

Both men nodded to the affirmative.

"Pity Burr shot Hamilton in a similar argument," Major Troutman reflected in a voice almost to himself. "You boys are going about this in the right way, and the debate *is* a course requirement. Fine, I'll schedule it first week of March." He rose from his desk, indicating the interview was over. "I'll get back to you gentlemen with the particulars."

They thanked him and left, each confident that their individual views would prevail in an academic forum.

XV

Recurring Dream

From his recliner he could make out an argument not far away. "*Atheists* . . . atheists in *heaven!*" the man sputtered. "Why, that's quite impossible!" He could make out a familiar southern drawl.

"You mean to tell me you haven't noticed until now?" his partner in conversation asked.

"I don't know *all* these people up here. Lord knows I have found few from my own congregation!" He snorted. "Surely, some have been saved . . . as they most assuredly expected."

"With all respect, sir, I don't think this place could have been *expected* . . . anticipated."

"What d'ya mean by that?"

Because of his listener's prominence and expectations, the man fumbled for the right words in answer. "First, no one here refers to this place as 'heaven' . . ."

"*What*?"

Several passers-by stopped in their tracks at the good preacher's resounding question.

"That's *blasphemy*, my son." He got up from the sofa they were sitting on and demanded in a high voice, "Where is He, anyway? *Where is Jesus*?" He turned around, staring beyond the onlookers. Those who knew of him were startled at his unfamiliar ire.

"Sir, Th . . . this place is known only as 'the Higher Plane.' You remember . . . from the orientation."

Still looking toward the horizon, the preacher uttered, "Yes, yes, the orientation that was given by that agnostic humorist."

"You have read him, sir?"

"Only when I had to . . . in school, I think. How in blazes did *he* get here?"

"As I understand it, entrance into this place . . . I think can be summed up by a bumper sticker I once saw."

The didactic preacher stood dumbstruck, allowing the fellow his say.

"The world is my country and doing good is my religion."

"A *bumper* sticker . . . this must be a bad dream I'm havin'" the preacher exclaimed, looking up.

His conversant was startled by the statement. "Surely you realize you're here because you were a good man."

"It's a *dream*, I tell ya. . . . must wake up now." And he pinched himself – and again, harder, "wake up, wakeup dammit," he demanded of himself. He turned to the man and asked, "Are you a religious man?"

"Why . . . I haven't thought much about it – now that you ask."

In a fit of frustration, the evangelist twisted in convulsion and threw his hands, wide-spread, into the air, "Why have You forsaken me, Lord?"

"We get a lot of that here . . ." Paul felt a hand on his shoulder and turned to see a diminutive man looking toward the growing spectacle. "He'll be gone from this place if he doesn't soon come to his senses."

"You mean . . ." Paul couldn't finish his sentence.

"I mean . . . the delusion must end somewhere! For many, if not most of us, it ended on Earth, without great expectations. Our new setting is so easy . . . comforting to us because we didn't anticipate something else . . . in an afterlife."

"This is the afterlife then?"

"Sort of -- as I think I understand it, and I've been here awhile-- it is an *after-death* thing where our mental momentum continues on toward an eventual cessation."

"Then the theologians were partially right in describing the soul?"

"Soul is a very ambiguous term . . . but for want of something better, they latched onto it and adopted it as fact. Really, it is the *mind* that seeks closure, the more robust, the more longevity of its winding down."

"And your name is?'

"Ed Teller. They call me Dr. Teller."

"The renowned physicist?"

"Some say that."

"*Wow* . . . then *you* should know the kinetics of the mind."

"I've talked a lot with Dr. Freud about it – and that's his take on things. Of course, no one really knows. Like we always say: 'it's purely academic.'"

The commotion beyond them died down and it appeared the preacher took his seat.

"Then, there is no rhyme or reason to our existence . . . to all of this?"

"We know very little more than we did while alive. If there is a plan, no one has discovered it. Most all of us wish to savor this time in accordance with what Thomas Jefferson once said."

"What was *that*?"

"I'll try to recite it from memory since I've reflected on it many times: '*Ignorance is preferable to error: and he is less remote from the truth who believes nothing, than he who believes what is wrong.*' That is from his '*Notes on the State of Virginia*,' I believe. Though we know so much about natural phenomena, we still don't know *why* it is. All we know is that there *is!* Few if any, here, would presume to foretell a purpose, or indeed, any prophecy – having seen foolishness, and the abundance of it, on Earth."

"Amen to that, brother! But your activities as a developer of the hydrogen bomb. . . wouldn't that make you less of a candidate for here?"

"A knee jerk reaction to your request might call for the affirmative. But, like Oppenheimer and Einstein, the development was of a redeeming nature – the denying the Fascists of that weapon." Dr. Teller looked deeply into Paul's eyes and exclaimed, "My conscience is clear . . . *our* conscience is clear! As your conscience is clear." "*My conscience?*" Paul asked in wonderment.

"Of course," the Doctor said matter-of-factly, "*You* wouldn't be here if your conscience wasn't clear."

What he was saying finally impacted Paul – it was all about *conscience*! "Thank you, Doctor. I think you've made my day.

"Anytime, dear friend." And he went away.

XVI

The Debate

The week leading up to the debate was full of hype. Classmates not preoccupied with their own debate requirements added their interest to the growing contest between the class's two high-profile protagonists. Students of other classes also expressed desire to view what appeared to be a cultural conflict of some proportion. Because of these developments, the debate's venue was moved to the auditorium.

Because of the course requirements, Paul and Lt. Stevens were required to have a second participant rather than be allowed to informally debate one-on-one. But Major Troutman did waive the usual protocol of: 1. Positive (*pro*) argument , 2. Negative (*con*) argument, 3. *Pro* rebuttal, and 4. *Con* rebuttal. Instead, to make the confrontation a bit more interesting, he would allow courtroom cross-examination tactics that would allow more in-your-face procedure. The foursome appeared to have been given top billing, being slated last, on Friday, the last day of debates. Of course Paul had chosen Erin as his partner, and she happily looked forward to the event.

That late winter morning, the dawn broke overcast but mild. The news program they woke up to included a flash about a murder of an abortion clinic doctor, and that the perpetrator may be headed in their general direction. The killer had struck late Thursday in the northwest Baltimore area.. "Not *again*," Paul uttered. "What's that make . . . three victims?"

"Yup." She got out of bed. "That guy is one of the reasons I've been sent to Carlisle."

"A religious nut or al-Qaeda?"

"What's the difference?"

"Touche." He raised his eyebrows. "What I can't figure out is: the Bible thumpers' protest against *Roe vs. Wade*. Even if abortion can be considered infanticide, the Bible mentions nothin' about it except the occasional time Yahweh gets his dander up and has a few women's bellies ripped open . . . like mentioned in the Book of Jose."

"That's Hosea 13:16." She corrects.

"I just can't get all those books right," he winced before adding: "You'd think those nuts would practice what they preach -- about not judging others -- and let God do the judging like the Bible says . . . in the New Testament, I think. And the pain thing . . . associated with the abortion, can hardly be noticed by the fetus any more than a fully developed infant boy's pain when the end of his pecker's cut off."

"But I get to see your buddy smiling *all* the time because of that."

"Yeah, well I wonder just how many nerve endings were lost in *that* procedure."

Ignoring his whining, she declared: "It's subjugation of women, *Paul*! Women should not be allowed to even *think* about terminating a pregnancy." She added with light sarcasm, while opening a box of cereal. "After all, it is a man's world!"

"That's a subject, for *another* day." Paul said wearily. "We gotta focus on today's debate."

"Hope the threatening sky is not an omen." Erin said , busy with dumping flakes into her bowl.

"You're not going to go superstitious on me at this late hour?" he asked from their bedroom. "We should have 'em by the short hairs if we keep our cool and stay on the *reason* track."

"Sorry to sound so negative, it's just that . . . few will admit to siding with us. We know we are right but *they* will hang on to their infantile delusion until the cows come home – and then some." She bit her lip in frustration. "It makes me wonder why we even try."

"Like we've often said before – it is too obvious a conundrum for us to deny our duty to try and save this experiment of government that the founding fathers started. We must be convincing in our argument that the *liberal* position is that politics can change our culture and save us from ourselves, as opposed to the *conservative* position whose politics is to preserve culture, even if corrupted, at all costs. I think Senator Moynihan said that"

"Yeah, it was Moynihan – but darling, you're lecturing to the choir."

"Just a pep-talk, honey . . . we must get our blood flowing to energize the audience to the *rightness* of our argument. We're so sure that theirs is all bullshit . . . we must convey some of our serenity, if not our happiness, into their bonnets . . . into their hearts." Paul hesitated as he tied his shoe. "This fight against the tide really keeps me pumped!"

"You sure were pumping last night," she said in a low purr, "as I remember."

"Oh honey," he blushed. "That was some lovin'. I have you . . . I have *everything*! – I'm so lucky!"

"I *love* you."

"I love you, too . . . but I guess that doesn't change the

fact that the religionists think we're zealots – cult members who disembowel sacrificial goats in ceremony. By the way, how *is* our supply of goats?"

With tilted head, she gave him an admonishing smile. "You're as bad as my brother . . . with the goat entrails thing."

"You mean . . . he believes that shit too?"

"He's not as bad as he used to be . . . he's done some reading -- and he's more mature."

"Has he gotten over the fact that you haven't any horns? I've searched every part of your body and I haven't found any."

It was her turn to blush. "I think you were looking for something else."

"Yeah . . . the only horn I found was on me."

You'd better get into uniform, lef'tenant . . . or I'll have your ass . . . *again,* tonight."

The various debates unwound -- the winners being judged by folded ballot from the matriculation that was required to attend. Some in attendance were from other classes whose interest had been piqued by the personality and cultural clash. And some were guests from off campus, invited by the contenders themselves. Arlee and Natasha and the Arabic doctor were invited from Erin's York group, as were several clergy and congregation from the nearby church that Lt. Stevens was attending while on TAD.

The final debating teams were introduced by Major Troutman, and the contestants took their seats behind the podium. "Lieutenant Stevens and Lieutenant Junior Grade Anderson will lead off arguing that religious morality is central to humanity's ethical system. Lieutenant Beckwith and his pretty wife, Lieutenant Erin Beckwith, will counter with the argument that the mind's conscience, *which can be independent of religious affectation*, is key to humanity's ethical system." The Major then turned to his left, addressing Stevens to commence: "you will have eight minutes for opening argument, Lt. Stevens—"

"Thank you Major Troutman, and everyone here today that came despite the threat of rain. I will be short because my premise is not a complicated one." He took a gulp of water and cleared his throat. "Morality is an overused word that attempts to gloss over much of what is wrong in today's world. Because of that, it has lost meaning to a great majority of people here on Earth. My opponents will argue that morality is not consistent when comparisons are made of the world's great religions, but that is a misperception on their part. Contrary to what they will contend, faith in a Supreme Being is absolutely requisite in the nurturing of the human spirit and its willingness to do good works. They will ask: 'So which Supreme being?' And we answer, 'Is it important? – sure different parts of the world have different Gods, but He is beseeched in the universal way . . . through *prayer*, my friends, through prayer."

"Whether you are Buddhist, Muslim, Jew or Hindu -- or Christian, prayer is the *time* honored tradition of communication. The world has not advanced to this point on the heavy forboding of pagans and atheists and their nihilistic, hedonistic, communistic, homosexual ways. Yes, changes have come in time through the ages, and the *great* milestones, the Ten Commandments, the Sermon on the Mount, the Magna Carta , our Declaration of Independence and Constitution took great periods of time to evolve. Change, as evidenced by those singular achievements, necessitates that it come slow – grudgingly slow -- to effect one of divine deliberation."

As the impeccably dressed Lieutenant droned on, Paul

thought to himself that Stevens would have made a very good minister. He was impressive with his three inches of height he had on him – and his blown-dry head of brown hair, though the same color as Paul's, was not as disheveled. His delivery was one of smooth, reasonable sounding *claptrap*. The kind that would be as hard to get a handle on as a pig covered with grease. The multitudes that have received similar weekly doses of ever thickening varnish -- that had been lacquered on their minds since birth -- would find his delivery comforting.

" . . . so in conclusion, it is imperative that our *heritage* not be denied in these perilous times, that *morality* -- the will to do good works -- is the one gift from above that recognition of *will* save this great nation."

There were a few "Amens" from the audience as Stevens withdrew to his seat.

Paul took Stevens' place behind the podium and surveyed the audience with a confident, knowing smile, thanking them for their interest and attendance. "Morality *is* key to the proper behavior of a society, no question. But where we differ from our opponents is that morality is not issued, not demanded from above, but comes from within our society, within us as citizens of society. We have evolved over millions of years as caretakers of our children who require special long-term care – much more so than any other animal species. That *care and nurturing* had extended to the others in the clan or tribe. For ages before recorded history, families have taken care of their fragile progeny, and they took care to help other families and progeny in their group. Anthropologists and archeologists, having studied primitive societies, are convinced that man has been taking care of his own kind for a good long while. Those primitive societies had found a basis for morality well before Jesus and Jehovah came onto the scene.

"Our opponent mentions several great milestones, but one was omitted for some unknown reason. The *Code of Hammurabi*! Hammurabi was a great leader that lived before Moses, in Mesopotamia, the birthplace of civilization. His reign is referred to as *the Golden Age of Babylonia*. His code consisted of nearly 300 laws that were beneficial to that society, code that came from *within* that society, attributed to his government -- not from a nebulous form in the sky!"

"Morality is extremely important, as I said, for the functioning of civilization. But it is presumptuous – indeed -- dangerously erroneous to deny *our own* involvement in its derivation." He hesitated, to allow his missive to sink in. "Morality is something that must be further developed by us, *for us*. Ethics *must* be taught to our children in the home, in school as well as in church. Unlike what our opponents propound, morality does not necessitate the worship of a deity – that is the business of religion! Morality is the code of conduct that humans show for their fellow humans. An omnipotent God has no need for our continual attention – *but humans do*! We need to *help* one another, giving to one another -- not God -- credit for *our* efforts and achievements. Some, more than others, are predisposed to thank God rather than *those* who, in reality, accomplish the wonderful deeds.

"It is arrogant ungratefulness to dun a god with such burdensome, often self-serving requests. *Conscience* will not allow me to subscribe to such prayerful begging." (There were a few moans from the audience). "It is *conscience* that matters to our condition – not some exterior guidance whose literature is rife with contradiction." (A yeah or two were elicited from down front). When I feel that I am more moral than the fickle and vengeful God of the Old Testament –and I say this in *good* conscience – then it is time I focus on delivering credit where it should be given – indeed, *where credit is needed*. This is not to say that worship of one's God is unimportant – it *Is*, too most . . . it satisfies *their* conscience. But to presume a national policy or public code requiring mandatory subscription to same, is not inclusive of all of our citizenry and is extremely regressive. The United States, the leader in establishing *freedom of conscience*, is dangerously on that track, backing away from its former accomplishments toward an unnecessary theocracy. This is really mass self-deception – a growing neurotic dependency on nebulous faith that has no upper limit in its demands, and may extend to extreme fanatical zealotry – all in the name of *morality*! Thank you."

The audience could be heard shifting in their seats and whispering an array of mixed feelings. Major Troutman then took the stand and, wiping his brow in feigned incredulity, uncharacteristically intoned, "Boy, Paul, you're tough!" Then he added, "And folks, if that wasn't enough, Lieutenant Beckwith's wife, Erin, will now follow with an eight minute first rebuttal / cross examination of Lt. Stevens' opening argument."

Erin took her place behind the podium and perfunctorily thanked everyone for their interest, before sipping some water from the ubiquitous plastic bottle. "In rebuttal, I want to correct Lt. Stevens in his inference that *all* of those milestones of human behavior that he mentioned – Ten Commandments, Sermon on the Mount, Magna Carta, our Declaration of Independence and Constitution – were God given. *Negative*! The first two are attributed to divine sources, of course, but the last three were derivations of the society in which they came into being. Oh, it is convenient for our opponents to lump them into their basket of 'evidence'" – she couched the word *evidence* with her arms raised outward and two forefingers of each hand bending as if to form animated quotation marks. "I wonder why they omitted the Early record of the *Old Testament* – but I'm not asking them *that* question.

"The Magna Carta was an effort by the populace, not God, to extract more humanistic behavior from the King of England. . ." she hesitated, knowing her critique was a bit lame because of her lack of knowledge of that event. With more confidence, she lit into her defense of the American documents. "Jefferson's Declaration is often cited by religionists as being ordained by God because of his mention of '*the Creator.*' Jefferson's Creator was defined at the time as the unknowable god of nature. Then, Deism was in fashion among the intellectual community . . . the *Natural Religion* it was called. -- A Creator who had set the Cosmos in motion, and then stepped aside allowing natural law to run things – a Creator that was indifferent to mankind as he was the fishes in the sea.. Prayer was of no consequence since mankind had *intellect* as his tool and was responsible for the wise use of same." Many in the audience murmured uncomfortably at her dismissal of prayer.

"Our *Constitution* makes no mention of God. It is a secular document in the strictest meaning of the word. It was written by a group of men who, for the most part, subscribed to the intellectual, natural religion of Deism. Certainly that can be said for the architect of that document, James Madison, who devoted a great portion of his political life winnowing away the hubris of indolent and misleading clerical babble. If our opponents find that hard to believe, I refer them to his '*Detached Memoranda*' and Edward Gibbon's '*Decline and Fall of the Roman Empire.*' Gibbon's history is one of many that Madison gleaned for information concerning ancient confederations, determined to design a

Constitution that would stand the test of time from the experience of others that had triumphed for a while, but then had failed.

"Those who say that '*Separation of Church and State*' is not in the Constitution want to remain blind to the interpretation of the establishment clause of the First Amendment. Why are these religionists so adamant to deny rulings time after time by the courts, based on *their* interpretation of that establishment clause? Because it *lessens* the authority of *their* church, *their* convictions, *their* god. To their way of thinking, God *must* reign supreme! But I *ask* our opponents where their church, or some other minority church, would be today without the protective umbrella of this nation's Constitution? Must not our nation's Constitution reign supreme in order to protect the beliefs of the various sects, and their god's long quietness? If our opponents could have their way, our political system would be turned on its head and become subject to the whims of the church. Then the church becomes the army, the government, and this nation becomes a theocracy – like that in Iran. Freedom of religion will suffer and may perish because the dominant church will eventually discredit the minor faiths – this is the way it has been *all* the years of the past.

"In closing I would like to read a quote of Robert O'Neil, founding director of the Thomas Jefferson Center for the Protection of Free Expression in Charlottesville Virginia – and, I might add – an active, practicing Christian: '*An Egyptian known as the philosopher of al Qaeda, Sayyid Quth, has given his reason for the truly dangerous element in American life: it was not capitalism or foreign policy or racism or the unfortunate cult of women's independence. The truly dangerous element lay in America's separation of church and state – the modern political legacy of*

Christianity's ancient division between the sacred and the secular.' In other words, the evangelical movement here in the United States to erode the wall separating church and state is *really* playing into the hands of the terrorist and the fanatically religious enemy!"

Erin hesitated, looking at the Major.

"Do I take it that there's a question in there . . . you're asking the other side?"

"Yes sir. My question is twofold: Why are religionists so adamant in denying the validity of the Court's many rulings concerning maintenance of church and state? And, who will provide the *real* umbrella of protection if in fact the church gets its way and God reigns supreme over and above our existing Constitution?"

"Do either of you gentlemen care to respond?" Major Troutman asked.

Lt. Stevens folded his hands, and countered: "I don't believe either question is relevant to this forum on morality."

"But, in your opening statement," Erin prodded, "you have cited the Constitution as one of mankind's milestones toward present day morality. It is at the very crux of our argument that the Constitution is the basis for all of our laws, thus our morality!"

"I think she is warranted an answer, considering she has effectively laid bare a link to that great document . . . and, indeed, its survival," the Major concluded. "Please answer the question."

The Navy Lieutenant's ploy had bought him some time. The two men exchanged whispers before Lt. Stevens commenced. He did not want to sound too critical of the Constitution he had sworn to defend. "We feel that the Judicial has ruled to our point of view in many cases, but has sometimes erred in interpretation in others. It must be remembered that too many of the Court's justices are not elected by the people. Too many of them are products of the elite, ivory tower universities and *that* mind set."

"Are you saying, Mr. Stevens, that our universities are *more* than intellectual, or just that? And are you proposing that other qualifications for the judiciary should be mandated in a future constitutional amendment?"

"Order, order, Mrs. Beckwith," the Major interrupts. "Those are two more questions, and Lt. Stevens is still occupied with the first two. Please let Mr. Stevens finish."

"Yes sir."

"Please answer her second question, if you will. You have two minutes."

"Of course the United States Constitution is the protector of *all* of its citizens." He hesitates, again with the folded hands.

After an interlude of quiet, the Major directs, "Go on, Mr. Stevens, I don't believe you have sufficiently answered her question. I too am curious how *your* god would sustain our nation's ability to protect everyone."

"God is doing *just that*, now! We are in his hands. We are blessed with his grace!" The Lieutenant struggled for words. "The Constitution does not need to be changed. His morality is seen in every thread of its text." He concludes.

Satisfied with his concession, knowing she would get nothing more out of him, Erin proceeded toward her conclusion. "Our opponents insist that change come grudgingly slow, as if our side likes change for change's sake. Let me assure them that we appreciate change that is *good, . . .* and for it to be good, we *must* be careful and *deliberate*!" It has been *their* hallmark to paint all things black or white, good or evil, but they will not admit that it was their hallmark, --religion -- whose definition interpreted evil in the first place. Evil was born of them to limit humanity – ecclesiastic law included many taboos that in today's world have withered on the vine through abrogation of ignorance. Diet and social taboos have been relegated to the dustbin of history as the light of knowledge has exposed their absurdity. No wonder religious texts condemn curiosity and the search for knowledge – *it exposes their modus operandi of thriving on the masses' illiteracy*!

"Many of us are a-theist, meaning we recognize no need for any of the religions on this planet. We do realize the folly of outlawing any of the religions because so many in the world are dependent on them for supplication. Atheists are not necessarily Communist – *atheism is a universal philosophy* that may be subject to approval or adoption by any of the world's political parties, but that is their business. Personally, I know of only one Communist atheist among the hundreds that I have met. And, I might add that it is legal to be a Communist in this country.

"For the charge of being 'hedonistic,' if enjoying one's self in *the pursuit of happiness,* at no one else's expense, then I suppose we're guilty. You see, if we don't look forward to an eternal heaven, we do try to make our existence heavenly, here and now. Not a hell, mind you, but heaven, *here and now!* And that has collateral affect on those around us in that we want very much to share our happiness.

But, to fundamentalists, evil overshadows good, and they can't see the goodness. That is such *negativity* in a world that should be appreciated for all of its positive attributes: the warmth of the sun; the many moments we are free from pain; our embrace of friends and books; the unfolding mystery of Nature and the Cosmos; and the comforts of family. We have a choice *now*, to either be hapless voyagers in the *dark*, or to be happy voyagers *toward the increasing light*. Should not oblivion be criticized rather than worshipped? What we know *now*, was once the basis of fear, *then.* We can be happy, and moral, at the same time!"

There was some applause in the hall as Erin took her seat – then a mixture of delayed, subdued response from the unconvinced.

"Lieutenant Anderson, you have eight minutes to respond to Lt. Paul Beckwith's argument -- and cross examine him if you like."

The Junior Lieutenant took his place at the podium and scanned the people in front of him. He felt that Erin had bloodied Stevens, and not able to come to his rescue at that time, hoped to make some comeback now.

"Our opponent's argument cited evolution as a reason for humanity's care and nurture of its own – that *evolution* was responsible for the roots of morality. But, in fact, those early people, too, depended on God's help in making it through the day and the long nights. It was fear of God and the reward of the hunt that kept them on the straight and narrow. To be sure, God was defined differently then -- worshipped differently -- and was not known to them as we know Him today. Evolution aside, mankind's first breath of consciousness recognized divine influence, to be sure. Their spiritual leaders then, showed them the important signs and guided them in their behavior toward one another. This we *know* as fact . . . evolution, well, the jury is still out on *that..*

"Our opponents cited the code of Hammurabi – that it was humanly derived. But was it not in fact divinely inspired, like the Bible? The Babylonians were religious people. God was known then as *Marduk,* who had great influence on the people. Their code was probably a manifestation of the Jewish Law that did come later . . ."

Man, is he out in left field, or what? Paul thought to

himself. *He is twisting the fact that the Jews borrowed from the Sumerians and Babylonians to write their Tome. But that is the way of the religionist: beg, borrow, and borrow some more, to preserve their delusion.*

"The good Lieutenant Beckwith would have us separate morality from religion! Absurd!

They go together like the song says: like love and marriage, and a horse and carriage. To separate the two, if that were possible, would constitute the undermining of our rich and lengthy heritage.

Traditions that we love and cherish today would topple in the chaos of liberalism. Change would become the norm rather than the exception – are we ready for that?"

The young man scanned his audience and could see some encouraging expressions among those he knew. Feeding on this energy of approval, he began his last critique. Morality and Conscience – what a match-up. Our opponents seek to define conscience in a different light than morality. Is that possible? Through some sleight of hand, Mr. Beckwith would have us separate them as he has tried with morality and religion. Here is a good example of how the tree of knowledge of good and evil has been used by the forces of evil to put their spin on things and take greedy advantage of seesaw opportunity." Anderson's eyes lit up as his delivery became more restrictive. "Of course they cannot be separated – they are the *same* and no amount of intellectual maneuvering can dispel *that* truth. Conscience, if anything, is a manifestation of morality. Morality is its guide and good deeds are done for His Glory." He took a sip of water and then added, "Thank you all for coming out today."

"You do not wish to ask the other side any questions?" the Major queried.

Come on, ask me a question, ask me a question, Paul was

thinking to himself behind clenched teeth.

"No sir…and may God have mercy on their souls."

At that, Paul thought he saw the Major wince. He knew Troutman to be Episcopalian as were many of the officer corps, and rather open to discourse even if there was a general dissection of religion.

The Major announced that that would conclude the day's program. Paul was itching for a cross-examination but the opportunity was not to be. He looked frustratingly at Erin, who, reading his thoughts, shrugged her shoulders. "What did you expect?"

"We won hands-down!" he said to her as they left the dais. "I could of tore that little shit apart . . . if he would have asked me only *one* question!"

"He knew that," she smiled at him. "That's why he didn't ask." They walked hand-in-hand across the campus in occasional sunshine. "They always retreat into a condescending fog.

They can't be – will not allow themselves to be – pinned down with detail. Obfuscation and passion are their reserve, and it's impenetrable in a reasonable debate."

"Do you think he really meant, " . . . may God have mercy on your souls?"

"It was a perfunctory statement -- I think . . . was given automatically. You have to understand that they are hardly more than robots with a fleshy exterior that they abhor. For them to be anything else . . . to question what they have been taught, and dunned through all their life, would be devastating. Their whole circle of existence would crash, and they fear they could not survive that, at the very least, mentally."

"*Wow* . . . but you're right. Look at us – both of us have just about completely changed our entire circle of friends, primarily because of the way we now think."

"I guess you could call it cultural shock!"

"But I feel so much happier . . . relieved of that incessant pressure to *prove* my devotion . . . and I found you, even though I wasn't really looking. And all of this *without* prayer!"

She squeezed his hand and said, "Let's go have pizza . . . and then make the bed fresh."

XVII

Killer in Their Midst?

The Saturday paper was full of news about the killer who might be nearby. The suspect's vehicle was found abandoned at an Emmitsburg, Maryland shopping center, just south of Gettysburg, where he may have met an accomplice.

"I wonder why they think that?" Paul said, commenting on the fact an accomplice might be involved.

"I guess there were no stolen vehicles reported in the area."

"What's interesting is his weapon of dispatch."

"Yeah?"

"A ball from a civil war era pistol."

"You mean, no lands and grooves. We know that . . . he's using Early tech. black powder weaponry."

"No ballistic marks?"

"Negative." She rolled her eyes, "That kind of weaponry is obtainable without any checks or permits."

"You *do* know something about this guy . . . you said you were sent here because of your unit's curiosity about these killings?" Without waiting for her reply he adds, "You're DIA, aren't you?"

"I'm in a liaison section between the military and the civilian Homeland Securuty Agency. I'm a research specialist."

"Ah, that's the librarian in you!" he yawned, "I know so very little about you."

"Yeah, short engagements have that disadvantage – or

advantage."

"Did you get any static from your superior, about getting married?"

"Honey, I'm not an *operative*. I'm just a four-eyed research schmuck wading through volumes of not-very-interesting literature."

"But you *do* have Top Secret clearance, right?"

"Like you . . . or we wouldn't be here."

"So, what's your take on this bad boy?"

"We have a profile of sorts. Conventional wisdom has it that he may have been a drop out from the *Concerned Christians* in the Philly area."

"The group that was ousted from Israel during that millenium debacle?"

"The same." She went on, "Because he may very well be a white supremacist, he became disillusioned by the passive nature of the CC and might have tried out other more militant cults."

"Mormonism?"

"Darling, Mormons haven't been considered a cult for the last fifty years or so."

"They're all cults to me!" he shrugged. "Anyway, they started out as a cult . . . and, once a cult, always a cult."

"Mormons aren't militant any more . . . strange maybe, but not militant." She continued, "He may well be acting on his own . . . might even claim to be one of your Phineas Priests."

"Now *that's* scary!"

"Yeah, they're lone wolves. He's probably holed up in the mountains somewhere with a wife he keeps barefoot and pregnant."

"Lots of sick puppies out there! So much negativity in the world . . . why can't people let other people live their lives?"

"It's the God thing . . . always driving the squirrel-like ones squirrellier. There is no end to their pious righteousness, even if it transcends the law of the land."

"But doesn't the Bible direct people to follow the laws of their nation."

"These nuts don't *read* the Bible, honey. Some infirmity within their brain latches onto a phrase or verse and ignites a passion to render those in seeming violation of that verse, target for rectification. They seriously believe they are doing what is right – and will martyr themselves if need be, to exact their end."

"Death, in the name of God . . . like the suicide bombers in the Middle East."

"Exactly!"

"It doesn't paint a pretty future for the human race, does it?"

"Not until religion is de-fanged and de-clawed . . . that is what the founding fathers wanted to do, and designed against with their efforts to separate church and state . . . like we argued in yesterday's debate."

"We won, you know."

"We did good . . . as attested by their reluctance to draw more fire from us."

"Well, there's precious little else we can do, without jeopardizing our career."

"We very well may have already done that."

"So be it. Sometimes I think I'd rather be a PFC . . . a poor fuckin' civilian."

"In *that* category, I think you would do just fine as a civilian!"

Coloring, as his heart skipped a beat -- he then kissed her on the nose before leading her back into their bedroom.

XVIII

A Special Introduction

"Welcome to 'THE WAY THINGS SHOULD BE – 101.'" Samuel Clemens drawled. "Mr. Madison has asked me to say a few things in introductory 'til he gets his notes together and gets out here. He's just like any congressman I ever knew – takin' forever to reach the floor – of congress, that is – and then goin' on about nothin' in particular until it's time to go home." He raised his eyebrows once or twice as if expecting something. "You can laugh now, don't take me so damn serious!" There was some laughter.

"I must admit, James Madison was not your ordinary run-of-the-mill congressman. He once lost an election because he didn't *entertain* enough – now that's rare. When he *did* get to congress, he took *control* of it and butted heads until most all the other congressmen thought the way he did on the way things should be. That guiding effort of *his* produced one of the most *profound* documents ever achieved on Earth, the American Constitution of 1787 – but I don't have to tell *you* that. Many of you out there probably know a lot more than I do about Mr. Madison."

Paul loved to hear Samuel Clemens speak and made every effort to listen to his presentations and lectures. He especially wanted to hear this classic introductory of one of his favorite American heroes, James Madison -- as well as Mr. Madison himself.

"Most politicians are extremely good orators," Clemens went on, "and can sell you somethin' you can't *even* use --

they're that smooth and convincin'. Not Mr. Madison . . . his voice was so weak he had to drop out of divinity school when he was young." He hesitated and looked to the side to see if Madison was in the wings. Then with his hand to the side of his mouth, feigning an aside to us, he added. "Now there's a choice of vocation for ya . . . preachin' or politickin' . . . you see why *I* became a riverboat pilot . . . *among* other things. Dodgin' them shifting and treacherous Mississippi River shoals was so much easier than flim-flammin' *everybody* about what generally amounted to nuthin'.

"Though young Madison couldn't speak worth a damn, he could write with convincin' persuasion. He did use a lot of abbreviations, though – enough that English teachers to *this day* give him hell about it. He was a maverick . . . with the written word as his weapon, you see. An,' as *you* know, what he wrote was no idler's fool-play – by the time of the Constitutional Congress he had devoured over a hundred – maybe 200 -- books that Jefferson kept sendin' him from Europe. Those books were mostly about histories and philosophies of long lost civilizations and confederations that maybe could be used to *derive* a new world order. With his recently acquired knowledge came confidence -- and he was soon arguin' and debatin' the best of 'em."

"Enough! That's quite enough, Sam." A short man of few distinctive features came from the wings. "You are very kind, though, in your remarks of my *ancient* past."

"Are you goin' to do that thing called '*Memorial and Remonstrance . . .?* " Samuel Clemens said in a cloud of cigar smoke. He then offered Mr. Madison a cigar, which the august gentleman promptly stuck in his coat pocket. "You probably have the very first cigar that I ever offered you?"

"Probably." Madison said matter-of-factly, turning to us with a faint hint of a smile.

Clemens, already facing us, added, "See what I mean about politicians – always taking somethin' and squirrelin' it away in their pockets.

"I'm saving them for a rainy day."

"It don't rain here."

"Then, it's better for your health if you give some of them away."

"Physical health is not a factor here."

"I don't think I'm going to win *this* debate. So, begging your leave, please let me be."

Clemens smiled triumphantly, then bowed, and left the stage, with considerable applause.

XIX

James Madison

"It is a privilege to be here with you today. Mr. Clemens questioned if I would be talking about my *'Memorial and Remonstrance* -- Against assessments for teaching *'Christian'* religion in the state of Virginia. Yes, that writing of mine seems to be popular, and I am asked to repeat it every now and again. It won't take too awfully long, but it has had a wearying affect on certain uninterested listeners. It is in effect a document that greatly assisted the passage of Thomas Jefferson's Bill for *'Establishing Religious Freedom'.*"

"I introduce this Memorial in the form of a letter I had written to General Lafayette in November of 1826." He then recited the letter:

'The Anglican hierarchy existing in Virginia prior to the Revolution was abolished by an Early act of the Independent Legislature. In the year 1785, a bill was introduced under the auspices of Mr. Henry, imposing a general tax for the support of "Teachers of the Christian Religion." It made a progress, threatening a majority in its favor. As an expedient to defeat it, we proposed that it should be postponed to another session, and printed in the meantime for public consideration. Such an appeal in a case so important and so unforeseen could not be resisted. With a view to arouse the people, it was thought proper that a memorial should be drawn up, the task being assigned to me, to be printed and circulated throughout the State for a general signature. The experiment succeeded. The memorial was so extensively signed by the various religious sects, including a considerable portion of the old hierarchy, that the projected innovation was crushed, and under the influence of the popular sentiment thus called forth, the well-known Bill prepared by Mr. Jefferson, for "Establishing Religious freedom," passed into a law, as it now stands in our code of statutes.

Memorial and Remonstrance
June 20, 1785

To the Honorable the General Assembly of the Commonwealth of Virginia

A Memorial and Remonstrance

We the subscribers, citizens of the said Commonwealth, having taken into serious consideration, a Bill printed by order of the last Session of General Assembly, entitled "A Bill establishing a provision for Teachers of the Christian Religion," and conceiving that the same if finally armed with the sanctions of a law, will be a dangerous abuse of power, are bound as faithful members of a free State to remonstrate against it, and to declare the reasons by which we are determined. We remonstrate against the said Bill,

1. Because we hold it for a fundamental and undeniable truth, "that religion or the duty which we owe to our Creator and the manner of discharging it, can be directed only by reason and conviction, not by force or violence." The Religion then of every man must be left to the conviction and conscience of every

man; and it is the right of every man to exercise it as these may dictate. This right is in its nature an unalienable right. It is unalienable, because the opinions of men, depending only on the evidence contemplated by their own minds cannot follow the dictates of other men: It is unalienable also, because what is here a right towards men, is a duty towards the Creator. It is the duty of every man to render to the Creator such homage and such only as he believes to be acceptable to him. This duty is precedent, both in order of time and in degree of obligation, to the claims of Civil Society. Before any man can be considered as a member of Civil Society, he must be considered as a subject of the Governour of the Universe: And if a member of Civil Society, do it with a saving of his allegiance to the Universal Sovereign. We maintain therefore that in matters of Religion, no man's right is abridged by the institution of Civil Society and that Religion is wholly exempt from its cognizance. True it is, that no other rule exists, by which any question which may divide a Society, can be ultimately determined, but the will of the majority; but it is also true that the majority may trespass on the rights of the minority.

2. Because Religion be exempt from the authority of the Society at large, still less can it be subject to that of the Legislative Body. The latter are but the creatures and vice-regents of the former. Their jurisdiction is both derivative and limited: it is limited with regard to the coordinate departments, more necessarily is it limited with regard to the constituents. The preservation of a free Government

requires not merely, that the metes and bounds which separate each department of power be invariably maintained; but more especially that neither of them be suffered to overleap the great Barrier which defends the rights of the people. The Rulers who are guilty of such an encroachment, exceed the commission from which they derive their authority, and are Tyrants. The People who submit to it are governed by laws made neither by themselves nor by an authority derived from them, and are slaves.

3. Because it is proper to take alarm at the first experiment on our liberties. We hold this prudent jealousy to be the first duty of Citizens, and one of the noblest characteristics of the late Revolution. The free men of America did not wait till usurped power had strengthened itself by exercise, and entangled the question in precedents. They saw all the consequences in the principle, and they avoided the consequences by denying the principle. We revere this lesson too much soon to forget it. Who does not see that the same authority which can establish Christianity, in exclusion of all other Religions, may establish with the same ease any particular sect of Christians, in exclusion of all other Sects? that the same authority which can force a citizen to contribute three pence only of his property for the support of any one establishment, may force him to conform to any other establishment in all cases whatsoever?

4. Because the Bill violates the equality which ought to be the basis of every law, and which is more indispensable, in proportion as the validity or

expediency of any law is more liable to be impeached. If "all men are by nature equally free and independent," all men are to be considered as entering into Society on equal conditions; as relinquishing no more, and therefore retaining no less, one than another, of their natural rights. Above all are they to be considered as retaining an "equal title to the free exercise of Religion according to the dictates of Conscience." Whilst we assert for ourselves a freedom to embrace, to profess and to observe the Religion which we believe to be of divine origin, we cannot deny an equal freedom to those whose minds have not yet yielded to the evidence which has convinced us. If this freedom be abused, it is an offence against God, not against man: To God, therefore, not to man, must an account of it be rendered. As the Bill violates equality by subjecting some to peculiar burdens, so it violates the same principle, by granting to others peculiar exemptions. Are the Quakers and Menonists the only sects who think a compulsive support of their Religions unnecessary and unwarrantable? Can their piety alone be entrusted with the care of public worship? Ought their Religions to be endowed above all others with extraordinary privileges by which proselytes may be enticed from all others? We think too favorably of the justice and good sense of these denominations to believe that they either covet pre-eminences over their fellow citizens or that they will be seduced by them from the common opposition to the measure.

5. Because the Bill implies either that the Civil Magistrate is a competent Judge of Religious Truth;

or that he may employ Religion as an engine of Civil policy. The first is an arrogant pretension falsified by the contradictory opinions of Rulers in all ages, and throughout the world: the second an unhallowed perversion of the means of salvation.

6. Because the establishment proposed by the Bill is not requisite for the support of the Christian Religion. To say that it is, is a contradiction to the Christian Religion itself, for every page of it disavows a dependence on the powers of this world: it is a contradiction to fact; for it is known that this Religion both existed and flourished, not only without the support of human laws, but in spite of every opposition from them, and not only during the period of miraculous aid, but long after it had been left to its own evidence and the ordinary care of Providence. Nay, it is a contradiction in terms; for a Religion not invented by human policy, must have pre-existed and been supported, before it was established by human policy. It is moreover to weaken in those who profess this Religion a pious confidence in its innate excellence and the patronage of its Author; and to foster in those who still reject it, a suspicion that its friends are too conscious of its fallacies to trust it to its own merits.

7. Because experience witnesseth that ecclesiastical establishments, instead of maintaining the purity and efficacy of Religion, have had a contrary operation. During almost fifteen centuries has the legal establishment of Christianity been on trial. What have been its fruits? More or less in all places, pride and

indolence in the Clergy, ignorance and servility in the laity, in both, superstition, bigotry and persecution. Enquire of the Teachers of Christianity for the ages in which it appeared in its greatest lustre; those of every sect, point to the ages prior to its incorporation with Civil policy. Propose a restoration of this primitive State in which its Teachers depended on the voluntary rewards of their flocks, many of them predict its downfall. On which Side ought their testimony to have greatest weight, when for or when against their interest?

8. Because the establishment in question is not necessary for the support of Civil Government. If it be urged as necessary for the support of Civil Government only as it is a means of supporting Religion, and it be not necessary for the latter purpose, it cannot be necessary for the former. If Religion be not within the cognizance of Civil Government how can its legal establishment be necessary to Civil Government? What influence in fact have ecclesiastical establishments had on Civil Society? In some instances they have been seen to erect a spiritual tyranny on the ruins of the Civil authority; in many instances they have been seen upholding the thrones of political tyranny: in no instance have they been seen the guardians of the liberties of the people. Rulers who wished to subvert the public liberty, may have found an established Clergy convenient auxiliaries. A just Government instituted to secure & perpetuate it needs them not. Such a Government will be best supported by protecting every Citizen in the enjoyment of his

Religion with the same equal hand which protects his person and his property; by neither invading the equal rights of any Sect, nor suffering any Sect to invade those of another.

9. Because the proposed establishment is a departure from the generous policy, which, offering an Asylum to the persecuted and oppressed of every Nation and Religion, promised a lustre to our country, and an accession to the number of its citizens. What a melancholy mark is the Bill of sudden degeneracy? Instead of holding forth an Asylum to the persecuted, it is itself a signal of persecution. It degrades from the equal rank of Citizens all those whose opinions in Religion do not bend to those of the Legislative authority. Distant as it may be in its present form from the Inquisition, it differs from it only in degree. The one is the first step, the other the last in the career of intolerance. The magnanimous sufferer under this cruel scourge in foreign Regions, must view the Bill as a Beacon on our Coast, warning him to seek some other haven, where liberty and philanthropy in their due extent, may offer a more certain repose from his Troubles.

10. Because it will have a like tendency to banish our Citizens. The allurements presented by other situations are every day thinning their number. To superadd a fresh motive to emigration by revoking the liberty which they now enjoy, would be the same species of folly which has dishonoured and depopulated flourishing kingdoms.

11. Because it will destroy that moderation and harmony which the forbearance of our laws to intermeddle with Religion has produced among its several sects. Torrents of blood have been spilt in the old world, by vain attempts of the secular arm, to extinguish Religious discord, by proscribing all difference in Religious opinion. Time has at length revealed the true remedy. Every relaxation of narrow and rigorous policy, wherever it has been tried, has been found to assuage the disease. The American Theatre has exhibited proofs that equal and compleat liberty, if it does not wholly eradicate it, sufficiently destroys its malignant influence on the health and prosperity of the State. If with the salutary effects of this system under our own eyes, we begin to contract the bounds of Religious freedom, we know no name that will too severely reproach our folly. At least let warning be taken at the first fruits of the threatencd innovation. The very appearance of the Bill has transformed "that Christian forbearance, love and charity," which of late mutually prevailed, into animosities and jealousies, which may not soon be appeased. What mischiefs may not be dreaded, should this enemy to the public quiet be armed with the force of a law?

12. Because the policy of the Bill is adverse to the diffusion of the light of Christianity. The first wish of those who enjoy this precious gift ought to be that it may be imparted to the whole race of mankind. Compare the number of those who have as yet received it with the number still remaining under the dominion of false Religions; and how small is the

former! Does the policy of the Bill tend to lessen the disproportion? No; it at once discourages those who are strangers to the light of revelation from coming into the Region of it; and countenances by example the nations who continue in darkness, in shutting out those who might convey it to them. Instead of Levelling as far as possible, every obstacle to the victorious progress of Truth, the Bill with an ignoble and unchristian timidity would circumscribe it with a wall of defence against the encroachments of error.

13. Because attempts to enforce by legal sanctions, acts obnoxious to go great a proportion of Citizens, tend to enervate the laws in general, and to slacken the bands of Society. If it be difficult to execute any law which is not generally deemed necessary or salutary, what must be the case, where it is deemed invalid and dangerous? And what may be the effect of so striking an example of impotency in the Government, on its general authority?

14. Because a measure of such singular magnitude and delicacy ought not to be imposed, without the clearest evidence that it is called for by a majority of citizens, and no satisfactory method is yet proposed by which the voice of the majority in this case may be determined, or its influence secured. The people of the respective counties are indeed requested to signify their opinion respecting the adoption of the Bill to the next Session of Assembly." But the representatives or of the Counties will be that of the people. Our hope is that neither of the former will, after due consideration, espouse the dangerous principle of the

Bill. Should the event disappoint us, it will still leave us in full confidence, that a fair appeal to the latter will reverse the sentence against our liberties.

15. Because finally, "the equal right of every citizen to the free exercise of his Religion according to the dictates of conscience" is held by the same tenure with all our other rights. If we recur to its origin, it is equally the gift of nature; if we weigh its importance, it cannot be less dear to us; if we consult the "Declaration of those rights which pertain to the good people of Virginia, as the basis and foundation of Government," it is enumerated with equal solemnity, or rather studied emphasis. Either we must say, that the Will of the Legislature is the only measure of their authority; and that in the plenitude of this authority, they may sweep away all our fundamental rights; or, that they are bound to leave this particular right untouched and sacred: Either we must say, that they may controul the freedom of the press, may abolish the Trial by Jury, may swallow up the Executive and Judiciary Powers of the State; nay that they may despoil us of our very right of suffrage, and erect themselves into an independent and hereditary Assembly or, we must say, that they have no authority to enact into the law the Bill under consideration. We the Subscribers say, that the General Assembly of this Commonwealth have no such authority: And that no effort may be omitted on our part against so dangerous an usurpation, we oppose to it, this remonstrance; earnestly praying, as we are in duty bound, that the Supreme Lawgiver of the Universe, by illuminating those to whom it is addressed, may on

the one hand, turn their Councils from every act which would affront his holy prerogative, or violate the trust committed to them: and on the other, guide them into every measure which may be worthy of his blessing, may redound to their own praise, and may establish more firmly the liberties, the prosperity and the happiness of the Commonwealth.'

"Please excuse the archaic form of the language which is no longer in fashion today. No one will take on a modernization for they say it is *prose*. I am deeply moved by such sentiment and I thank all of you for your interest.

XX

The Aftermath

Paul and Erin's Classes were winding down. The warmth and happiness they found in each other more than offset the coolness of some of their colleagues at the war college. Religious tolerance, it seems, extends only to those of other denominations – not to atheists: the one discipline hated by nearly all believers of ghosts and supernatural deities. Indeed, many *lay* people think of them as Devil worshippers, never having known an atheist other than the description of them handed down from the pulpit. Generally speaking, proceedings and events were quiet as they awaited their grades – *and orders.*

A few of their classmates, not so immersed in pious unreality, continued to treat them with congenial civility, as did Major Troutman who awarded their debate project with an 'A+.' and an 'A' for the course. But they were effectively shunned by most of the officers, even as they, themselves, maintained their personal and military secularism. The young couple affirmed the fact that non-recognition of their philosophical persuasion was probably the last major discriminatory frontier. Being the '*Trekkie*' fans they were, they referred to the prejudice as the *final frontier.* They were *Bohemians* in a regulated society; they were gypsies in a sea of non-rational rationality: the Trinity makes sense to those claiming to worship only 'One Deity'; the virgin birth, miracles and resurrection makes sense to a few of the scientific minded; guns and war makes sense to those

Christians that seem unaware of Christ's passivity; greed makes sense to those Christians that seem unaware of Christ's charity.

Their frustration with the constant mixing of faith with fact by many in their special course irked Paul to exclaim to Erin one day, "We are studying about over-zealous religious nuts in a classroom that has zealous religious nuts in it!"

"Yeah, except ours are better clothed, better smelling, and more convinced of their intellectual ability – more so than their faith in any hereafter."

"Whatd' ya mean by that?"

"The religious zealot in *this* country is not nearly so ready to give up his or her life for their faith, as the Muslim types in the Middle East are."

"*That's* true." Paul was continually amazed at Erin's deduction of subtle nuances of the superstitiously infected. "But maybe that's because they don't have much in this life."

"Life is certainly cheaper over there . . . and easier to disdain than our very commercial society – and the Judeo-Christian community calls *us* hedonistic!" She squinted her eyebrows together and continued: "After Sunday services they're off to the lake in their expensive jet skis and power boats to make noise, endangering wildlife and friend, alike."

"It does seem, given all the fundamentalist's lip service about Heaven, none of them want to rush toward concluding their life here on Earth. And they willfully maintain their earthly existence by exorbitantly funding the World's largest military machine to defend against their premature demise – at the expense of social infrastructure like education, health-care, and welfare. '*Thou Shalt Not Kill*' I guess means 'Thou Shalt Not Kill Thine Own – To Hell With The Others,' seein' that we don't mind killing a lot of people in Iraq as we rearrange the sand dunes over there."

"It's another indication of their irrational rationality, darling." She fluttered her eyes, seeming to say the seriousness of the conversation had gone on long enough. "What do you say we go to bed and practice our own irrational *rationality*?"

3-14 -06

The next morning, the papers were full about another killing – this time multiple – in Pittsburgh. An abortion clinic in the South Hills section had been bombed, killing a doctor, a nurse and a patient the previous afternoon. News wire reports indicated that it was a homemade bomb constructed of aluminum casting and fused in Ted Kaczinski fashion to explode when the UPS parcel was opened. There was no immediate indication about the perpetrator or perpetrators, but it was suspected that it was the same man or organization who had killed abortion providers on three previous occasions in the past two years.

"He's definitely a religious nut . . . out to save the fetuses." Paul observed, sipping his coffee.

"It certainly appears so."

"You think it's a lone wolf, or maybe some organization behind all this?"

"If it were an organization, there would've been messages . . . notes promoting the reasoning behind their nefarious but redeeming efforts."

"*Redeeming*?"

"Yeah, the end justifies the means! But I think in this case it's a lone wolf that hears God talking to him . . . either by hallucination or in dreams."

"Like, we've compared – dreams that reinforce, never condemning, our *own* beliefs?"

129

"Exactly. Dream interpretation studies have indicated that they are a mosaic of our subconscious thoughts – what *we* believe . . . not some unknown entity sending us messages, that we know nothing about."

"And some sixth grade dropout with a room temperature IQ, not apprised of that fact, allows dreams to control or at least influence their actions?"

"Pretty much; they are self fulfilling prophecies" She reached for an envelope on the table. "Did I mention that my orders were in yesterday's mail."

"I saw the official envelope but forgot to ask. Mine should be coming along sometime soon." Hopefully, he reached for her hand. "So, do you get to stay in school . . . with me?"

"I don't know. I have to go to Philadelphia to find out . . . according to this, I gotta be at headquarters Monday morning." She showed him a travel voucher.

"So . . . I was thinkin' . . . They say Philly is kind of nice this time of year – want an escort?"

"Absolutely!" and they partially embraced, each holding a coffee mug.

XXI

Quakers

She came from the inter-office after an hour-long interview. He had been waiting in the anteroom, contemplating *his* future as his orders had arrived two days after hers. "Whew, honey, let's get some brunch." She remarked.

"So, can we stay together, or what?" he asked with a look of concern on his face.

"Cheer up, sweetie . . . I'll tell you over bacon and eggs."

"Yes -- and no. I can stay where we're at but I must do full time research and be on call for this developing situation in our area."

"You mean the killings?"

"They call it: 'developing situation'. That's all I can say. Rather cryptic, isn't it?"

"It's more than *I* expected. I was hoping they weren't going to send you to some remote place . . . far away from me."

"We always knew that would be a possibility."

"So, I get to stay in school . . . and you are now on a hush, hush assignment. *Cool*! We can still play house together."

"So, what d'ya want to do . . . see the Liberty Bell?"

"Why not . . . and we could inquire 'bout getting re-married in the old Quaker Meeting House."

"You're such a joker!"

"Hey, I'm serious! He said between sips of coffee, "If I was forced to accept any one faith, I would probably sign on to the *Society of Friends*."

"You *are* serious, aren't you?

"No preachers to soil the quiet of the meeting house."

"But they believe . . ." She began.

"But they don't proselytize. They let you be . . . whatever you are."

"Still sounds rather church-ish to me."

"Certainly, but there are many agnostics, humanists and free-thinkers out there that still need a quiet place for reflection and perhaps worship."

"Oh, Paul. I'd re-marry you in a heartbeat . . . but not in *any* kind of church."

"I was just kidding."

She gave him *that* stare. Then, in a lighter voice, she asked: "This meeting house . . . you've been there before?"

"Yeah, when our college geology department had us on a field trip to the Franklin Institute. Sunday morning we were free to see the city. Walking up Arch Street from Christ Church, I stumbled upon this rather plain brick building which had an historic placard out front." He could see that Erin was all ears.

"Go on."

"People all dressed up were entering, and – not realizing it was a church – I went in, too. I was curious, and there didn't seem to be any charge for admission. All of the people inside were sitting quietly until I heard a man behind me several rows away say that he was thankful for the wonderful day they were having. Then another across the large room got up and remarked his thanks for his and his family's good health. And on it went for about an hour or so. No overbearing preacher, no disparaging remarks, no fire and brimstone."

"Why don't we hear more about these people?"

"I told you . . . they don't proselytize!" He looked into her eyes with a serious look on his face. "Had I been raised a Quaker rather than a Baptist, I think I might not have questioned so much, and stayed a Christian."

"Really?"

"It was the hell-bent-for-leather, fire ant preaching that got to me. I just couldn't *stand* it anymore."

"Isn't it funny how fickle fate is?"

"Did you know that William Penn's Philadelphia was for a decade or so, the only place in the British Empire where Catholics could hold Mass?"

"How do you know that?"

"When I left the Meeting House that morning, I gathered up some of their literature in the entrance hall, and read about it on the way back to Kentucky."

"Anything else of interest?" she asked, reaching for his hand on the table.

"Well, their numbers are decreasin' . . . there's only about 14,000 of them left in the Philadelphia area. And, strange as it seems, the country of Belize -- or is it Honduras -- has the most Quakers of any nation."

"Why?"

"As I remember, they went en mass . . . to form a colony. He shrugged his shoulders, "That's all *I* know."

When they got back to the privacy of their apartment at Carlisle, she confided more to him about her orders. "You may as well know . . . they said it would be okay if I told you . . ."

"Tell me what?"

"That I am to research any and all information on this serial killer, to ascertain that he is a lunatic fundamentalist or if he's an al-Qaeda operative."

"You once told me they're one and the same."

"I know, I know . . . but that was *me* talking!"

"You mean your superiors don't know the diff'rence?"

"Like you say . . . it seems *everyone* is in denial. Anyway, I'm just a lowly pencil pushing junior officer."

He remained quiet as he looked into her eyes.

"If he's a lunatic – that's one thing. But if he's an operative . . . the plot thickens." She continued.

"Will you be in any danger?"

"Who knows . . . they don't seem to think so – unless, of course I get too close to this guy."

"*Too close*?" he spat. "Whad'ya mean, too close?"

"They gave me a list of newspapers . . . I'm to check there archives, interview their reporters . . . anything to get a lead as to where this guy is coming from, or where he might be holed up. Right now they believe he might be located in the Somerset area."

"*Kentucky*?" Paul blurted because there was a Somerset not far from his hometown.

"No, darling. Somerset County, . . . here in Pennsylvania. They showed me on the map that it appeared to be the center of his beaten-zone"

"West of here, I guess."

"Yeah, about 100 miles . . . in the Laurel Highlands."

"The Allegheny Front." He unconsciously muttered.

"What?"

"I'm sorry, sweetheart. It's a geological dividing line – north and south -- that separates the Allegheny plateau from the Ridge and Valley mountain system."

"You sound like a geologist."

"The Allegheny mountain starts at the Allegheny Front . . . runs all the way from Tennessee into New York State."

"Like the Appalachian Trail?"

"They're parallel to each other . . . The Front is farther

west."

"Plenty of places to hide?"

"*Oh, yeah,* baby! Plenty of places." He said in a doleful tone.

"One horror scene that he's suspected of is that mixed-racial couple found hacked to death on the Appalachian trail last summer."

"Oh boy. Honey, you don't need *me* to tell you that I don't like your orders."

"You can come with me, when you can get away from your studies."

The conversation continued into the late hours. Then, slowly, he rubbed his chin with his hand and he began to nod off . . .

He didn't hear her soothing voice ask, "Are you tired, Honey?"

XXII

The Long Thin Thread
(or Spark) of Reason

"I don't need to tell all of you out there, that the great country, the United States of America, didn't just come about out of *thin air*. There were movers and shakers that set the stage to make it a possibility. And not just on this continent but over across the big pond, in Europe. Though most people through history seemed to be content with minding their manners and existing comfortably within the status quo, there were a few who were not *quite* so satisfied."

Paul was again drawn to a lecture – this time on history – narrated by the uncompromising, intrepid voice of Katharine Hepburn. Like so many people, he had admired her accomplishments on the silver screen. He was in total agreement with TIME magazine's millenium poll; of the top 100 actors of the twentieth century, she was voted the best of all actresses.

"From Lucretius through Aurelius, Bruno, Spinoza, Voltaire, Paine, up to Jefferson, a thin trace of *Reason* threaded down through history. Like the undying spark of a cooling emba', those gentlemen's sage influence have kept alive what most of you in the audience know as *objective sanity*." Her voice was as vibrant as ever in its undulating, never predictive, never modulated tone.

"Life, sweet life, was their progenita', the driving force to question the limits imposed by the shamans and pious old men. They emboldened and supplemented the mathematicians and scientists of their day, like Euclid, Khayyam, Gillileo, Copernicus, Newton and Franklin, to pave the way through the long darkness toward a growing light of the futcha'. But it wasn't so much their wonderful accomplishments that enabled Reason to continue to glow, but the *mistakes* of the negative, the misadventures of piety and ignorance that failed to *snuff out* that spark."

"Nerva, Trajan, Hadrian and the Antonines produced the Golden age of Rome, as did the Greek philosophers, who in *their* great civilization, categorized the human psyche. Their histories transcended the fall of their civilizations, to *catch fire* again in the Renaissance – it was the moors and naïve monks of the long Dark Age that kept that spark alive. Their efforts were subtle, though, compared to the Status Quo's later initiatives to eradicate *evil*. Not mentioning the indiscretions that took place during that Dark Age, it *was* the Crusades that brought Christianity out of its fiefdom squabbles to vent its righteousness in a truly global way. At the suggestion of Pope Urban II, in 1095, two centuries commenced of hysterical, murdering rampages of the '*Holy Lands*', but produced nothing. Finally, the kings and another Pope terminated that series of outrages -- after that insanity had accounted for tens of thousands of deaths, and casualties and destruction indeterminate."

"Then, shortly thereafter, it was determined that all *heretics* be ousted from Spain and Portugal, giving rise to the Great *Inquisition*. In this, the dominant culture of Roman Catholicism did prevail, and the Iberian Peninsula was swept clean of apostates, which was then preserved for the *majority's* peculiar brand of irrationality. But England was having *its* problems with ecclesiastic policy, after Spain's not so subtle victory over the heretics. It seemed King Henry, VIII, was more in love with Anne Boleyn than he was with

---

the *One True Church* and had Rome's outreach program terminated, much to the consternation of the remaining Catholic countries. Spain, feeling flush from victory over the moors, thought to take matters in its own hands when that redheaded, bastard daughter of the late King and Ann Boleyn became Queen of the misty isles. That southern Catholic nation amassed the greatest armada of all time to attempt to bring England back into the swaddling fold of submission. However, it was promptly whupped by more reasonable men who were better experienced in seafaring. Though Spain considered itself a much more righteous kingdom, God did not make Himself available to them in *that* quarta', but, in fact, allowed storms to wreak havoc in the North Sea that week, and the northwest coast of Ireland the next, as the floundering Armada attempted to escape back to their mild waters of home. More reasonable men had sensibly prevailed by using their *knowledge* to defeat their *prayerful*, doleful enemy."

'I *agree*, I agree with everything she is saying' he thought to himself, unaware that this was a dream, and dreams out of the subconscious only reinforce the dreamer's conscious beliefs.

'Some might think she is being too hard on the Latinos – that it's not politically correct to pick on one section of the world community, but *go-to-it*; -- giv'em hell –they deserve it, the unthinking, unquestioning blobs on humanity!'

"Some might think I am being too harsh in my condemnation of the Latins." She looked in Paul's direction. "But I assure you, in all my heart, they deserve no less than the criticisms I have offered. Even, as I left the World, Catholics, which are the dominant religious sect of America, were whining about being discriminated against, as indeed they have been whining since the second century! Even in

138

the wake of the recent and universal child molestation scandals, that church continues to whine!" No one got up to leave, but there was a murmuring of approval.

"The thread and the spark lived on to become the Golden Age of England, with Elizabeth's reign lasting forty-five years. In England as well as the remainder of the World, Protestantism, a modified form of irrationality, survived the more numerous but more stumbling devotees of Catholicism."

She smiled and paced a bit, back and forth. "The scene unfolds on isolated, but not quiet, England and her new found confidence. After thousands of Protestants had been killed in the religious transition, a wariness crept into that nation's political ambivalence. Protestantism gave rise to Calvinism, Puritanism, and a society of friends called Quakers because of their unorthodox worshipping practices. Internecine bickering and persecution occurred between the dominant Anglicans and the emerging sects. But, that aside, where would the World be without the maturing discipline of English Law? Order took precedence over chaos, and arbitrary actions of the monarchy – thanks to the new law's roots in the Magna Carta – were curtailed. English jurisprudence was far from perfect, but it provided a sub-base of foundation that could and would be built upon. Its evolution exceeded that of the constantly squabbling neighbors, and in its strength and liberalism set out to influence, and conquer the World."

Smiling confidently as if she was Elizabeth reincarnated, Hepburn pronounced: "She *did* just that – conquered the World, setting up outposts of English Law in the not yet formed United States, India, South Africa, Australia Canada and many smaller nations. The Sun never set on the British Empire, it was boasted. Yet, in spite of its broad, sometimes heavy-handed colonialism, there came a festering from within that was manifested in the agitation for yet more freedom of religion, and of conscience. The thirteen colonies that gave birth to the United States of America were settled primarily by religious misfits, contrary to established British religious mores. Massachusetts was settled by the Puritans, Pennsylvania by the Quakers, Maryland by Catholics and Georgia by Huguenots, to mention a few."

"The Connecticut Yankee looked about her captivated audience, visibly exhibiting her trembling emotionalism, "So what did the Puritans do when they set up housekeeping in the New World? They promptly showed *their* intolerance to those others who interpreted Scripture different from *themselves*. One individual in particular, of probably many, was asked to leave the province because of his refusal to take an oath for public office. At the time, Roger Williams, remarked that for him to give an oath before God which was contrary to the dictates of his conscience, would be the same as taking the Lord's name in vain. He emigrated south into the wilderness and founded a community based on *freedom of conscience.* He wrote a book blasting Puritanism, whereupon Cotton Mather wrote a book critical of him, having the same title with the addition '. . . *Washed White in the Blood of the Lamb.'* The exchange continued with a tome from Williams, further extending the title, and infuriating the xenophobic and pious Mather."

"Roger Williams's newly founded community was named Rhode Island, which became civilization's first known effort at separating church and state, with the ancient exception of Babylon. Williams passed on in 1683, at about the time William Penn founded Pennsylvania. As a Quaker, his people too, sought refuge in the wilderness after suffering persecution back home. But, unlike the Puritan experience, he welcomed diversity, recognizing value in what the immigrants to his colony brought. Among the immigrants was Ben Franklin,--out of Massachusetts Bay Colony – and later, the very industrious plain people from the Lower Palatinate. Because he recognized *freedom of conscience* as a human necessity, he welcomed immigrants' religions – or non-religion, allowing their churches, temples and libraries to be built. "Needless to say, this flourishing port of Philadelphia became the largest city of the colonies, and the focal point for the establishment of America's freedoms. The ember had flared into broad flame once again. And those flames would be fanned to intensity by a few gentlemen farmers from Virginia. The thread had grown to the size of a cord, and through the auspices of Thomas Jefferson and James Madison, it would become like a rope. First, there was the successful gaining of independence from Britain, and the high-wire walk of juggling the loosely formed Republic.

"Hardly a sideshow in all this was Madison's efforts in the support and success of Jefferson's Bill *Establishing Religious Freedom* in Virginia. This culminated to produce the World's first de-clawing of religion in policies concerning the consciences of *all* the people. In 1786, Madison wrote to Jefferson after they prevailed in debate over that State's populist, Patrick Henry: '*The enacting clauses past without a single alteration, and I flatter myself have in this Country extinguished for ever the ambitious hope of making laws for the human mind. . . .*

Adieu affectly –'

"The rest is, as they say, history. The newly adopted U.S. Constitution became the World's prototype for reasonable government, copied and mimicked by governments seeking Democracy. Until *now*, that is – and we are not able to assist in its continuance."

XXIII

Erin

The second part of the special course on 'Politics of Terror' was also under the direction of Major Troutman. Paul had made the cut with his "A", and Lieutenants Stevens and Anderson were privileged to stay, as was the condition of *their* scholastic assignment. Erin was busy traveling the aged Turnpike, and the hilly roads connecting the small towns of south central Pennsylvania, interviewing editors and reporters of their papers. She hated the worn and truck congested Turnpike, but too often, it was the only direct route to her required destination. The old Lincoln highway was but a series of hairpin turns that cut across the rugged mountains south and west of Carlisle, but did offer a change of scenery in its routing through verdant forests and breath-taking overlooks. 'So many places for a killer to conceal himself' she thought to herself on those challenging drives. She had heard horror stories of people sliding off highways, down steep slopes, in mid-winter storms, only to be found several days later.

Fog was always a problem on ridge tops with the change of weather, and on other occasions, after a lot of rain, it was the valleys that were thickly blanketed. She took note of the many jeep trails that were everywhere, pealing off from the main road into the dark green timber tracts, reminding her of the frustrating manhunt for Eric Rudolph in the North Carolina mountain forests. It sent chills up her spine on those long drives trying to anticipate the mind of a deranged lunatic and his path to self-preservation so he might be able to strike a blow another day at the Godless 'baby killers' or the sinning hedonists.

What business of it were theirs, of decisions a woman makes in her trek through life? she often reflected. What is that eluding mechanism that transforms a few written words of an ancient text into instructions to *kill* those who would interfere with the divinity and sanctity of life, even it its formative stage? Is it not the sole business of the woman to make the decision to nurture or not to nurture an egg of hers that was inescapably fertilized by her husband or lover – or even a rapist who violate her most precious of privacy. Was she an instrument of God, a tool of God, who had *no* say whatever, or was she an entity who was, like the opposite gender, free to enjoy the pursuit of happiness in all of its manifestations. Was the human race an *endangered* species, where every fetus must be protected? Were women just baby mills, spewing forth offspring for the glorification of God, or were they to be responsible, caring mothers in an enlightened world of *real* hope? Where does the arrogance of Eric Rudolph and this present maniac get off making that decision for her and so many others. They violate their own religion's tenets to enforce some nightmare they once had – interpreting the bad dream as god-speak of what they *must* do.

And the population thing is out of hand – out of control – with the Catholic Church, led by its voluntarily impotent hierarchy, enforcing by omission its subtle law against birth control. Mothers of third world nations affected by such insidious policy, continue having babies that must die because of lack of available nourishment. Always, pious old men and stupid young men in positions of power, making decisions for virile young women of the world. What *business* is it of theirs that a woman, not necessarily in concert with the gender imposed upon her, chooses a path of independence from the dictates of the orthodoxy and mentally infected, to live out her life as she has decided. It *is* her right in this country!

Their minds are as narrow, as their noses are long. Their tolerance is exemplified by their mental dysfunction. Their intelligence is as apparent as the hole where they hide. And their respect for their country is diametrically in opposition to what they claim. Though women are protected by the laws of the land -- if *Roe v. Wade* is overturned, then that protection becomes less as their health becomes more endangered. Was it not Madison who once said: *'(I) have in this Country extinguished forever the ambitious hope of making laws of the human mind. . . .'* and yet congress insists on doing just that, paving the road to the rescinding of that decision -- and in making laws that guarantee public subsidy of church run education and faith based assistance.

Erin continually reiterated to herself, as she drove her government car, the reasons why she had left the confines of her family and community's tradition. It was all about *freedom* – freedom of her mind, and body. It was *her* right, too! In America, that was an *inalienable* right, over and above the dictates of her former church, or any church for that matter. This was a nation that started out with the brazen assertion that this is the *'the land of the free, and the home of the brave!'* and *' . . . with liberty and justice for all'*— the latter Pledge of Allegiance having been altered to include only those who believed in some god. It now seemed more like the land of the ninnies, and the home of whiners. Individual freedom, especially for women like her, was being jeopardized by a growing insistence that the U.S. become a Christian theocracy so as to reap the full protection of God.

She made that point very effectively in the debate at the

War College, but it was small consolation in the face of rising hysteria that ' . . . we need and pray for more protection by the Man *above*.' What man – god was always a man – and where was 'above' anyway? She, Paul, and her friends at York weren't so fearful – they didn't seem afraid at all. And they were just as giving – maybe more so – than many Christians she knew. Thoughts of death didn't scare her like it had in the past, because she had put the concept of burning in Hell out of her intellect. Christians were so *terrified* of death -- probably because they weren't convinced themselves that they had enough faith in the mysterious Spirit that supposedly craved the undivided attention of their souls.

It was so wonderful to live without fear. Her new found courage opened doors to the unknown, and much happiness was experienced in the unfolding discoveries and challenges. The life that others had sought to control for her, was now her own, giving her the satisfaction of meeting responsibility head-on and ignoring all the naysayers. If there were a God, this is the full life He or She intended to be lived. *Living*, not cowing, is the ultimate of this opportunity of existence. She felt not as a piece of dirt, but as a tiller in the garden of Nature, growing the notion of truly enlightened civilization rather than just waiting for her piece of dirt to be probed by worms and trampled by idiotic shamans.

XXIV

Paul

While Erin was away during the first week of her 'assignment', Paul busied himself with the new class work. Hardly more than token courtesy acknowledgments greeted him as he went to-and-fro from classes. He generally took his lunches alone, interrupted on singular occasion by someone curious as to where Erin was. He could only generalize his answer thereby making communication with others even frostier.

At the apartment, he became more aware of his neighbors, especially the Army Captain who lived with his wife and two children next door. They were rather cool toward him, likewise, and he felt he stuck out like a sore thumb without his mate's presence. His average height and nondescript features never allowed him to be a 'Mr. Personality' but, oddly enough, he didn't feel lonesome – his confidence in himself was rock solid, and he kept his vision focused on what lay ahead, not on what had happened or would have happened if he had done things differently. Primary fears had been allayed in his matured ascendance to total self-responsibility.

He now looked incredulously at those colleagues he probably would have deferred to earlier in life. Happiness was no longer some event that occurred as a rare blip on a mundane plane of low ordinate. Even with Erin gone, everything was *light* – and he made light of circumstances that would have devastated him ten years before. It was as if he had achieved Nirvana – that final beatitude that transcends suffering – without dying. Now, depression was a rare blip on the high plane ordinate of self-understanding.

He overheard the neighbor's children playing one day, as he was taking his garbage to the Dumpster -- the boy, about ten or twelve, telling the younger girl that "He's an atheist!" It reminded him of the movie '*Chocolate*' where the heroine, a Gypsy mother, charmed a town in France with her many different preparations of that sweet, enticing commodity. Young children would peek beneath the drawn shades of her house to see her busy at her confection. "She's an *atheist*," one child said, and the other answered with a question: "What's an atheist?" Of course that child had yet to be carefully *taught.*

A few days later, the boy was selling magazine subscriptions and knocked on Paul's door. Upon opening the door, the boy began to ply his wares: "Are you interested in buying any magazines, sir?"

Paul, realizing it was the neighbor boy, was not inclined to turn him away. "Maybe . . . Whad'ya got?" and he invited him inside.

"Here's a list, Mister." The boy said handing him the colorful brochures. Paul noticed the boy's stare as he perused the lists.

"Let's see . . . we get TIME now." And he studied the list again, intent on choosing something for the boy to make a sale.

All the time, the boy stared at him with the widest of eyes.

"I think I'll take NATIONAL GEOGRAPHIC . . . how much would that be?"

The boy studied his chart and gave him a price for one, two and three years. "It's cheaper if you buy three years . . . cheaper a copy that is."

"All right – three years it is. Put me down for three years."

"You don't have to pay me now," the boy stammered. "They'll bill you later."

"Yes, I know. They'll bill me later." And he escorted the young salesman to the door.

As he was closing it, the boy suddenly turned and blurted: "My mom said you wouldn't buy anything, an' prob'ly slam the door in my face. But you seem like nice guy!"

"Well . . . did she say why she thought that way?"

"'Cause she says you're an atheist . . . and atheists don't do any *good* for anybody." He screwed up his face, and asked: "Don't you believe in God, mister?"

"I used to. When I was your age I did."

"You don't seem to be any dif'ernt than other people around here . . . and you wear an American Army uniform like my dad."

"It's a long story why I don't believe in God . . . maybe sometime we'll talk about it. But you better be getting on home before your mother gets worried."

"I think she worries too much 'bout everything."

"If she asks, you tell her that we atheists try to be good, upstanding, helpful citizens too."

"I will . . . 'cause I believe ya." And he disappeared out the door.

We lack good PR, he thought. But where does one start? Every clergyman, priest, rabbi and Imam vilify us every chance they get. He supposed they had that attitude about non-believers because it was bad job security to *say* otherwise. And everybody seemed to want to believe it when they said such patently false lies. The fact is, he reflected, he'd trust an atheist before some religious person. An atheist is honest enough to admit he has serious doubts about a

Supreme Being – at the risk of losing old friends, a place in Heaven and maybe a good job. How many religious people would admit *their* doubts to their fellow churchgoers? With an atheist, you knew exactly where he or she stands; with a religionist you don't know if they are sincere or just talking the *good* talk to gain your confidence, business – or vote.

Too many atheists keep quiet about their unbelief -- so as not to offend sensitive feelings of acquaintances. *Why is that?* he thought. <u>They</u> are the ones who should be most assured in their faith – or, maybe more likely, they aren't so sure of their faith at all! Think about it! On what foundation is faith built? With Christianity, it is built on a series of stories in the four gospels of the Bible, stories handed down by word of mouth for from forty to sixty years before someone thought to put them to paper. This so-called evidence would be inadmissible in a court of law because it would have been judged as here-say! Yet it is called *gospel truth* – a sin to dispute. He had heard quite enough of gospel truth in the form of snake oil and real estate salesmen – among others -- in the hills and hollows of Kentucky.

All the major religions have their beginning-of-time stories, and the line between myth and oral history is extremely blurred to say the least. Each of them is considered by its constituents to be the only *true* accounting, but in fact, differs in considerable degree from the others. And their squabbles have spilt over national borders to the extent of cruel behavior leading often to bloodshed. In fact, there are at least four such conflicts raging in the world today. If these major denominations cannot pacify and control their minion's passion, why should he subscribe to *any* of them? They are to each other as children fighting over candy or toys – not deserving of serious attention. Few dunderheads want to admit that the founding fathers, especially Franklin,

Washington, Jefferson and Madison saw quite clearly the pitfalls of allowing religion to influence the secular and neutrally designed American government.

Yes, he knew about the condescending nuances of the above four: Jefferson's mention of the Creator in the Declaration; Washington's inaugural address; Franklin's condoning Congress's opening with a prayer; and Madison's allowance of chaplains in Congress and the military – but, for Chrisake, they were flesh and blood politicians who had to tread quite carefully lest the sensitivity of the naive, and *uneducated* citizenry be hurt. And that blurring fog has continued to this day with the printing and stamping of our money with a new motto '*In God We Trust*'– tacked on at moments of national *fear.* The same was true with the Pledge of Allegiance – religionists not being satisfied that the original version was quite adequate for half a century, with no one protesting it. Fear of Communism in the McCarthy era precipitated its change to include ' . . . *under God*,' a beseeching or prayer for God's protection – which strongly smells of a violation of the First Amendment

Those fearful changes caused a cleft in the unity of America's citizenry. In both cases, in their original form, there were perhaps less than one percent who found '*E. Pluribus Unum*' and the omission of God in the Pledge lacking – and they were mostly clergy. Now, with the inclusion of ineffective pious servility, 15% and 30% of the population, respectively, feel that those additions are inappropriate – those inclusions now divide the once solid consensus of Americans. Pat Buchanan, the obtuse fundamentalist who started the Cultural War, would put a different spin on it. He would say that the majority of people in America wants and *needs* those changes – that the majority's wishes should prevail. In the grossest sense of

Democracy, he would be right. But the *Bill of Rights* – the first ten amendments to our Constitution -- neutralizes that grossness, providing warranty to the minorities certain rights and due process. This qualification seems to confuse, sailing over the head of, most fundamentalists. But it is those pesky ten amendments that the Judiciary is charged with studying and interpreting when they hand down many decisions deemed unpopular.

And what about the Cultural War? Paul found it strange that a Christian would start *any* kind of a war. True, there has been no spilled blood yet – or *has* there? What about the murders of gays and lesbians and abortion providers, like the one currently on rampage – are they directly linked to Buchanan's war, or only indirectly. And if that blood is not on his hands, Surely the war in Iraq is on George Bush's hands, invading that country on false and misleading information, killing thousands to vent his spleen. Another war started by a Christian, even against the wishes of the leaders of his own denomination -- and the Vatican!

Yet, he and Erin and other atheists were the *strange* ones in their reluctance to fall into lock-step with the unthinkables. They were the weird ones to be shunned and their voices to be drowned out in the cacophony of holy gibberish and mumbo-jumbo. It was looking more and more like humanity had painted itself into a corner, with no way to retrieve itself without getting soiled. But the metaphor is *mild* compared to the unreal *reality* that awaits the detoxification of vast numbers of humanity. Indeed, it is very questionable that humanity can survive the withdrawal from its mental opiate – even if it consciously wanted to do so!

'Why is it that we cannot face the simple truth? Religion is at best unsubstantiated superstition.' Says Massimo Pigliucci, an evolutionary biologist at the University of

Tennessee. Perhaps if we could face that truth, we might be surprised that the '*internal misery*' that Catholic theologians insist are our ordained lot could melt away. And then '*ideal happiness*' which was supposedly lost in the Garden of Eden, could be again found for those willing to go for it – when their neuroticism has melted away. But the tenets of most all clergy say this isn't possible – that what Paul has experienced in his self-reliance is '*false happiness*'. Paul thought that he would gladly accept whatever happiness comes his way.

XXV

Explosion

Erin was back at their apartment in Carlisle for the weekend. Friday nights were a joyous, consuming reunion for the two lovebirds, and they love wrestled in bed to the early morning hours. They could not keep their hands off each other as the touch of one anywhere on the other's body excited neuro-paths of sweet enjoyment and anticipation. Sexuality peaked time and time again as they lay cooing in each others' arms whispering of love endearments and appreciation. Their intimacy was *total* without confining, neurotic notions of restraint. Their lovemaking was a dream fulfilled -- beyond their wildest expectations. And their love spilled over into their daily routines, each helping the other with the chores. Paul's appreciation of Erin moved him to do for her, even *beyond* what he expected from her in return – and vice versa – Erin likewise, could not do enough for Paul. But their love was not blind, and each did not stumble in the way of the other in their show of affection.

They slept in, Saturday morning and, after another bout of love play, read the paper over a brunch.

"Honey, look at this!" Erin nearly shrieked.

He looked over her shoulder at the shocking headlines: "**Atheist Center Bombed**."

"The Atheist Union in Gallitzin has been bombed . . . they think it might be the work of my serial killer."

"Is that the place where those two at the Solstice party, dressed as nun and priest, were from?"

"Yeah, but they must be okay because it says here no one was in the building . . . no deaths, but a few injuries in houses nearby, and a bartender who was closing his pub."

"Wow! This guy is a one man inquisition . . . *it is* one man?"

"It appears so, from all accounts. Two men leaving the bar said they saw some stranger near the Center around 3:00 A.M."

"So, where's Gallitzin anyway . . . with a name like that it *must* be in Pennsylvania."

"You've been to their Web site . . . you know – *ASK ELMO?*"

"Oh, atheiststation.org. . . . Somewhere near Altoona . . . right?"

"Yeah, up on your Allegheny Mountain . . . where the railroad's mainline goes through the tunnels."

"I bet I know where you'll be going Monday."

"Yup . . . unless somebody tells me otherwise."

"Are you thinkin' about looking them up . . . whut's-their-names?"

"I think so . . . I've got their e-mail addresses in my palm pilot. I think they live in Altoona."

"Wasn't much of a building as I recall . . . though I understand it was the brightest, most colorful building in town."

"Yeah, I believe the lady – was it Adrienne – got the building from her mom and then they refurbished it, putting new siding on with the intent of renting it."

"That's right. And because of the lousy economy, they couldn't find a renter . . . then her and her group thought it would make a great meeting place for local atheists and other free-thinkers." He remembered from talking with them at the party.

"Honey, that was a blow against the very people we know and admire!"

"It's getting to be kinda like Northern Ireland." He choked. "Don't they realize that this could be a call for retribution."

"Honey, this seems to be only one man – not a gang of teenagers from the town."

"Yeah, I s'pose you're right. But didn't they say that they had *some* trouble from vandals in the past?"

"Nothing real serious . . . but it kept the town's policeman hopping from complaint to complaint."

Monday morning, Erin drove directly to Altoona to meet with Adrienne and her retired husband, Ben. She had called the night before, after an exchange of e-mails assured her of an invitation to a friendly base in that city. They welcomed her with open arms and commiserated over the terrorist's deed.

"We knew it was going to happen sometime!" Ben said as they sipped coffee. "But we expected it to be a local effort by whacked out religionists in the area."

"Yeah. Many of the people in Altoona and the valleys are fundamentalists, while the Catholics live mainly up there on the mountain. They all are pretty xenophobic . . . don't question anything except, "Why are we here?" They don't see *our* fundamental mission: that *we* exist too, and have undeniable rights in this country so long as we stay in accordance with the law. We have to *advertise* our existence so that these people know we are here and are not going away anytime soon. If we don't exercise our rights, we're afraid we'll lose them by default."

"You say all that on your Web site . . . so I wonder what his problem is?"

"He's *sick* . . . that's what his problem is." Ben piped up.

155

"Probably had a dream where God told him to do it."

"So you think he has a computer and knows how to access your Web site?"

"Or he gets his information from somebody else," Adrienne added. She offered other points of the assailant's character profile.

" You talk as if you've had some experience . . ."

"I was in law enforcement a long time ago . . . in the Southwest – Amarillo Police Academy, 1976." She smiled and said, " . . . and I read a lot of mysteries."

"Yeah, we were in New Orleans several years ago sitting on a park bench overlooking the River. I was enjoying the view of the ships coming and going when she nudges me and said we just saw a drug deal go down. She saw it – I sure as hell didn't. I looked around and saw this well-to-do guy walking fast, away from us. She's got eyes like a hawk . . . when she has her glasses on."

"You guys know this area real well?"

"Yeah, I'm a traveling notary and Ben is a retired surveyor. I know the roads and towns up on the mountain 'cause I was born and raised there."

"Raised a Catholic, huh?"

"Yup . . . I think most of the ones in our group are former Catholics, with the exception of my honey."

"Yeah, that seems to be the case in the York area, too." Erin turned toward Ben, asking: "What about you . . . you were formerly a Protestant?"

"That's right. I guess I made the jump when I was about twenty-five. I had studied civil engineering and worked for the Navy's Ocean Science program as a hydrographer after college."

"What's a hydrographer?" Erin asked, wondering what that had to do with his losing faith.

"We were surveyors . . . of the sea. We made charts . . . all over the place. International travel opened my eyes, especially when I visited the Catholic countries of Italy and Latin America. The poverty and the politics impressed me as a direct result of the Church's ubiquitous involvement with everything in the lives of those people, from cradle to grave," he said with a look of chagrin.

"But you were Protestant from a wealthy Protestant country – why should you care?"

"I see what you're asking. I suppose my travel experience confirmed what I had already subconsciously suspected – that religion was superstition, and that was the long and the short of it. It was boring, it was embarrassing, it was confining, and few really good people existed in its fold. Through my education and travels I met perhaps six or eight avowed atheists and was stunned by their integrity and trustworthiness. To a fault, they were honest and caring people leading me to suspect the claims of the clergy . . . as good as *they* let on to be. Not one large incident can I recall – many, many small incidents that accrued over the years to give me a bitter taste in my mouth for religion. Today, at my advancing age, that taste has become even more acrid when I see the likes of our Senator, Rick Santorum – or that other asshole from Connecticut – espousing their religion in order to gain the confidence of voters."

"Wow, you sound very discouraged!"

"I'm sorry, Erin. Really I am quite happy with life . . . I am so lucky to have a wonderful gal by my side like Adrienne . . . to kick me in the ass now and then." He smiled at his wife and reached for her hand. "And I vent my spleen with what I write on our Web site."

"What do you write?"

"He gets his kicks writing '*ASK ELMO*' Adrienne

interrupted, " . . . among other things."

"My husband likes ELMO a lot."

"It's a hoot making fun of all those serious, long-nosed, glum bastards out there." Ben added. "No one takes our point of view seriously – the *Altoona Mirror* has stopped printing my letters – so that is the only way I get to have fun!"

"Why won't they print your letters?"

"I s'pose my letters were affecting their circulation. They won't print two-thirds of the letters Adrienne sends in either. So, there you have it, freedom of speech is truncated in rural America by the likes of editors similar to that young shit, Steve what's-'is-name."

"We have better luck in York." Erin said. "The two newspapers there seem to welcome the give and take."

"This is beautiful country, here in the hills of Central Pennsylvania, but so many minds are closed to anyone who doesn't glorify Jesus." Adrienne added. "We've lived in many parts of the country and like it best here – so we both agreed: we're not moving."

"It's funny . . . religion is like surveying – you see the very worst side of people if you question their faith -- like you see the worst side of people if you find the property line six inches over on them from where they thought it should be."

"You've done so much with Atheist Union."

"It *will* live on . . . on the Web. We are *not* going away!"

"So there haven't been any negative messages . . . threats of any kind?"

"Nothing out of the ordinary. Once in a while we get a: '*You are sick*', '*You're going to hell*', or '*Why don't you get a life?*' They can't understand that this *is* our life, trying to maintain, through this holy terror, the tenets of Madison's and Jefferson's Republican Democracy."

Adrienne then added, "What I don't understand is, they have God on *their* side, and they feel threatened by a small group like us, yet we have no such God-like powers."

Erin wanted to get away, up to Gallitzin, but found it difficult to leave the two unbelievers: "I have talked to many people that have *never* met an atheist – that is a big part of the problem! For *that* reason if nothing else, we must make our presence known – to show that we *are* good, law abiding citizens too. They would like very much not to hear from us - - so I think what you are doing with your Web site is very appropriate, if not reverent. As Paul says, 'we must get in their faces'. We are not breaking any law but their ancient code of blasphemy, which has never been codified by this nation." She got up and offered her hand. "They'll get over it, and if they don't, they have all of eternity to get over our miniscule efforts of preservation."

At Gallitzin, she stopped by the Borough Hall, which also housed the police station. The town was unimpressive in its drabness and was dominated by the two huge Catholic churches on (what else?) Church Street. The Town Hall was a neat, single story building overlooking a huge railroad cut leading to two of the town's three famous tunnels. The recently constructed building also included the Borough's library and a small gift shop that sold mostly railroad memorabilia and knick-knacks. Across the parking area was a small public lookout area from which rail fans could view the heavy mainline traffic. It was complete with a decommissioned Pennsylvania Railroad caboose, which commemorated the days when that auspicious name meant the '*Standard of Railroads*'. From where she stood at her car, she could see in the distance the rubble of where a good size explosion had taken place. Ben and Adrienne had shown her photos of the late and humble building of Atheist Union that obviously had been taken from very near where she now stood.

Not expecting much in the way of information, she went in and was greeted by a frail, smoker's-voiced woman who was the Town's mayor. They were soon joined by the Town's policeman who indicated that he had pretty much been pre-empted in the explosion's investigation by the State Police. Ben and Adrienne had warned her of the Town's reluctance to pursue vandalism in the past.

"They pretty much ask for what they get," the heavyset, middle-aged policeman said.

"Why is that?" Erin asked, knowing full well what the answer would be. She suppressed her vision of a plate of donuts before him.

"This is a Christian town."

The mayor added, "Why did the atheists have to come here to set up shop?"

"Aren't they law-abiding citizens, too?"

"They . . . they believe in Communism . . . and that our Lord was a faker."

Erin nodded her head, realizing the futility of offering a counter opinion.

"'Whatever thouest sow, thou shall reap,'" the mayor added.

Typical small-town reaction, she thought to herself, evoking reports of the Scopes Monkey Trial eighty years ago. She felt a sudden urge to escape back into the sunshine from the burning stares of the two municipal officials.

"What is your function in all this, Ma'am?"

"Army Liaison to the Department of Homeland Security." She handed them her card and got up to leave. "The man who was seen by the two drinkers . . . was he a complete stranger?"

"It seems that way, Ma'am, though they noticed the cars plates – if it was his car – started with PP," the policeman offered.

"A vanity plate?"

"It's remotely possible, but much more likely to be a random prefix."

"Thank you for your time," she said, shaking their hands, wondering what their reaction would be if they knew she was atheist. That temptation passed when she considered the sensitivity of her professional position.

"Good luck and God bless." The mayor intoned as Erin left the office.

After stopping by the crime scene, she drove to the State Police Barracks at Ebensburg. It was Early afternoon and the Sergeant was in a meeting, so she took a seat in the small waiting room. The license plate prefix "PP" absorbed her attention. *Phineas Priest* kept coming up in her head – was there a connection? Surely, the state's records would show if it was a vanity plate. The fact that the guy noticed the prefix at all was unusual – unless he had a vanity plate *himself,* which might be the case.

Her reverie was interrupted by the duty officer's voice. "The Sergeant will see you now, Miss."

She was escorted through the door into a small office that reeked with duty to public safety. "Welcome to the front lines of the State of Pennsylvania," he said with a smile, obviously referring to her uniform. "It isn't often we see Army personnel around here . . . especially pretty women wearing the uniform." He offered her his hand, "Bob Melesko at your service."

A charmer, she thought. "You're very flattering, Sergeant."

"What can we do for you today? I understand you are

working with Homeland Security on the Gallitzin bombing?"

"Yes, Sir. I've been assigned to find out if there is any connection this madman might have to international terrorists."

"al-Qaeda?"

"Exactly."

He leaned back in his chair and ran his fingers through his graying hair. "So far, we've come up with nothing."

"What about the license plate?"

"Has to be out of state! There are no two letter prefixes on automobiles in this state."

"The witness didn't recognize it from being out of state?"

"As a matter of fact, he did. The plate he saw was on the front of the car and, as you know Lieutenant, Pennsylvania is one of the few states that has no front plate requirement."

"Could it have been Maryland?"

"Maybe . . . *they* have a two letter prefix code on some of their plates."

"You didn't check with Harrisburg to see if a vanity plate was issued with a "PP" prefix."

"No, but I don't see the point . . ."

"Please . . . would you?"

"PP, followed by a set of numbers -- highly unlikely!"

"But, it *is* possible . . . that if it were a vanity, they would be exhibitionist enough to have a duplicate made privately, for the front?"

"Sure," he shrugged his shoulders. " Sit tight, and I'll see what we can come up with." He left the office.

A short while later he returned with a printout in hand. "There were two plates issued in 1999, both of which are still on the road." He highlighted the printout and handed it to her.

She read the designation: PP MAP 1 and PP MAP 2,

registered to Philip and Margaret Ann Popovich of Erie. "Hmm," she studied, thinking to herself that this was not a likely suspect. She sensed the Sergeant's doubt of her alacrity, and was feeling uneasy that she was allowing her personal sentiments to influence her objectivity in the case. "You're right, Sergeant. Maybe it's Maryland. It's just that my superiors think this guy is holed up in the mountains of PA."

"The mountains of Maryland aren't far away . . . and Homeland Security has already shared their sentiments with us!"

She left feeling her pushing the tag issue was a wild goose chase. They knew what they were doing and had probably already checked pertinent Maryland tags. And if they found anything that pointed toward a Phineas Priest, she was out of a job seeing that a Priest would be the arch enemy of an al Qaeda operative. . . zealots at both extremes, and she was the neutral in between, hardly a friend to either as a freethinking atheist.

XXVI

On The Beat.

She spent the remainder of the week poring over maps in the evenings, and traveling the roads she had studied during the day to familiarize herself with the area and its terrain. On the probable notion that Sergeant Melesco was correct, she expanded her area of interest south into Maryland, northern Virginia and West Virginia. If she thought the hills of Pennsylvania were spooky, the mountains south of the Mason – Dixon Line were incredible, in their height and steep slope. The Interstate highway, I – 68, finished in the nineties, traversed thirty miles of mountainous terrain east of Cumberland Maryland in modern, freeway style, slicing through Sideling Mountain, one of the world's deepest manmade cuts.

Stopping at the visitor's center at the east toe of the cut, she remembered talking to the curator who was a geologist. "This excavation reveals millions of years of sediment deposited on the ocean floor prior to being heaved in the air by cataclysmic tectonic forces." She thought of how Paul would have appreciated talking to him.

West of Cumberland, I – 68 topped Mount Savage at an elevation as high as any mountain in the Keystone State. "During the winter, whiteouts occurred frequently on the Allegheny Front, between Cumberland and Frostburg," the curator had said, in his description of that geological division line Paul had apprised her of before. And south of I – 68 in West Virginia, U.S. Route 50, began its steep descent down the Front, at Mount Storm, with a panorama to the east hardly equaled anywhere. *That* area atop the plateau was dotted with crusty coal towns and clear-cut strips in between verdant forests.

More and more she realized this was not al Qaeda territory. Her killer was not al Qaeda, but some deluded hillbilly who took his dreams, and his preacher, too seriously. For that reason, she wanted to stay on the case to seek out this warp-minded pimple on civilization. It was interesting she thought, how the extremes of one religious sect were interpreted by people of other faiths as completely whacko, and the zealots of *their* faiths were just orthodox soldiers that walked and talked with God. *Allah* walked and talked with Osama bin Laden, as *God* did with George Bush – doesn't anybody recognize the insanity of their claims? Oh sure, bin Laden is the crazy one we say, but Bush is the *crazy one* to the Moslems of the world. And the split is *complete*! There is no reconciling of the two largest religions on the planet, even as they strive to discredit this planet in favor of a much more wonderful place that exists in their imaginations. *And they sprang from the same ancestor, Abraham!* What was God thinking when he allowed *that* to happen?

Back in Carlisle, she luxuriated in Paul's love making and innovative embraces, free of all concern whatever. "They were so lucky – so *free"* they remarked to each continually in the passions of their union. Conversation of the week's events was interposed between their episodic lovemaking and post-coital slumber. Saturday and Sunday mornings were to them like the Elysian Fields, in their satisfying and glorification of each other. They struggled to interlace each of their torso and extremities as much as possible with the other, for that ultimate thrill of intimacy. Then they would breathlessly lose consciousness while still embraced.

"I love you, Erin." He said upon awakening.

She returned a similar refrain, then kissed him warmly.

"Are you taking care to keep your distance from the bogeyman?"

"Darling, I'm supposed to *close* that distance."

"I don't want you getting too close – your not *trained* as a cop!"

"Well, I'm no where near him, yet . . . and it doesn't seem that I ever will."

"Why do you say that?"

"For one thing, he's not al Qaeda. And as soon as I confirm that fact, I'm off the case."

"And you'll be back here with me."

"That would be nice." She said, smiling provocatively. "So how are your studies? She asked, not wanting to talk anymore about her unproductive week.

"It's been quiet. I miss the give and take of college bull sessions. It's like Stevens and Anderson rolled over and are playing dead."

"We got to them, darling. They can't hold a candle to objective rationality . . . and they know it."

"But . . . why *is* that?" He looked into her sparkling blue eyes. "Why is it so plainly obvious to us, while they hang on to their threadbare encumbrances?"

"Remember how tough it was for *us* to break away from that security blanket?"

"Yeah, . . . it *was* tough!"

"I think that there comes a point in everyone's life when, if life is comfortable, and unchallenging, people stick with what they know . . . what they've been taught. Why give up a tradition that has carried their ancestors into the 21st century. *Better the God you know rather than the one you don't know*." She propped her head up with hand and elbow, prominently displaying the fullness of her breast. "That's why people of substance and standing are so intertwined with their religion – they *have* so much to be thankful for. They *need* to owe their good fortune to an Almighty because so much was handed to them, either in the form of money or in physical endowment. I think that is why so many athletes do their kneeling and crossing, showing their humility and thankfulness in moments of triumph."

"You should've been a psychologist."

"I've had a few courses." She smiled, then asked, "So, is Troutman allowing you to pursue your political project?"

"Like you, he thinks it a bit quixotic." He pursed his lips indicating his waning confidence. "He feels the electoral process is just fine and can't be improved upon."

"That ignoramuses should get away with conning the public into a false sense of security -- Selling them a bill of goods like the war on Iraq, or questionable Medicare reform and education reform here at home?"

"It's up to the electorate . . . and all their wisdom" He smiled. "You're not playing the devil's advocate very well, honey."

"But, you *do* have a point in your premise. Even Plato had considered it."

"Thanks, I'll rewrite my proposal pointing out all the damage that was done in the Bush Administration. There's enough material evidence there to convince a gaggle of koala bears.

"And Republicans?"

"Unbiased, informed Republicans! Those who are more in tune with history rather than hysteria. Those who are more in tune with their conscience than their pocketbooks."

"I get the picture."

"Trouble is, the picture is in color and I need to make it

black and white."

"Is Troutman Republican?"

"I have *no* idea . . . but I s'pose, to be on the safe side, I should assume so."

"If such a proposal is to make it into law, you will have to convince those who have played the confidence game to perfection. How do you propose to surmount that formidable obstacle?"

"Honey, I'm such a rube!" and he covered his face with his hand.

"It's *still* a worthwhile effort . . . maybe something will come of it." She ran her hand through his hair. "Darling, don't let it get you down." Then, moving her hand elsewhere, she added: "I know something that will *come* in a little while if we cuddle some more. I like my men to be a little on the quixotic side." And she kissed him.

XXVII

Profiles in Courage

"I appreciate you coming today to hear me jabber again. I *do* enjoy talkin', more so than ever . . . now that those days are gone when I *had* to do it for a living." The effervescent Clemens was again center stage. "I know you were expectin' Phyllis Diller to introduce our speaker today, but she was unexpectedly detained . . . probably in consultation with engineers about her face lift!"

There were some groans as well as some chuckles from down Front.

"I s'pose I should apologize for that unkind remark . . . it's just that, looking upon her reminds me of the street plan of Boston." There was a pause as if waiting for some response. "I see, few of you have been to Boston . . . well, I have -- and that was before the city had subways."

Another pause and a cloud of smoke. "But I'm not here to talk about Boston, but to introduce to you one of its favorite sons, President John F. Kennedy. You can say what you want about the man, and many have -- even with *clenched* teeth, but there were certain distinguished traits about him that no one can take away." He looked piercingly out at the audience with heavy, drawn eyebrows.

"It cannot be taken from him, that he gave his all for his country – even though he *was* a politician, and you know how I feel about politicians! Somehow he exuded a sense of youthful altruism, not only to those in the U. S. but throughout the world. He was an idealist, even if he came

169

from an in-idealistic background – a family whose fortune was unceremoniously gained taking full advantage of the prohibition era. But in America, I think, *still* to this day, the sins of the father do not become those of his sons, and the sons have served well that country, without blemish."

"The first, and only, Catholic to reach that high office, he promised in his campaign that the vision of separation of church from state would be maintained, with no influence whatsoever from the head of his faith's Church in Rome." He took a long puff on his cigar, and continued. "Many suspected that that might be the case, and his election to office was extremely close, over the consummate politician Richard M. Nixon, who, I might add, has not been seen on *this* plane. I do believe *that* man's fears overcame his sensibilities."

"Anyhow, without further ado, or embarrassment, I give you the 35th president of the United States of America, *John F. Kennedy.*"

That solid figure many in the audience knew so well walked out from the wings "Thank you, Sam." Turning to the onlookers of thousands, he thanked them also.

"They call you Jack, don't they." Clemens pried from behind a cloud of smoke.

"Yes sir, they do." Kennedy answered, waving futilely at the tainted air.

"Is it true, Mr. President . . ."

"Call me Jack."

Clemens hesitated as if it was beyond him to take such liberty with so distinguished a guest. "Isn't that a bit confusin' . . . with your wife's name bein' '*Jackie*'?

"She doesn't mind."

Clemens looked aside at the audience, in puzzlement -- to their amusement -- then recovered, continuing his inquiry:

"Is it true, Jack, that your fine book, '*Profiles in Courage*' was not written by you but, in truth, was ghost written?"

"Who told you that? I want to know who leaked that information . . ."

"Come now, Mr. Pres. . . er, Jack, everyone suspects that to be a fact."

"Well, look at you," Kennedy said, taking a hands-on-hips stance.

"What d'ya mean?" Clemens looked with mouth hanging open.

"I had the courage to put *my* name on a book that I admit I had a lot of help with . . . but you wrote *many* books, and put someone else's name on *them*."

"I can explain that." Clemens said in a quieter tone and a puff of smoke.

"You don't have to, Sam," Kennedy smiled at the crowd. "Jus . . . just lay off me, will ya – next you'll be asking questions about a certain movie staa."

"I don't know what you're talkin' about."

"Oh, that's right . . . you passed away long before *that* happened."

"Ouch!" Clemens feigned being hurt.

"Anyway, I bet you made more money with your story telling than I made telling other people's stories."

"I had to make a livin' somehow. Besides, you just said a run-on sentence."

"You could have stuck to being a sailor – like I was during the war."

"Riverboat pilot, Jack, not a sailor – there's a dif'rence."

"So . . . you want to hear about some of the profiles in my book – I've had a chance to read it!"

Quietly, leaving a trail of smoke Clemens backed off the stage – to much applause.

"Mr. Clemens is partly right. As he intimated, my book *'Profiles in Courage'* was researched and assisted very ably for me by Theodore Sorensen. However, I did choose the individuals to be profiled, from my studies while in college and in the hospital recovering from back surgery. I was wealthy enough, but very busy, and wanted to write more but didn't have the time. It was necessary, I thought, to tell the truly courageous stories of a handful of senators that refused to compromise their high integrity. They're efforts in most cases were career ending. Others survived and won the day. I produced this book to counter the growing antithesis towards political candidates – a sort of guide to the would-be politician -- to be *courageous and take the high road* when national interests are at stake . . ."

Paul awoke with a pressing urge to use the latrine. Walking in a daze, he kept trying to remember details of his dream to tell Erin. She was intrigued by the vividness of his recurring dream adventures. The dreams were of such good, positive quality that they seemed in every way to reinforce his philosophical path in life. There was a time, way back, when his dreams were very disconcerting, except when he was experiencing much stress in his college studies. Crawling back under the covers and snuggling up against Erin's cool backside, he hoped to continue the dream by trying to recall more about what he had read in Kennedy's book. He was trying to recall . . .

"John Quincey Adams's senatorial career was truncated after one term because of his virulently independent attitude that his nation come first over the dictates of his party. He was a Federalist but voted for many important things that Jefferson proposed as president, and his constituents recalled him, electing another candidate after his one term of office. Ironically, his independence later propelled him to the White

House for a one term presidency – and he was fired again – only to be asked later, by his community, to stand for election again, as their representative to Congress.

"He acquiesced, specifying that he should never be expected to promote himself as a candidate and ask for votes; and . . . that he would pursue a course in Congress completely independent of the party and people who elected him. On that basis, he was elected by a large vote, and served in the House until his death. He had recorded in his diary of that last position: 'No election or appointment conferred upon me so much pleasure. My election as President of the United States was not half so gratifying to my inmost soul.'

Kennedy's gaze scanned his listeners with watery eyes and remarked: "Is it any wonder that politicians are held with such distrust today. With the exception of Senator Jefford's abandonment of the Republican Party to become an Independent several years ago, how many congressmen can you name who have taken such a stand?"

He continued after a respectful pause. "Daniel Webster, the unequaled orator, also from Massachusetts I might add, did much the same thing, abandoning his constituents' wishes in order to save the Union. Because of his brazen and autonomous stand, his career also ended, terminating any hope of his achieving his life long ambition to become President. His 'March 7th speech in 1850' was his swan song packing the House galleries, and enabled Henry Clay's Compromise of 1850. A compromise that delayed civil war for another eleven years – allowing the North to grow significantly in population, industry and transportation in the interim.

"Two southern senators, Thomas Hart Benton and Sam Houston, also bucked their party and constituents to cast the deciding votes for the Compromise of 1850. Neither would submit to sectional politics, claiming the Union must be maintained. Benton's thirty-year career (the longest service of any senator) was reluctantly ended because of that vote.

"Sam Houston's plight was particularly sad in that he was considered Mr. Texas, having beaten Santa Anna at San Jacinto, winning independence from Mexico. He was president of the new Republic of Texas and then its first senator when Texas entaad the Union. But with the vote on the Compromise, he, too, fell into disfavaar and was recalled. Even so, he regained popularity, and in 1859 was elected Governor of Texas without any party affiliation. But Texas had become a significant slave holding state and when Lincoln became President, secessionists ruled the day ignoring his advice and warnings about leaving the Union. He was again removed from office, this time because of his refusal to take the oath of the new Confederate state. When asked about his honest opinion of the secessionist leader, Houston replied: 'He has all the characteristics of a dog except fidelity.'

"Aftaa the Civil Waar, with Andrew Johnson stepping into Lincoln's place as President after the latter's assassination, Northern Republican's were outraged at the policies and vetoes of the new President. Though of different parties, Lincoln tapped Johnson to be his running mate in 1864 because of his undying devotion to maintaining the Union. As a Tennessee Democrat, he was the only senataa of a secessionist state to stand against the South's whirlwind withdrawal from the Union, and Lincoln requested his presence in his bid for re-election with the hopes of reaching out a conciliatory hand to the border state Waar Democrats.

"But the profile I offaa now is not so much that of Johnson, and his trumped up impeachment, but that of one young freshman Senator from Kansas, Edmund G. Ross, whose vote preserved the institution of the Presidency. At the time, Radical Republicans wished to impose punishment on the defeated South and submitted bill after bill for just that purpose, many of which were vetoed by Johnson. Soon theaar was a movement afoot to remove the obstacle, Mr. Johnson, by impeachment proceedings, so thaat the South could be propaarly trampled.

"Of seven Republican Senators who would not go along with the kangaroo court, Only Mr. Ross kept his sentiments to himself until the very last minute. During the long run-up to the day of the Senate's vote, he was queried, cajoled, threatened and bribed to insure his vote for condemnation. It wasn't enough that his voting record had been counter to Johnson's southern protection and that his dislike for the new President was well known, but his party demanded that he confirm his enmity beforehand. The Senate, acting as judge and jury, requiraad a two-thirds majority of 36 votes to remove a sitting President – and it fell one vote shoart of dooming the Office of the President to one of future impotence. Of course, Mr. Ross was vilified by most all the northern papers, his party colleagues and the citizens of the new state of Kansas. Suffice it to say that none of the seven Republicans were returned to office from their respective states.

"Again, Kennedy's tear-impregnated eyes looked out to the quiet audience. "Of course it is too late to right a wrong . . . and history will repeat itself, yet again. There is nothing we can do here but to marvel at the folly of it all! It is interesting to note that four of the above mentioned five Senators, as well as the remarkably conscientious Lucius Q. C. Lamar of Mississippi, were affected by the split between the North and the South – that split affecting nearly all the first half of the nineteenth century"

"In Lamar's case, it was about economics after the 'Crash of 1873', that his efforts nipped in the bud the inflationary thought of 'free silver'. For his stand against the expeditious attempt to bolster the short term value of ever increasing quantities of silver, by coining it upon demand, he would suffer the enmity of his constituents who saw it as slap in the face of their recovery from the war.

"In the twentieth century there were two Midwestern, Republican Senators who stood squarely against the tide, and acted on the dictates of conscience: George W. Norris was a conservative from Nebraska whose sentiments slowly changed to independence and then to progressive as his illustrious career unfolded. In 1910 and again in 1917, he cold-cocked his party with deserved insolence, yet survived termination, unlike the six above profiled Senators. In 1910, The young Representative was instrumental in unseating 'Czar Joseph Cannon' from the House Speaker's position, in adept strategy and moments of vulnerability. Even though Speaker Cannon was of his own party, he explained his motives to the people back home: *I would rather go down to my political grave with a clear conscience than ride in the chariot of victory as a Congressional stool pigeon, the slave, the servant, or the vassal of any man, whether he be the owner and manager of a legislative menagerie or the ruler of a great nation. . .'*

"As a Senator in 1917, he spoke out against the Merchant Ship Armament Bill, convinced that its inception would hasten the United States into a war that armament and industrial manufacturers were itching for. Though the country was brought into the war several months later, his stand at the time met with mixed feelings back home, allowing him to survive. Then, in 1928 as a progressive, he broke from his conservative constituency to support the

Catholic, end prohibition, Tammany Hall candidate for President, Al Smith – even though he was a Protestant, and a 'dry' Republican. He had explained once: *'. . . sure of my position . . . unreasonable in my convictions, and unbending in my opposition to any other party or political thought except my own. . . . One by one I saw my favorite heroes wither . . . I discovered that my party . . . was guilty of virtually all the evils that I had charged against the opposition.'* . . . Said the intrepid Norris

Robert A. Taft, son of President William Howard Taft, had aspirations of himself one day becoming President. But he, too, was endowed with the individualism of those mentioned before. It was 1946 and the Nuremberg trials were winding down, with death sentences meted out to eleven Nazis convicted for 'waging an aggressive war.' What piqued Taft's concern was that these Nazis were tried on an *ex post facto* law that was hastily adopted after the defined offensive act was perpetrated. His concerns met with little sympathy but, in defense, he explained: *'I question whether the hanging of those, who, however despicable, . . . will ever discourage the making of aggressive war . . . About the whole judgment there is the spirit of vengeance, and vengeance is seldom justice. The hanging of the eleven men convicted will be a blot on the American record which we shall long regret.'*

"I leave you at this time with this: Without belittling the courage with which men have died, we should not forget those acts of courage for which men have lived. A man does what he must to further improve the condition of *all* men – in spite of obstacles and dangers and pressures. And that, ladies and gentlemen, is the basis of all human morality."

XXVIII

Re-assignment

"Sweetheart, the phone's for you." Paul announced. It was Monday morning and he was preparing to go to class. Gathering his things together, he noticed how intent Erin's facial expression was. She soon hung up the phone.

"Was that your Colonel?"

"Yeah."

"Can you talk about it . . . I've got a few minutes before I must leave?"

"I think I should. You need to know that they want me to see Sergeant Melesco this afternoon . . . something's come up and they want me on the scene . . . for what reason, I have no idea."

"Sounds intriguing. I wish I could go with you."

"I know honey; I wish you could too." And she stepped into to his enfolding arms.

"Don't forget . . . I'm just one phone call away – You have your cell phone, right?"

"Yes darling, she purred, her voice barely audible as he crushed her to his uniform. "And you . . . you'll carry yours to class?"

"Absolutely . . . everywhere I go."

"The Colonel's voice was so cold . . . his message so cryptic."

Silently, they found reassurance in each others' embrace.

"Everything's going to be okay. For god's sake, the Pennsylvania State Police is on your side, backed up by

Homeland Security!"

"I know, but I'm not an *operative.* I'm just an over educated library researcher – what could they want from me?"

"Maybe more research."

"Yeah, I hope that's *all* they want!"

"He loosened his embrace.

"Hold me a little longer . . . I feel, I need some of your strength."

"My strength?" You're tough as nails!" I'm a pussy-cat . . . with big ideas, that's all."

"Look how tough you were in our debate."

"Not as tough as you, with your devastating cross examination."

"You'll come if I call you?"

"Honey, when have I not come, when you called . . . or do other things to me."

"Not that, *silly*!" she removed her head from his shoulder and smiled at him. "Can't you ever be serious?"

"Well, I thought maybe that would cheer you up . . . thinking about all the times you made *me come.*"

"It does cheer me up, sweetie. What do you think I think about when I'm driving all over creation."

"That's wonderful. Oops, I'm getting' tight down there, I better get going – or you won't be safe havin' me around."

"I'd rather have you . . . the devil I *do* know, than the one waiting for me out there that I don't know."

"Cheer up, sweetheart. Think about our next weekend coming up."

"Okay, soldier boy. I love you very much!"

"I love you too . . . Please be careful, and give me a call . . . whenever."

Her drive out the Turnpike was lost in her reverie of the

past weekend's love making with Paul. She felt so alive in his embraces and kisses. Life was so exciting and she couldn't imagine being any happier. She knew that he felt the same way about her, too; the way he took his time to assure her of her experiencing ultimate pleasure. And it was so obvious how he reveled being with her, too. It seemed what he enjoyed playing about her, she enjoyed the playing immensely, also – and vice versa when she played with him. She couldn't understand why so many in life disdained such wonderful expressions of intimate love as being lustful and the devil's temptation – an evil to be avoided if possible. She recalled knowing pious maidens, enraptured in thoughts of being with God rather than a man, in some imaginary, safe, virgin cocoon, for eternity. Catholic nuns were considered chaste enough to be '*Brides of Christ*', married to a spirit, but unfulfilled of their natural biological demand. She thought that maybe fear of the real world drove those poor women into the refuge of the convent.

In their many conversations on the subject of sexual abstinence, unlike her, Paul *had* experience of embarrassing torment when his easily excited organ insisted on bulging his trousers at inappropriate times. She remembered not being so easily excited when she was at that tender age – but then her genitals were not exposed to inadvertent, everyday rubbing as was the male organ. Paul had told her how about when he was in high school, doing his homework late at night, he would experience a twinge of something like a gentle but demanding sensation between his legs, and, trying to put it from mind, the suppression only made that excitement increase all the more. Finally, and *guiltily*, he succumbed to masturbating – if only to relieve the condition so he could return to his studies. A wonderful release to be sure – but the guilt associated with it was complete. There were so many stories about how a boy could lose his eyesight, or even his sanity, if continued to indulge in self-play. He related to her that his early neuroticism probably stemmed from such over-riding guilt – masturbation being totally banned in the Bible.

Today, science has debunked such self-relief as being perfectly normal. Indeed, *not* to relieve such natural and powerful urges is considered unhealthy -- both physically and mentally. She knew of studies that have proved that the more frequent the male orgasm occurs, the healthier his prostrate gland remains – leading to a longer, *fulfilled,* happier life. Her husband's unconcern about how they experience his orgasm, now, has all but banished from his psyche the naïve, mind-gripping guilt and debilitating repression. How dare such long nosed busybodies drive pubescent young boys into despair over a natural urge they can hardly deny! Unknowingly – or *do they know?* – the Church drives innocent young men into mental dysfunction -- or an early, rushed marriage at the least, and at most, into suicide, *or* the violation of young women to avoid '*spilling their seed on the ground*'. Incredibly, the Church says that it is the devil's temptation that provides the engine of lust, yet, if a non-complying woman is raped and is impregnated, *then* it is God's will – God's creation of a child, that to abort would be a sin. Where is the rationale in such conflicting blather?

As she neared her exit, and the last fifty miles of her journey to Ebensburg, her thoughts drifted to Sergeant Melesco. What was it in their less than functional conversation a week ago that tweaked his interest? She was convinced she had fumbled the ball in her representation of her office, and that he was polite but defensive of his department's handling of the affair. At any rate, she felt her involvement in discovering the killer's whereabouts were moot since she had, herself, diagnosed the perpetrator's intentions, and they were hardly in coordination with al Qaeda.

At the State Police Barracks, Sergeant Melesco did not keep her waiting long. Hesitantly, she took the offer of his hand and sat down opposite his desk. After the exchanging pleasantries, he leaned forward with elbows on his desk and hands folded under his chin, he stared into her eyes: "His car has been spotted again. You were right . . . in your assumption that his front plate was a vanity – not an official tag, but one produced privately."

"Wow." She uttered, though she suspected this was not the reason for her being summoned. "Then . . . he is a Phineas Priest?"

"If that is what the "PP" stands for."

"You'll be making the arrest soon, then . . .?"

"If only things could be that easy."

"You don't have a make on his tag?"

"Unfortunately, no."

"So, why have you requested me to come out here, since . . ."

"Because, I have a plan, and with your cooperation . . ."

"My *cooperation*?" she fairly blurted. "My involvement has ended with the. . ."

"Please hear me out Lieutenant." He insisted with a look of commanding seriousness. "It was something *you* had said at our last meeting that got me thinking."

"Thinking what, if I may ask?" she said sardonically.

"I'll not beat around the bush, Lieutenant. But I got the impression from talking to you before, that you might not be too serious about religion."

"So, what makes you think that?"

"The way you rushed to Atheist Union last week, interviewing the owners – it was as if you knew where to go .

. . that you knew them from before!" He cleared his throat, and went on: "But when you made the comparison of al Qaeda with religious fanatics in this country, it dawned on me that that view is not often, if ever, heard. Are you what they call a free-thinker, or an atheist?"

"What if I say no?"

"It doesn't matter. What I have in mind will work either way, that is, with *your* cooperation."

"You want to use *me* as bait, don't you?"

"We have your Colonel Simmins's permission." He smiled confidently. "If you are an atheist, I know you would like very much to see this fanatic apprehended. Colonel Simmins thinks you are somewhat of that bent, and he has the greatest confidence in your abilities."

She saw the trap closing. "I *am* a-theist, but I'm *not* a field operative . . . why aren't you calling in one of your own, that is trained in enforcement?"

"Because you've been to school on this guy. You've been researching him for over a year . . . and because you have a vested interest in *getting* him."

"Because I'm an atheist . . . and a woman." She said matter-of-factly.

"Exactly. I think you'll agree that he's a misogynist."

Wow, law enforcement grunts using such big words, she thought. "You have no atheists in the State Police?'

"I don't know any who are full blown." He shrugged his shoulders, "I know of many who are doubters, to some degree . . . don't go to church – that sort of thing."

"What about the F.B.I.?"

"What about them?" he asked with a hint of going defensive. "They're *involved*, of course."

"An atheist friend of mine is with the Bureau."

"So . . . you're suggesting that a trained F.B.I agent who

is an atheist be called in to play, here?" He squared his shoulders and sat very erect. "Do you have any idea, Miss Beckwith . . ."

"That's Lieutenant Beckwith, if you'd mind."

He nodded with reluctance, and went on, "*Lieutenant* . . . the difficulty of drawing your friend into this case at this late hour?"

"I can imagine," she said with an air to avoid a hint of insubordination. "But I'm just a tad reluctant to get into the line of fire of what you're asking – I hope you can understand that."

"Yes Miss, Er, Lieutenant. I *do* understand your concern for your personal safety."

She heard herself saying: "I would be glad to undertake this effort with a Special Agent of my choosing and, like you say, beliefs."

"I see." She could read his thoughts on his facial expression -- that *nothing is easy.* "I'll have to get back to you on this . . . Where will you be staying?"

"At the Ramada, in Altoona."

"What's your friend's name?

"Ted McAuliff."

"And he's in Washington?"

"His residence is suburban Virginia."

"Please consider our talk here today, as confidential." He said as he got up to escort her to the door. "Thank you for coming out here on such short notice."

"Orders are orders."

"There's something I don't understand." The police Sergeant said while opening the door for her. "I was curious as to why you keep saying a-theist instead of atheist?"

"The word atheist has been dragged through the dirt for ages and is synonymous with evil by the ignorant and superstitious minded. I use the emphasis on the *short* 'a' to qualify the word of its rightful meaning, that is: *not being* theist. Another example would be the word: *atypical*, meaning *not being* typical."

"Í thought it means the irrevocable belief that there is no God ."

"That's true . . . some of us feel that way – many others are simply not theistic but indifferent to the fact that God or gods might exist. They, including my husband and I, would rather be categorized as being atheist rather than recognize any of the world's religions."

"Then you *do* think it is possible that a god exists?"

"It's *possible*. Never say *never*! Of course it's possible, but I believe it's highly unlikely . . . and if there is one, he or she is not taking prayers or interfering with the laws of Nature. It's up to us to find this killer – you know that! When was the last time God led you personally through to the successful conclusion of a case?"

He stood in the doorway, wanting to say something, but couldn't.

"It's your forensic science, the singular efforts of the gumshoe on a stakeout, ballistics analysis and medical examinations that solve your cases – God doesn't help you much, does he?"

She drove down the mountain to Altoona, but did not stop to visit with Ben and Adrienne, lest she inadvertently divulge sensitive information. Instead, she immediately checked into the Ramada, on the south end of the city, and collapsed onto the bed. She lay there staring at the ceiling, considering a myriad of possibilities: would McAuliff be available? How much of this could she relate to Paul over the phone? Would her orders to cooperate with Melesco stand if McAuliff wasn't available? Would she resign her Commission rather than get in harm's way? And how would Melesco's plan interface with the killer's itinerary?

The last item sent a shiver down her back, and it wasn't the kind of shiver she experienced with Paul in close proximity! She lay, taking deep breaths – decompressing from the exciting, if shabby, invitation of a challenge. Isn't this why she joined the Army – for the excitement that it might offer? Melesco was right – she *has* a vested interest in seeing this guy brought to justice. If he was a Phineas Priest, *she* would represent to him everything that is *despicable* on this planet. She would be the ideal bait in her apostasy and her flinging away of Eve's *original sin*.

A little later, Erin reached for the phone and called her husband and talked to him as cryptically as possible. Then she sat at the desk with pen in hand, thinking of ways to turn disadvantage into advantage.

XXIX

Erin's Terms

The phone burped four times before she realized it wasn't in her dream. "Hello," She managed.

"Caught you sleeping in, eh?"

"Oh, Sergeant Melesco?" she yawned. "What time *is* it?"

"Seven fortyfive." He answered. "And I've got good news for you!"

"You've caught the deranged son-of-a-bitch!"

"Well . . . not exactly *that* good. But . . . Lieutenant, I'm surprised to hear you talk like that."

"But you wouldn't be surprised if it were coming from a male?"

"Touché, Lieutenant . . . but the good news is that agent Ted McAuliff is on board and will be in Pennsylvania first thing tomorrow morning."

"Tomorrow – that's Wednesday morning, right.?" She wasn't fully awake and yearned for some hot black coffee.

"Yes, Lieutenant," he said with just a hint of testiness. "Tomorrow morning is Wednesday."

"Can I call you back after I eat a bite?" and she took down his number in case she had misplaced his card.

Getting dressed, she realized that she had gotten to first base and felt safe knowing that Ted would be looking out for her. After breakfast, she called Sergeant Melesco back and they discussed the particulars of their meeting. She would not be returning to Ebensburg, but instead was given directions to the State Police Barracks at Somerset. She was to check out of the Ramada and bring all her gear. They would meet at 0900 to discuss a plan of action. Those in attendance would be herself, Melesco, Sergeant Peters of the Somerset Barracks, Agent McAuliff, Colonel Simmins, and the State Police Commandant, Colonel Brubaker.

Her unit commander was right after all, she thought, designating the Somerset area as the focal point of interest. She noted that the Sergeant referred to the killer as *Sick Bear* over the phone – probably for security reasons. Somewhat relieved over the turn of events, she looked over her wish list.

In the Pennsylvania mountains, there was no such thing as a straight line route between many places -- Altoona to Somerset being no exception. She experienced, too often, the local's answer to her request for directions, *"You can't get there from here"*—because of the terrain. As the crow flies, the direct route to Somerset was 47 miles, but by expressway down I-99 and out the Turnpike, the distance was 70 miles – 'out' always meaning going west. The clerk at the desk said she could cut maybe eight miles if a certain short cut was taken, but she disdained the idea from fear of making a wrong turn.

The long hour's drive passed fairly quickly as she thought how nice it would be to see McAuliff again. She smiled at the way Arlee poked fun at him at the last Solstice party, calling him Ted McAwful, because he had unfortunately divulged the fact that he was sometimes called that at the Bureau. He was a tall, handsome fellow with boyish features, that she had considered going after – except that he was already spoken for. But her nondescript Paul – average in every way, except mental – now, fulfilled all her requirements. But Ted was a hoot to be with, too.

The meeting took place in the small conference room at the county seat's Barracks. Barracks 'A' it was called, as all

Pennsylvania State Police barracks were designated by some letter of the alphabet. She was ten minutes early and everyone was there except Ted. Introductions and pleasantries were exchanged, as they each took a seat at the plain rectangular table. Protocol dictated that the Commandant sit at the head of the table, with Colonel Simmins taking the chair to his right, and the two Sergeants opposite Simmins. It was difficult to be casual in a room full of rank, and she found herself wishing to be a 'PFC' as Paul had appropriately defined the acronym.

The Commandant had been staring at her for some length before saying, "You sure drive a hard bargain, Lieutenant . . . Your Colonel and I had pull a few strings to get McAuliff up here."

She thought Pennsylvanians' use of colloquialisms to describe places 'up here', 'out there', 'down east' charming. The part of Pennsylvania where she came from was relatively level and not nearly so dependent on such necessary adjectives; she realized that Barracks 'A' might be the highest elevation in the state, situated on the east rim of the Laurel Ridge. "I thought the *circumstances* warranted full guarantee of my safety."

"And your concerns have been noted and, I hope, satisfied."

"They will be . . . when I see Agent McAuliff in this room." She found herself saying.

"Surely, Lieutenant, you agree we are all on the same side."

"I've heard *that* before-- too many times." At that moment there was a scraping at the door as Ted pushed into the room with his briefcase -- and close-cropped hair.

"Sorry I'm late, but my flight into Cumberland was delayed." He looked around, and seeing Erin, smiled, "Erin, we have to stop meeting like this."

She and Colonel Simmins surrendered a chuckle as the remainder of the group perfunctorily motioned Ted to a seat opposite Erin.

"So, Ted, are you an atheist too?" the Commandant asked.

"Yes sir."

"And the Bureau let you in?"

"There are no religious tests, sir."

"I was being facetious, Special Agent."

"Of course you were."

Erin subdued the urge to chuckle again.

The Colonel, uncomfortable with attempting any more humor, went straight to the point. "What we have here is a golden opportunity to bring *Sick Bear* – that's the killers code name by the way, in case you haven't been informed – into the light of day. Lieutenant Beckwith, here, has volunteered to act the part of an atheist -- as bait, if you will --, to see if we can get Sick Bear to strike in a controlled environment." He then asked Sergeant Peters to distribute copies of what appeared to be a rough game plan. "Take a coupla minutes and study this outline of action – coffee is available . . . right Sergeant?"

Sergeant Peters rose from the table, opened the door and shouted to the duty officer to bring a coffee tray, while the group studied the paper.

The paper revealed that the killer's car was seen at a Meyersdale convenience store, by an emergency management volunteer for an adjacent municipality. He had noticed the front tag of an Early ninetys brown Ford Explorer, having the distinctive "PP" on it, and while calling police, the suspect had gotten back into the vehicle, driving off without the spotter seeing the rear license plate number.

"The guy sure didn't sort out his priorities very well, did

he?" Colonel Simmins remarked.

"Shit happens," Commandant Brubaker replied.

"He could have followed him."

"And do what?" He didn't have a cell phone or a radio."

"I thought you said he was an EM."

"A lot of those guys aren't wrapped real tight . . . mostly, they tool up only if there's an *emergency*. Besides, he was waiting for his bacon cheeseburger."

There was a period of quiet until Brubaker asked McAuliff if he was pulled off anything important.

"No sir, I was catching up on paperwork . . . that's all."

Erin breathed easier knowing her request had not rearranged the universe.

"Had I been on an important assignment, I doubt they would have allowed your request."

"As you know, this lady, here, is adamant that you in particular assist us in protecting her."

"I understand. I'm flattered that I am thought of so highly."

"It's because you're an atheist, like her . . ." Brubaker looked in Erin's direction. "She doesn't seem to trust any of us *common* folk."

She remained quiet, letting the sarcastic remark go. This was not a forum to explain why she distrusted many Christians because of their potential for irrationality -- as secular as they may seem.

"Erin and I go back a ways." Ted apologized, trying to defuse the animosity.

"There's just not that many of us that have come out of the closet." She said, finally. "We have to choose our fights . . . our stands. And when we fight, we must be on the high ground. Being offered as bait in a lunatic hunt is hardly being on high ground, but more like wading through a swamp."

"Spoken like a true tactician." Colonel Simmins came to her rescue. "I am immediately responsible for those under my command and the Lieutenant here is one of the clearest thinking personnel I have . . . I hope the developing circumstances haven't taken her out of my control!"

"You have my assurance, Colonel, that as American law enforcement, we will consider *all* in this mission as brethren in one, regardless of anyone's beliefs. That is the American way – and predjudice be *damned*!" Colonel Brubaker's countenance was burned into every face in the room.

Erin and Ted looked at each other across the conference table, each raising their eyebrows in mild astonishment.

"Ladies and gentlemen, I give you until 1500 hours to build on this outline, at which time we will compare notes as to the best way to proceed. Are there any questions?"

The meeting adjourned with few pleasantries. Erin and Ted withdrew to the parking lot where they agreed they should see to motel accommodations, and a bite to eat.

"You need to bring me up to speed on this, ASAP."

"Of course . . . Pancake house or breakfast Burrito? I'm buying."

"Burrito, in Somerset – *really*?" without waiting for an answer he quickly added: "I think I'll go for pancakes."

At breakfast, they compared notes on the history of the terrorism between tidbits of personal life and news. They were buddies in a cadre of like-minded thinkers, devoted to each other in their ultimate quest for understanding and appreciating life. They were like two giddy school kids, now assigned to a class project. She *loved* him, like she loved *everyone* of the PAN members at York. They were such a delight to talk to, to be with . . . so free from banal chit-chat and defensiveness.

Colonel Simmins had recommended to Erin the Penn Alto

hotel where he was lodging, and they proceeded there to get a room. A year before, she would have been open to suggestion, should it have been brought up, that they share a room, but that was before either of them had married. Even then he would have been fair game though he was engaged. She didn't know his wife, and assumed she wasn't one of their kind, since she never came with him to PAN meetings. She was probably a back door Christian, ready to snatch him back into the fold after weakening his independence – Erin could only suspect.

Their rooms were on the same floor but not adjoining, since the hotel was nearly booked for some Laurel Highland pageant event. Though going to bed with a hunk like Ted would have been an erotic thought in the past, she now longed for her Paul to be with her – the randy-ness of her old self was gone.

Back at the barracks that afternoon, the group reconvened, getting down to business.

"The question is: how do we have Erin interface with the subject?" Colonel Brubaker commenced.

"Sick Bear always seeks out his prey, so the Lieutenant, here, must advertise her presence, and her disgust with the subject in his bombing of Atheist Union. "

"Very good, Sergeant Peters."

"She must be given total media exposure throughout the region." Sergeant Melesco added.

She thought to herself how unusual *that* would be: getting total media coverage! Usually, the media is standoffish with atheists, fearing retribution from all their readers of faith. Erin was, however, in agreement with the tactic of advertisement. Indeed, this is what she had *wanted* in making out her wish list last evening. Atheists get precious little air time and *very little* of what they have to say ever gets out to the public, thereby complying with the clergy's wishes that atheist existence remain as mysterious, nonconforming, and in-the-closet entities. In their policy of rebuking atheists existence, they continually expound *their* self-preserving lies: 'You can only be happy by knowing God,' 'The ACLU's agenda is out to destroy religion,' 'Patriotism and religion are one in the same,' 'Evolution is a fabrication,' 'America was founded as a Christian nation,' and on and on through ad nauseum. A Nazi general once said if you tell a lie often enough, it becomes 'truth.' That is one of the basic premises of religion.

"Lieutenant Beckwith, what are your thoughts?"

"I agree that advertisement should be effected on a broad spectrum."

"You don't mind going public?'

"I don't see any other way! As a matter of fact, I relish the idea."

"I see . . . it gives you a chance to hawk your propaganda." Brubaker said half facetiously.

"That's unkind, sir . . . especially in light of the fact that churches never miss an opportunity to hawk *their* propaganda." She looked over at Ted who gave her a wink of understanding. "I see that I was right in my suspicions concerning our own cultural differences."

"Okay! Okay, everyone." Colonel Simmins broke in. "First and foremost – we *are* all on the same side – the same team – so let's start acting like it."

"Erin's got to come across to the public, and Sick Bear, as a true poster child of atheism."

Ted McAuliff piped up. "Surely the religious people will have faith enough to weather what she has to say."

"So be it" Colonel Brubaker said. "Sergeant Peters, arrange a press conference as soon as possible, making sure we get blanket TV coverage. Make damn sure they understand we need full blown coverage . . . with little or no editing."

"Yes sir." And the Sergeant left the room.

"What about a special feature in the Sunday Altoona or Johnstown paper?" Sergeant Melesco offered.

"Very good idea." Brubaker agreed. "Get on it right away!"

The Colonel looked at Erin and said: "I guess you'll be up to all of this?"

"Absolutely, sir."

"Why don't you get started then." He then looked at Ted and Colonel Simmins. "The rest of us will stay in meeting to discuss strategy and contingencies."

XXX

The Setup

She was back at her room, busy working on her outline of things she wanted to bring to the public's attention when Ted knocked on the door.

She let him in, smiling. "We're finally going to get a public forum – I can't believe it!"

"Hold on a minute . . . we've come upon a problem of which atheist group you'll be speaking for – and do you realize this could make you into another Madalyn Murray O'Hair?"

"What's wrong with that? I happen to admire Madalyn O'Hair!"

"Then you're affiliated with her group, *American Atheists*?"

"Of course, I am!"

"What about the Freedom From Religion Foundation and the Secular Humanists?"

"I get both their publications, too – great stuff!"

"I thought you did . . . but wasn't sure."

"Did they give you a rough time?"

"Brubaker's pretty conservative for being a Presbyterian; he's not a happy camper."

"Maybe we'll turn some of their heads when they see my *stuff*."

"I hope so." Ted sat down on the bed. "So who will you be speaking for?"

"I understand American Atheist's directorship in

Pennsylvania is up for grabs, now that Liz has resigned." Erin looked at him with wide eyes. "I could call Ellen and volunteer for the job."

"That's a thought," his boyish expression revealed his approval. " . . . a *good* thought.! You could lead into your Article as being the 'new State Director for Pennsylvania.' You girls get all the fun."

"Yeah, right!" she said sarcastically, thinking about all the work Liz found herself involved with.

"Being State Director would give you the flexibility of living anywhere in the state."

"I hadn't thought about *that*."

"We wouldn't want to make a location too obvious to Sick Bear . . . not too easy, but not a difficult location, either."

"Paul will be apprised of all this – right?"

"Absolutely! So you might consider renting a domicile somewhere between here and Carlisle."

"You mean . . . we'll have to move again?"

"Nah, it probably can be arranged that you keep your quarters at the College. Just a few things, that's all."

She visibly shuddered.

"What's the matter, Erin, you're shaking like a leaf."

"You'll be nearby, won't you?"

"I'll be near by." And he took her hand as they stared into each others eyes. "And I know Paul will be with you at every chance he has."

"I guess we better start looking for a place?"

"Don't worry about it . . . Sergeant Peters has already detached two troopers to find a place that can be observed and protected – between here and Carlisle. How would you like the Huntingdon area?"

"Awfully churchy!"

"So what place isn't? We aren't in Scandinavia." He opened a map of the state. "One of the troopers is checking out Everett also . . . because of its access to the Turnpike. And troop 'T' turnpike contingent is based there." He added.

"That sounds safer."

"We don't want things too safe – or Sick Bear won't come *calling*."

She shuddered again. "I wish Paul were here to help in the arrangements."

"Do you want to call Paul now? . . . Maybe meet 'im halfway and have dinner?"

"Yeah, good idea. I'll give him a call right now."

"And see if you can get hold of Ellen . . . about the directorship. I'll go tell Simmins what we're up to."

The drive out to the Turnpike's Sideling Hill Rest Area took hardly an hour. The new mountain-view rest facility was Pennsylvania's answer to Maryland's I – 68 cut through that same forbidding mountain. It housed several restaurants and a huge truck stop amidst the canopy laden, extensive forest. The 'Hill' had been one of the great barriers of the early migration to the west. She wondered why some of the largest mountains in the state were nominally called hills, or knobs, like Sideling, Laurel Hill and Blue Knob, the latter two being the highest points in the Commonwealth.

Paul arrived shortly after, and they went into the restaurant that had the best view -- the long evening daylight offering a stunning view of the mountains to the east. Ted brought Paul up to speed as the married couple held hands opposite him. Paul could only shake his head in bewilderment upon hearing the developing circumstances.

"Ellen Johnson was glad to hear that I wanted to volunteer for Pennsylvania State Director's position."

"You can still do that and be in the military?" Paul asked,

unconvinced.

"She agreed that it would be temporary, if I were reassigned out of the area . . . or if it became a problem."

"You *were* careful not to mention the prime motive for your volunteering?" Ted asked.

"Of course." She smiled and squeezed Paul's hand, "You don't think I'm a schmuck, do ya?"

Just then Ted McAuliff's cell phone rang melodiously, breaking into the conversation. "McAuliff here. Yes sir . . . yes sir." His eyes went back and forth between Erin and Paul as he listened intently to the caller. "We're just finishing dinner now. Yes sir, we'll meet you at Barrack's 'T' . . . just drive through the PennDOT maintenance gate -- which will be open. Got that Colonel." He rolled his eyes, "Yes sir, we'll be careful crossing the median."

"What was *that* all about?" Erin asked.

"Colonel Brubaker wants us to come back to the Everett barracks right away. They've found a house for you guys, just off the Pike's northern right-of-way." A silly grin spread over his face. "He wants us to be *careful* crossing traffic -- where we're to turn in to the barracks – it's on the south side of the Pike, right next to the state's maintenance shed."

She looked at Paul. "Honey, we can sign a lease on our *first* house!"

"Yeah . . . it's so romantic, having it picked out for us by a State Policeman."

The two lovebirds followed Ted back to Everett. Erin was exuberant one moment and then apprehensive the next. Paul could understand and feel her mood swings – his stomach was churning too. In a little while they saw Ted's left turn signal and they slowed into the extra lane that looked convincingly like an after-thought than proper highway design.

"How old *is this* highway?" Paul asked, as they sat, buffeted by huge trucks from both directions, waiting for a break in the traffic.

"It's the grand daddy of 'em all . . . I think the Pike is nearly sixty years old in this area."

"Why'd they build a superhighway in the middle of nowhere . . . way back then?"

"Because of the war . . . World War Two – they needed a link between Philadelphia and Pittsburgh to carry war materiel . . . most of the tunnels had already been bored some sixty years before by a railroad that was later disbanded. They call this string of small towns through here the 'Turnpike District."

"Wonderful! 'Our first house was along a noisy highway in the *Turnpike District*, picked by a policeman, 'specially for us,' we can tell our children . . . there's no end to the romance."

"Oh, Paul. You're such a kidder?"

"I'm worried . . . worried about you, Erin."

Just then, Ted's car moved forward, turning into the maintenance yard. They followed quickly behind, as more trucks could be seen hundreds of yards away, bearing down on them from the west.

"That's quite a thrill – that turn across traffic – isn't it?" the uniformed officer beamed.

"To say the least!" Ted answered.

"It's our emergency access for Pike cruisers and winter maintenance trucks." And in the same breath while offering his hand. "Sergeant Piper, Troop 'T' – I understand you'll be requiring our services."

"Crossing traffic like that reminded me of a question I have always wanted to ask:" Erin said. "Me being from eastern Pennsylvania, and all."

"Shoot, ma'am . . . but I'll have to ask you for your name first."

"Oh, I'm sorry." And she made the introductions around.

"And your question?"

"Do you guys get hazardous duty pay for working the Turnpike?" She suppressed the urge to add if this was purgatory for duty failure in other districts.

"No, I'm afraid not. You see . . . duty here is a kind of purgatory for those who want advancement at any cost. This was the only way I could make Sergeant at the time." The tall, winsome fellow added, "we do have a chiropractor in house for upper back and neck adjustments, neck spasms mostly . . . for those conscientious enough to keep an eye on traffic zipping by at close range."

The threesome smiled, relieved to meet a not-so-serious trooper for a change.

"Colonel Brubaker is reviewing our records – he doesn't get out here very often. So follow me and we'll interrupt 'im."

The Barracks reunion was not a warm one. In the small conference room, Commandant Brubaker filled them in on their efforts with the media.

"The Altoona *Mirror* turned us down about a Sunday feature because they say they already have something prepared." He turned his head and absently scratched at a non-existent itch under his eye, and muttered: "The editor mentioned somethin' about our request being just another ploy by atheists in the area to bring attention to themselves – that their coverage of Atheist Union efforts in the past has cut into their Christian readership."

"What about Cumberland and Johnstown?" Erin asked.

"The Johnstown *Tribune-Democrat* will do a feature . . .

for five thousand dollars, mind you." He looked at them and wrinkled his nose as if there were a stench nearby. Pursing his thin lips, he went on: "The Cumberland paper will have a reporter at the press conference, and make a decision on what they hear. The press conference will be at 0900 in the morning at Somerset's Barracks."

'Well, at least it's a start,' Erin thought to herself, suppressing the urge to call the Altoona *Mirror* a bunch of anachronistic, delusion preserving *candy-asses.*

"About this rental unit you'll be visiting shortly – it appears to be an ideal location for lure, entrapment and security." All eyes were on the Colonel as he continued. The lure being the offer of easy access / quick get-away via the Pike . . . similar to a plot used by a bank robber twentyfive years ago when he parked his car on the berm of the Turnpike in Bedford, went down over the embankment to rob a bank a hundred yards away. Then, retracing his steps to his car, he fled west on the Pike."

"Did he get away?" Paul asked.

"Yeah, the Bedford exit was just two miles down the road and he escaped before we could get there. We got 'im later, though"

"But in this case, we'll be about equidistant between Bedford and Breezewood exits . . . what, twelve, thirteen miles away?"

"True, that's to Sick Bear's disadvantage – if he takes the lure. But the whole idea is to lull *him* into a false sense of security – that his comings and goings will be completely unknown so there is no need on his part to race to one of the exits in get-away. Unbeknownst to him, Erin here, will have on her person at all times, a sensor that need only be pressed for an alert to be sounded, here at the duty desk, and on your beeper, Special Agent."

"The signal will be a distinctive audio?"

"That is affirmative."

Sergeant Piper spoke for the first time. "Lieutenant, when you press the sensor, the amount of times you press will indicate the level of danger you are in. Once- you suspect presence of the intruder; twice- confirmation of intrusion, three times- contact is imminent, four or more presses indicates the level of danger."

Paul could see Erin's eyes widen at each level of explanation.

"I see." She said quietly.

"Our advantage in all this is, the situation will be fully monitored with a cruiser being within a mile of your house at all times."

"On both sides of the Pike?"

Piper looked at Brubaker, who nodded in the affirmative.

"Yes sir. There'll be *two* cruisers – One in town and one at the ready . . . at our gate."

Paul and Erin were directed to go with a plain clothed trooper to the house picked out for them.

"Isn't it rather short notice to sign a lease this time of month?" Erin asked.

"I think they're desperate to rent . . . the noise and all, along the Pike."

The trooper answered. "The place has been on the market for several months."

"Great!" Paul winced in resignation.

"Darling, it's only for a little while! She took his hand, "you'll still come to me when you can?"

His eyes rolled top right and he smiled, bussing her on the petite nose.

"There are evergreens in the backyard . . . to filter the noise." The trooper swallowed.

"I'm sure it'll be all right" Paul gave in return.

They followed the trooper out of the PennDOT compound by the official entrance and, by what seemed to be a very circuitous route, crossed under the Turnpike heading toward the downtown business district, then another two left turns put them on a street that had a '*No Outlet*' sign. The subject house was two doors back from what might have passed as a cul-de-sac in the fifties. 200 feet behind the house was the Turnpike's right-of-way fence barrier that was twisted and collapsed at various points because of its weathered age. The trooper was true to his word about a row of mature blue spruce trees breaking much of the din of passing trucks.

"That's the first time I've ever had young couples check out the back yard before looking at the house." The real estate agent remarked as she engaged them. "I'm Trudy," she said while pumping Paul and Erin's hand. " . . . and this is a real doll house for a young couple just starting out."

The trooper made the introductions, having already initiated contact as a friend of the couple. Ted McAuliff was introduced as a brother-in-law.

The agent wore a rather large Cross on a gold chain, around her neck, almost dominating her business suit. They followed the sales agent through the door into the small one bedroom bungalo.

Paul's thoughts echoed that of Ted and Erin -- that the saleswoman's medallion invited their skepticism of the woman's veracity. The question always arose that the Cross might be used as a subtle tool to gain the client's naïve confidence. In many instances, it didn't hurt business to wear one's religion on their sleeve – the first relay of potential customers being one's congregation.

Erin was reminded about what Ted had said earlier: 'this is not Scandinavia,' where national law often limited the number of churches in any one area. Then she recalled reading about the incident right here in Everett, when the local Representative to Congress went ballistic in a speech attacking Dr. Michael Newdow's petition to have the words '*under God*' removed from the Pledge of Allegiance. What Ninth District Congressman, Bill Shuster, said scared her: In a knee jerk reaction to a list of several thousand signatures that had been presented to him -- defending those words in the Pledge -- he vowed to fight the 'Tyranny of the minority' – that, ' . . . they [the Judiciary] can't stop us!' His words were demagoguery in its most blatant form.

It was a sorry state of affairs that our educational system had not more completely informed our children of the proper intent of the Constitution and the important functions of the three branches of government – the checks and balances of each upon the other. There was little, if any, emphasis on the history of the founding fathers – and how the debates then, just as now, were fought between liberals and conservatives: those who wanted radical change, and revolution, as opposed to those who would demand only subtle change, preserving the status quo.

And the 'under God' issue – how many school children were aware that the Pledge served a good fifty years in its original form, not mentioning God, until President Eisenhower prevailed upon Congress to implement the two additional words? They were hardly aware of the Presbyterian minister who had inspired Eisenhower in a 1954 church sermon, George M. Docherty, who was quoted on the fiftieth anniversary of his coup as saying: "God save the Queen was commonly invoked in my Scottish homeland . . . why not 'under God' here in America?" But at the founding of this nation, weren't we breaking *all* ties to the mother land, including the foibles and circumstance of the monarchy?

The four of them combed the house for advantages and disadvantages it offered in setting up a trap – a trap that offered ingress and egress of the subject and the lure, respectively. Erin and the trooper occupied the sales rep with questioning of details as Paul drifted off with McAuliff to sketch out the floor plan so as to analyze its potential. His training in making field sketches and impromptu maps on a clipboard greatly facilitated Ted's reconnoitering of all possible entrances, windows and utility services.

After thoroughly scanning the full basement and upstairs three rooms, they went into the rather large kitchen where Erin was nodding at the continual sales pitch offered by Trudy.

"What d'ya think, guys?" Erin was almost aglow.

After seeing Ted's nod in the affirmative, Paul said, "It's okay by me – if this is what you want, sweetheart."

"Do you have any references that we might call?"

"Ma'am, I've known these people a while," the trooper spoke up with his pre-arranged spiel. "I'd stake my reputation as a police officer, that you'd never have a problem with Erin and Paul."

"You say you're from the Turnpike Barracks?"

"Yes ma'am."

"Could I see your I.D.?"

"Certainly." And the trooper pulled out his wallet."

"Well now – that's looks good enough for me. Let me jot your name and badge number down, just for the record."

The lease was signed and a cash deposit made on the spot, and the sales woman went to her car. She said the keys would be available as soon as they dropped by her office to pay the first month's rent.

"Tomorrow, sometime." Erin found herself answering, as Trudy prepared to drive off.

"Whew, what a charade!" She whistled trough her teeth.

"You done good, darling."

"Yeah – I haven't acted like this since my high school play!"

XXXI

The Interview

The news media had been apprised of the situation and cooperated with the State Police as well as they could. The press conference took place on the back lawn of the Somerset Barracks with questions ranging through the spectrum of civility. Erin was introduced by Sergeant Peters, as the Pennsylvania Director of American Atheists. McAuliff, Brubaker and Simmins stayed in the background, the two Colonels biding their time when they could slip back to their respective offices in the east. Paul had driven back to Carlisle right after He and Erin had signed the lease.

"Was this attack on Atheist Union a religiously motivated act?"

"Yes . . . absolutely!"

"The police think the bomber is the same person who has struck in Baltimore, Pittsburgh and on the Appalachian Trail – do you agree?"

"All of those cases highlight the perpetrator's zealous efforts to enforce certain passages of the Bible. They seem connected in that way – he may be a Phineas Priest"

"Do you think the Bible is an evil book?"

"No – I think it is a mosaic in prose of early attempts to establish moral law, complete with example after example of fearsome retribution and legendary stories -- historical, maybe to some degree – designed to warn of supernatural wrath if the moral law is violated."

"What is a Phineas Priest?"

"We think it is an individual who acts out biblical admonishment to the letter – as was the case when Phineas slayed two lovers of differing tribes with one thrust of his sword as they lay in union, a mixed union if you will. I believe that's in Chapter 25 of The Book of Numbers. If there is a society of these individuals, it is not evident, for there is no information available concerning recruitment. They are essentially lone wolves, acting maybe with one or two empathetic parishioners."

"You say parishioners – are they Catholic?"

"That may be the wrong word – *like-minded zealots* might be better. Catholics are not as well versed with the Bible as, say, fundamentalist Protestants. It is thought that the Phineas Priesthood follow Christian Identity teachings."

After a while, Ted overheard the two Colonels remarking to one another that it would have been impossible for anyone other than an atheist to play the necessary part of lure in this setup. Satisfied that the proposed operation was well on its way toward implementation, they departed for their cars and left the area. Ted continued to observe, marveling at Erin's astute handling of the questions.

"Do you feel *hatred* for the religious people who show their disgust for your philosophy?"

"No – I feel pity . . . that they've been flimflammed into leading a life of fear and forced mediocrity. Many religious people are afraid of death because they don't know if they've prayed enough, had enough faith, been *good* enough – to stay out of Hell."

"What do *you* know about Hell?" one reporter asked with a trace of sarcasm.

"The only thing I know about Hell is, that it exists right here on Earth, produced by greedy, narrow-minded charlatans and bigots, sometimes in the guise of piety. Clergymen are

209

always reminding us of Hell, as if they have first hand experience of it – but where was the concept of Hell *before* there were priests and shamans? –There was none!"

"Isn't atheism really a religion, itself?"

"It's a philosophy for living, like people's use of religion as a philosophy of life . . . but it's not a religion! Religion is the belief and worship of a supernatural deity usually in the form of a great parent that can give you things and take things away from you, as if you were a child."

"What do you think about most American's belief that monotheism is the ultimate mark of civilization?"

"If eliminating the need for many gods is a mark of progress, then atheists have gone one better . . . and have need of zero gods. We feel the problems of the world, and in our own personal lives, are our responsibility and must be solved using resources that come from within, not from without."

"Then you feel that you are really god?" Another reporter asked. " – that god is within us all?"

"I believe we all have the potential for playing God – and we do everyday, in rearranging nature and destroying our fellow man. We are the ultimate that Mother Nature has conceived and it is our responsibility to act accordingly, or we'll probably perish in our offal."

"Then you consider Nature to be your God?"

"In a sense, that is correct. It is the magnificent, yet subtle, warmth of the Sun that sustains us. If *anything* should be worshipped, it is the Sun."

"Then what created all the wonders of Nature?" the reporter asks, throwing his arms wide.

"*Good question.* Fundamentalists ask me that question all the time, and I answer with my question: 'then why do you disdain life on this planet as being too worldly, and yearn for even a better place . . .' Erin looks toward the sky, '. . . up there?' To me, that seems like such an ungrateful criticism of the gift of life."

"Do you think creationists are full of malarkey?"

"Let me put it this way: I might have more respect for their arguments if their agenda was less transparent. Do you notice that every creationist is trying to preserve the images and teachings of his religion, which is almost always fundamentalist?"

The sarcastic reporter asked: "Do you then consider Americans to be irrational when they find comfort in their religious beliefs?"

"Yes. I think they are being very irrational when they pooh-pooh the intellectual revelations of science and experiences of history . . . yet believe in hearsay that was at least forty years old before it was written down, describing all sorts of supernatural events. Then culminating such adoration in rolling on church floors and talking in 'tongues' that would even make those on the floor of Congress blush."

"Don't you agree that religion does some good?"

"Of course it does some good. It is a ready-made package that provides comfort and solace to those experiencing bereavement. To the naïve, it is a shortcut to understanding the meaning of life, and gives all the answers to all the questions – *no thinking required*! The clergy will do the thinking for you – some Christian religions will even underwrite a collateral amount of badness known as sin, if you sign on the dotted line that *Faith* will rule your life no matter what. There lies the rub – you shall receive all the benefits, on *condition* that you maintain the Faith. Yes it is a shortcut – but really more like a short circuit!" Any future thinking is discouraged and in its place is put mindless dogma and sectarian ideology. *'Ignorance is bliss'* is what comes to mind when one surrenders one's intellect for a smooth, good feeling sales pitch of a product having a very small price tag – in the beginning."

"So, what's the matter with that?"

"For one, it is nearly the same thing as a child abductor offering candy and sweet sayings to lure the unsuspecting child into his or her car. People who, without thinking, sign on for the 'answers for everything and sweets for all – who truly believe' package have relinquished their right and care for any further life. Curiosity – the engine that drives pursuit of knowledge – is curtailed, and the engine seizes up because of rust. No wonder people infected with mediocre expectations of life experience a glum existence and mark time until they are taken to a much better, if less interesting, place. People who don't know what to do with themselves on a Sunday afternoon now, yearn, without thinking, for a blissful eternity of *having nothing to do*."

"So what if you are wrong in your beliefs?"

"You are inferring that I will then burn in Hell for my apostasy. Close to two billion in the west now live in that fear – wondering if they have *enough* faith to make the cut." She took a swallow of water and reflected happily that she was finally doing what many atheists and agnostics really want to do – to have intelligent conversation about these very issues. Even the debate at the war college lacked intensive question and answer dialogue that seeks a common denominator known as *truth*. Usually, after a question or two, the religious walk smugly away muttering 'I will pray for you'. Many debates on these issues wind down with the opposition preaching rather than rebutting with rational argument – that's no fun. " . . .Then we have 1.7 billion Muslims living with similar fear – and hope -- of an afterlife, in the Middle East. Though these two contesting factions have common roots in Abraham, they are far from agreeing on anything except they claim a singular God –not the *same* God, mind you, but monotheism."

"Which one is right? All of the religions have different messages, different protocol – and they are forever cutting each others throats. One needn't be a rocket scientist to figure out that it's all conjecture . . . speculation . . . wishful thinking! I truly believe that if there is a God, he or she would reward atheists for not playing the game. After all, we didn't ask to be born. What callous entity would provide eternal misery for those who refused, out of common sense – out of conscientious use of the brain they were born with -- to take sides in the religious and irrational bickering of the culturally enflamed?"

"So, what happens to us when we die?"

She smiled at the male reporter and said: "We are buried, and the worms eat us up."

Several reporters and photographers hung around for a one-on-one opportunity, which Erin gladly obliged. Then, just before lunch, she answered questions in depth for the Johnstown Tribune-Democrat team who would do the Sunday spread.

After lunch she went second-hand shopping for basic homemaking items to furnish their new abode.

XXXII

In Transition

Back at school, Paul found his preoccupation with thoughts of Erin and the danger she was inviting was interrupting his studies. But the week was drawing to an end and, this time, he would be making the trip west to be with her in their bungalow by the Pike. Major Troutman tried to draw him into classroom discussion, but found Paul uncooperative and standoffish. After class, he asked his top student if there was something wrong. And Paul replied that he was worried for Erin, who was on a difficult assignment.

"I see. Hush hush is it?"

"Yes sir. –Thanks for askin', I hope someday we can all laugh and joke about it."

"Your wife has a good head on her shoulders. She'll manage okay." And the Major gave him a pat on the back and walked toward the hall exit.

Friday came and he handed in his class proposal concerning electoral examination. He knew it was lame and Polly-Annish, realizing by now that the successful candidates for political office learned -- or should learn -- about what they didn't know from good, expert advisors on the campaign trail. Still, there seemed a need for an overview, since political advisers are often flawed or self-serving as what appeared in the most recent Bush administration.

In the case of President George W. Bush's dismal use of the language and his disdain for history and even science, many of the electorate remained unconcerned. Bush was '*one of them*' and as long as he professed Jesus to be his most influential philosopher, what more do they need in a leader – Jesus was quite all right with them. The fact that he had procured his one term presidency with significantly less popular vote than his Democratic opponent, hardly made a dent in his conviction that God put him in office to deal with the events of 9-11-01. He would not recognize that it was a political fluke -- the deciding vote in the Supreme Court, concerning Florida's dysfunctional counting of ballots, being cast by the 'swing vote' moderate Republican, Sandra Day O'Connor. In 2000, The Democrat controlled Supreme Court of Florida was trumped by the Republican controlled Supreme Court of the United States – talk about state's rights!

Major Troutman was correct in their discussions about candidate's intellectual integrity. 'Egghead' Adlai Stevenson lost to Eisenhower because intellectuality was not in demand so much as the famous warrior general. Harry Truman may have been our last intellectual President, being a self-taught man like Abraham Lincoln. His down-home Missouri drawl and plain manner struck a common chord with many Americans. Troutman and others in class discussion, kept mentioning that Intellectual competency was *not* a requirement for high office. It was unfortunate, but true, that a pretty face, an imposing presence and a smooth, disarming demeanor was all that was required for a candidate to be successful. A nicely wrapped package on the outside that conceals a lot of unknowns inside.

He remembered what Ayn Rand had said: "that everybody, to some degree was an intellectual," yet most of the general population, out of self deprecation, would not be enthused about claiming such a label. Intellectual endeavors were generally distrusted because of MSS, Mad Scientist Syndrome, among other fried brain stereotypes. He

215

remembered in his undergraduate days at Kentucky, of the Cross-bearing art student who exclaimed to him that "Science sucks!" It is very true that science, with its cold, calculating predictability, is hardly a warm, lovable, feel-good topic, but without its rigorous Scientific Methodology where would civilization be today?

With the exception of a few Nazi doctors who experimented with humans in the World War II concentration camps, where does the notion come from that scientists and intellectuals may in some nefarious way conquer the earth? Many scientists really are introverts, concerned only in answering questions that Nature poses. But in many ways scientists *have* conquered the earth: in medicine, in transportation, communication, meteorology, geology, engineering, and agriculture, making our species one of relatively comfortable existence. And other intellectuals are busy with analysis of where we've been and where we are going , with curiosity -- the tabu of the religious afflicted -- their driving engine.

'Ah,' he thought, 'The definition of the Cultural War! The path of curious inquiry through reasonable analysis of all that surrounds us, versus the anachronistic know-nothings that forever cling to contradictory, chaotic and sometimes vulgar and violent Scripture that came into being at a time when humans learned to write. And who started the Cultural War – like we needed another war anyway – It was Pat Buchanan, the epitome of anachronism – the fire breathing fundamentalist that hates everything to do with the world except to make sure that there would be Hell here. Was it rather unbecoming for a Christian to start a war? "Yes" a *good and true* Christian would say, but a precedence had already been set with the actions of Pope Urban II, in 1095, when he aroused Europe to go and smite the infidel Muslims that lived in the Holy Lands.'

'Hitler had used Christianity to advantage during his war mongering days, while purging Europe of Jews. And now Bush, the Christian, has started a war in Iraq on drummed up charges that were "irrefutably supported by intelligence" – the same intelligence that failed to warn us about 9 – 11. What ever happened to the pastoral teachings of Christ and his efforts at charity? What use is religion if some of its loudest expounders are using it in an atrocious manner?'

His thoughts carried him onto the Turnpike, and he headed west to be with Erin.

At their newly adopted but humble nest on the Southern outskirts of Everett the two young lovers reviewed the dwelling for temporary housekeeping – and defending, if all goes according to plan. Ted tried to prevail upon Sergeant Piper to have the locks changed and additional dead bolts placed on all doors to the outside. The Sergeant countered that this was a controlled entrapment situation and security must allow the perpetrator access to the lure. Paul did not like it one bit, until Erin showed him the little electronic sensory button she was wearing between panty and stocking.

"Electronics have been known to fail, you know," he said touching the warm, smooth mesh leg covering."

"I have backup on the other side," and she showed him. "But, right now, I want you to take these off."

"I thought they were to stay on you at all times, except when you shower."

"They will, silly! What I want you to do is take off my stockings . . . they are sooo confining." She blinked her lashes provocatively.

With little resistance to her immediate wish he fumbled at the task, deliciously savoring every touch of her silky textured thigh. "I love you, Erin." He heard himself say as he brought the stocking down, replacing the uncovered flesh with kisses.

"I love you, too, darling." She purred.

Before he started the other leg, he picked her up and carried her into the bedroom, placing her on the bed.

"I hope you like soft, honey."

"Sure do," he said pressing the inside of her other thigh.

"You crazy! I meant the mattress . . . I already know what you think of my thighs."

"Oh! I hope it's not *too* soft."

"Like our bed at the apartment."

"Well, let's try it out." And he zipped her other stocking off in half the time, planting a few less kisses.

"Soldia boy, has it been a long time?" she cooed.

"You know damn well how long it's been!" and he ran his fingers slowly around the waste-band of her panties, in preparation of their removal."

"What about my buttons?"

"Honey, I know where *all* your buttons are . . . just give me time to get at 'em."

"No . . . I mean my electronic sensor. Will it be okay for you . . . where they are?"

"I'll treat them like that little mole on your left tit."

"Oooh, your so sweet . . . I love the way you circle it with kisses – among the other things you do so well."

"I can see how *they* feel, already . . . your not wearing a bra, are you?"

"Why should I when I know my love-deprived husband will be coming through the door at any moment."

"You know how I love removing your bra."

"You can put it on me – then take it off again, if you like." She said, tonguing his carlobe.

"The only thing I want you to put on -- is me!"

"Darling!" She exclaimed looking at him in full length. "It looks like I've already put you ON . . . turned you ON, that is."

He looked down and feigned amazement at seeing his rock hard alter ego. *"Ooh, scusi maddam,* it seems something of mine has gotten out of hand."

"Non necessary, Monsieur, I don't mind." And she craddled him in her hands and kissed his glans as moisture dropped onto her wrist.

"Such a juicy boy! –And he's safely back in hand."

"You *know* how messy I can be."

"That was *not* a complaint – I assure you." And she took him fully into her mouth.

"Oooh, ooh!" he exhaled. "If you do that much more, I'll explode."

She let him go, saying, "We'll not rush things just yet. Here, let's crawl under the covers and check this bed out – I got it for a steal."

They were soon snuggled together between the sheets in total embrace kissing one another. Their tongues were jousting as he crushed her to him in a spasm of ecstasy.

"My! You *are* horny, aren't you?"

"I've been a week from my love – whad'ya expect?"

"I've missed you, too." And they more or less wrestled -- jostling each other until she was ready to allow him to find his way home -- to perfect their love for each other.

XXXIII

Ayn Rand

"No, you old fool. I don't need your damn introduction . . . and further more you stink of   cigars." Ayn said as she made her way toward the curtain. She turned to a stage hand and muttered, "What is it with him now-a-days, that he's got to muscle in on *everybody's* action, any way. If I needed an introduction, I would have had Phyllis Diller – she's so much funnier."

"Your on in five, Ms. Rand," the smiling stage hand answered, sheepishly putting his hands in position to pull the curtains. "The auditorium is full."

"Oh, my. They didn't hear me complaining just now, did they?"

"It's no big deal," he smiled. "This isn't Carnegie Hall." "I don't know *what* it is – but I'm sure as hell glad to be part of it!"

"*Sure as hell* – what do you mean?"

"Oh, be damned!   Please forgive my outburst of thoughtless superstition."

The stagehand shrugged his shoulders and began opening the curtains.

"Gentlemen and ladies," she began, looking out at all the faces. "I am so honored that you chose to be here at this time. I was hoping that Phyllis Diller could break the ice, so to speak, but I understand she is still incommunicado – probably something to do with that facial re-make she has been contemplating for a while." She clasped her hands and looked in a different direction with a deadpan expression. "You don't think she's ugly, do you?"

There were a few gufaws among the chuckling.

"Actually, on the inside she is a very beautiful woman, and her self deprecating monologue is just a gambit to do what she does best – to entertain. I know her husband, Fang, and he is certainly not the man she makes him out to be in her routine." She screwed up her face into a grimace and said: "He does need dental work, though! Phyllis should be extending her efforts in that direction rather than her own – unless of course, they enjoy kinky sex."

Some more chuckles could be heard.

"Like me, Phyllis Diller is atheist – or an atheist – however you interpret that word/ phrase." She wiped her brow with an imaginary tissue. "It is a delight to be able to use that word without seeing any hand-wringing gestures or hearing any moans, like we experienced on Earth. Out there among you sit atheists, Christians, Jews, and others of different persuasion – all good, open-minded people that have come to this plane – congratulations to us all!"

"Now, I'm here to talk to you about my thoughts on *Objectivism* that many of you have probably heard of and are curious about. My immensely successful novels, *Atlas Shrugged* and *The Fountainhead* outlined my early concepts of Objectivism, and later, in my book, *For The New Intellectual,* I developed the fundamentals of it more fully. It was my brazen effort to re-invigorate the lagging discipline of Philosophy. Philosophy should be more in control of things, but has inadvertently relinquished its responsibility through the divergences of the classical philosophers, becoming an apologist and rationalist for the clergy -- which I hath dubbed *Witch Doctor.* Descartes, Kant, Hume, Hegel, Marx Comte, and Nietzsche in varying degrees got it wrong, corrupting

Philosophy's pristine virtue. Religion is *unmistakably* a philosophy for living, yet what Witch Doctor would admit to his beliefs being a sub-order to Philosophy? This is, indeed, a good example of the tail wagging the dog.

Philosophy started out in Greece on such a high note, defining and cataloguing all of man's endeavor. Aristotle's philosophy was the Intellect's Declaration of Independence. Aristotle, the father of logic, should be given the title of the world's first *intellectual*, in the purest and noblest sense of that word. He defined the *basic* principles of a rational view of existence and of man's consciousness: that there is only *one* reality, the one which man perceives – that it exists as an *objective* absolute – that the task of man's consciousness is to *perceive*, not to create reality – that A is A! The fact is: every rational value that we possess – including the birth of science, the industrial revolution, the creation of the United States, even the structure of our language – is the result of Aristotle's influence. Never has so many owed so much to one man.

"But in relatively recent times Philosophy has become more of a lackey -- a servant of the clergy, rather than the latter's guiding institution. I proposed that the *New Intellectuals* rectify this conundrum and start using everyday common sense – across the board, without exception. The *sacred cows* of polite conversation are to be ignored and supplanted with seeds of *reason* in its most unadulterated and pure form. Truth must again be known as *truth* and not some wish-wash symbol of the unknowable.

"The other players of Objectivism, besides the Witch Doctor- the agent of feelings; are: *Attila*- the agent of force; and the *Producer*- who is the agent of reason. I have now described the three players: the mystic; the brute; and the thinker.

"From the beginnings of tribal order, and in some

instances even now, Attila and the Witch Doctor form alliances and divide their respective domains. Attila rules the realm of men's physical existence – the Witch Doctor rules the realm of men's consciousness. Attila herds men into armies – the Witch Doctor sets the armies' goals. Attila conquers empires – the Witch Doctor writes their laws. Attila loots and plunders . . . and slaughters – the Witch Doctor rules by means of guilt, by keeping men convinced of their innate depravity, impotence, and insignificance. When men do not choose to reach the conceptual level, their consciousness has no recourse but to default to its automatic, perceptual, semi-animal functions. If a *missing link* between the human and the animal species is to be found, Attila and the Witch Doctor are that missing link – the profiteers on men's default.

"The great treason of the above mentioned philosophers was that they, the thinkers, defaulted on the responsibility of providing a rational society with a code of *rational morality*. They, whose job it was to discover and define man's moral values, stared at the brilliant torrent of man's released energy and had nothing better to offer for its guidance than the Witch Doctor's supposed morality of human sacrifice – that of: self-denial, self abasement, self-immolation – of suffering, guilt and death.

."The first society in history whose leaders were neither Attilas or Witch Doctors, but a society dominated and created by the *Producers,* was the United States of America. The moral code implicit with its political principles embodied in its Constitution were not the Witch Doctor's code of self-sacrifice or Attila's blank check on brute force."

"America's Constitution was devised to protect against these primordial ambitions. The founding fathers were neither passive, death-worshipping mystics nor mindless, power-seeking looters; as a political group, they were a phenomenon unprecedented in history: they were *thinkers and producers* who were also men of action. They had rejected the soul-body dichotomy, with its two corollaries: the impotence of man's mind and the damnation of the earth. They had rejected the doctrine of suffering as man's metaphysical fate, they proclaimed man's right to the pursuit of happiness and were determined to establish on earth the conditions required for man's proper existence, by the *unaided* power of their intellect."

"Capitalism came into its own with the founding of this brave new country, eventually spreading throughout the world. Capitalism wiped out slavery in matter and in spirit. It replaced Attila and the shaman, the looter of wealth and the purveyor of revelations with two new types of producer – the *businessman* and the *intellectual.* The businessman is the field agent of the army whose lieutenant-commander-in-chief is the *scientist.* The professional intellectual is the field agent of the army whose lieutenant-commander-in-chief is the *philosopher.*

"The businessman, driven by profit motive, succeeded immensely in utilizing science to produce and build bigger and better things. Slowly but surely the general populace was lifted out of the seemingly endless drudgery of thumb pressed existence as more and more of remuneration and improvements came their way. This is not to say there was no abuse and exploitation of the worker – there were. But it is very obvious that Capitalism had advanced the general human condition.

"On the other side of the coin, the professional intellectuals have not done their part to improve man's incentive to think – other than to help turn a profit. The philosopher's insistence on re-establishing metaphysics alongside or, in support of reason, was as if they were afraid to assert themselves in the vacuum left in the defeat of the Witch Doctors. It seemed they were determined to elevate conception to the level of perception – to make philosophy as complicated and as slippery as its subordinate, religion, is.

"If the American Experiment perishes, it will perish by intellectual default. There is no diabolical conspiracy to destroy it: no conspiracy could be big enough and strong enough. Such egotistical but scared, neurotic, mediocre politicians find themselves pushed into national leadership because nobody else steps forward: they are like pickpockets who merely intended to snatch a welfare-regulation or two and suddenly find that their victim is unconscious.

"The New Intellectuals must assume the task of building a new culture on a new moral foundation, which, for once, will not be the culture of Attila and the Witch Doctor, but the culture of the Producer. The New Intellectuals have an inestimable advantage: they have *reality* on their side. The difficulties they will encounter on their way are not stone barriers, but fog: the heavy fog of passive disintegration, through which it will be hard for them to find one another. They will encounter no opposition, since, in this context, an opposition would have to possess *intellectual* weapons. As to their enemies, they should comply with their enemies request – and leave them to heaven. But there are two principles on which all men of intellectual integrity and good will can agree. These two principles are: *a.* that emotions are not tools of cognition; *b.* that no man has the right to *initiate* the use of physical force against others."

XXXIV

Feature Story

Paul woke up with a start. "Sweetheart, what a dream I had!" he exclaimed, watching Erin open the blinds.

"Another visit to 'the Upper Plane'?"

"Yeah, and this time I was at an Ayn Rand lecture."

"I must say, I wish my dreams were as interesting."

"And *you* were there with me this time!"

"This *is* an after-death thing, right?"

"Yeah." He hoped that she wasn't thinking of that being an omen.

"Doesn't it occur to you that it sounds a little like heaven?"

"Yeah . . . it does." He propped his head up with his elbow. "But it isn't!"

"You're starting to sound like an attorney."

"Well, it is a heaven of sorts, but not an anticipated, wished for, religious final resting place."

"Oh yeah?"

"Good religious people are there, too, along with atheists and secularists and people who have a wonderfully positive outlook on Nature's universe."

"How about the atheists, Joseph Stalin or Pol Pot?"

"I don't think so."

"But it sounds so supernatural?"

"That may be – but it is not a requirement or a condition to believe *that* way. It is an award of the individual's psyche to be there – no strings attached other than the possession of a positive, productive and optimistic attitude."

"That leaves me out!"

"Honey, you say you're a pessimist – but you are actually a realist." He looked deeply into her eyes and continued: "The way you show your love for me is anything but pessimistic! What is more positive than that?"

"Nothing, I suppose." And she crawled back under the covers beside him. "You sure have a knack for saying the sweetest things."

In the afternoon, Ted stopped by to compare notes about the progress of implementation. "How're you two lovebirds doin'?"

"We're makin' out, er, it." Paul answered, untying the knot in his tongue.

"I'm sure you were right the first time." Ted said, smiling at Erin.

Both of them colored a bit, and then held hands. "You *know* how it is: newly weds, new house and all."

"Yeah, but I hate to tell you kids . . . the honeymoon is over." Ted sat down on the bargain store armchair across from them. "We've got to get serious real quick."

"Has something developed?"

"Nothing specifically." His eyes were piercing, accentuating his lean, clipped countenance. "But your press interview is all over yesterday papers in a hundred mile radius of here. Our boy, *Sick Bear,* is now aware of your apostatical presence."

"I don't think that's a word, Ted." The librarian in Erin said.

"Heretical, then."

"That's better."

He held his gaze, but didn't smile. "I want you to spend your time together doing less of what I think you're doing, and more about the project at hand. I love you guys, and I don't want anything to interrupt the mechanics – anything that might make this operation fail."

"Got it!" they answered almost in unison.

"As you know, the tap was put on the phone after it was installed yesterday, along with the trip wires; I'll initiate their operation today, before I leave."

"Wire trips?" Paul asked.

"Sensors have been placed at all windows and doors that will trip audio pickup and transmit same to the Barracks."

"No wires then?"

"Old bureau terminology – everything is photoelectric in the ultraviolet range."

"Will I have control . . . to shut it off if I trip it by mistake?" she asked.

"Like coming through the Front door? –of course. Just say 'Delta' for deactivation."

"What if I want to activate?"

"Press the button on your person once. That will activate the audio for fifteen minutes. If you press twice: thirty minutes. If you press more than twice, the audio will continue until you command 'Delta'. But we'll be in here by then."

"I see."

He pulled out from behind his sport coat a small automatic. "I'll leave this Kel-Tec P-32, with you Erin – you know how to use it?"

"I fired the Glock at OCS."

"Good – here are two clips of ammo. I sincerely hope you need not have to use them."

She could see the concern in his eyes.

"Sorry we don't have a clip with more than seven rounds – but this is small."

"I'll be careful to keep count." She replied, biting her lip.

Sunday morning, they went out for breakfast and picked up two Johnstown papers.

"The nerve this fish wrapper has to demand the government pay $5,000 to print my story!" Erin protested.

"Well, that's a good indication of the sorry state back-water papers are in, these days."

"It'll probably be rife with misspellings and grammatical errors . . . like those books my friends in York pay to get printed."

"Pay . . . to get published?"

"Oh, yeah. No one wants to touch the subject of atheism with the exception of a few publishers around the country – like Prometheus Press in Buffalo. Even *they* require money from an author if they feel it will not readily sell."

"Then why are you surprised that the *Tribune-Democrat* would charge?"

"Regardless of the circumstances, it *is* a news worthy story that should be disseminated to the public . . . or the locals' xenophobia will only get worse."

"They're afraid of their readers sentiments, I suppose." Paul finished his coffee and gathered up the check. "I guess religion is the only life many people have – their friends, their social life – their color of the world. The local papers are probably reluctant to take that away from them for fear of subscription cancellations."

"That's exactly right . . . and I don't have a problem with it. It's just that . . . when they start with getting their hooks into our government – the government that protects them as it is supposed to protect us – I fear their meddling is a potential threat to *our* way of thinking – our *very existence*, and our form of government!"

Back at the house, they studied the feature story in minute

detail, hungry for the meat that would explain to the surrounding communities why atheists believed the way they did. The feature was re-capitulation of the many questions she fielded at the press conference, but they were most interested in her personal history and comments, that were the cement of Erin's discovered freedom:

' . . . Atheism isn't for everyone – make no mistake about *that*! It can be summed up by reading Dostoevsky's *Grand Inquisitor,* a parable of some twenty pages in *Brothers Karamazov,* that attempts to explain the cause and the power of the Inquisition's high priest at the prospect of having *Christ,* upon his return to Earth, imprisoned in his cells. The priest explains to Christ that in his absence of over a thousand years, the burden of mankind's confusion and fears have been borne squarely on his and his colleague's shoulders – without so much as a whisper from above. No direction or guidance offered. Had it not been for the policies instituted by him, those contemporary and before him, and the ever evolving Church, where would the Lord's flock have turned to?'

'The Inquisitor's story illustrates in a sort of prose -- in what some call a poem -- the seemingly inescapable need of the masses for a Higher Power to give them hope that their meager existence and suffering is not for naught. Before Christ – before Religion -- these concerns arose in the gathering consciousness of early homosapiens . . . as they do to this day. It can be compared with Linus's security blanket: a soft, warm, fuzzy entity always at one's fingertips! It is easy for everyone to laugh at Linus's insecurity, blind that they too demand such assurance, only in a different, all encompassing form that lasts for eternity. It really is an uncontrollable opiate, as inoffensive as it may seem.'

'American Atheists have no problem with any of this – most of its members are for repealing the war on drugs, a kind of prohibition that didn't work in the 1920s and is not working today. What we *do* have a problem with, is the *continual* attack on the word atheist. Too many religionists say we are attacking religion. It is not an attack – it is a *counterattack*, in the defense of our way of life, our values and beliefs. They are not content with 'Live and let live,' but must purge any and all sign of what *they* interpret as sin, from existence. They are not content with their assertions that heaven awaits them with open arms, but must bolster their vulnerable and fragile faith with their war on *all* sin – that that will make them even more guaranteed of God's welcome in the hereafter.'

'We are not proselytizing their ranks for converts – science and time will do that for us. But their efforts to eradicate us – and we are sin incarnate to them, simply because of our unbelief in things they believe very much in – is counter to the American way! They are frustrated to no end because courts have ruled time and time again in support of the First Amendment. They don't, and *won't*, understand that the Constitution was derived with respect to *all* of its citizenry – that it was derived to be *neutral* to anything concerning religion. Why? Because there were so many variations of religious belief out there – and more in the Old World that might immigrate to our shores later. That neutrality is in very big danger today, and that is why we are finally stepping out of the closet and facing off with those who would be rid of us!'

Lastly, without the tentacles of religion choking civilization, consider the following questions: Would there be an Arab / Israeli conflict?

Would there be a Protestant / Catholic conflict in Ireland?

Would there be a Cultural War?

Would there be a war on drugs? (tax and regulate it like

alcohol and tobacco)

Would there be a verbal conflict between creationists and scientists

Would there be, in fact, less wars?

Would Women have more control over their bodies and lives?

Would there be less hypocrisy?

Would there be less superstition?

Would there be less teenage suicides and less mental illness?

Would there be less fear of death?

Would there be less obstacles in developing medicine and other sciences?

Would there be less wasted time getting important tasks done?

Would there be more property available to share the tax burden?

Would there be less cemeteries and more efficient use of real estate?

Would Population control become viable?

Would ethnic nationalism be as important?

Would a neutral, secular form of government such as ours be less vilified?"

Ethics and manners *can* be taught in our secular schools every bid as well as in any Sunday school!"

"*Wow*! Sweetheart . . . good for you! I like it! I like it! It's worth five thousand dollars to see this in print for general consumption. I'm going out and buy another dozen copies."

"But then – that'll be a dozen people who won't get to read it."

"Oh, pshaw, I guess you're right. I'll pick up a few papers when I leave for school."

"Don't show them around the college. I don't want my

cover blown just yet."
    "Exactly."

XXXV

Paul's Insight

He lost himself in his studies, and class project, to keep from thinking about the impending danger that his soul mate was facing in the mountains. Especially distracting were the dreams he was experiencing. He had read Ayn Rand's *For The New Intellectual* when he was in Iraq, and her book was a big influence on his decision to come out of the closet and challenge the hobbled status quo and the omnipresent fairy tales of religion. That he would choose to do so as a junior officer in a military hierarchy was unconventional to say the least, but reflecting back on his path through life thus far, he found he had no regrets of being unconventional.

There was something in the dream -- Ayn Rand's speech that came to mind, then, fleetingly, it was gone. A fertile notion that intrigued him, but he couldn't seem to grasp its content. Then, while emerged in his studies, it would come -- and vanish, again. It seemed to have something to do with a protocol, an *order* of things. An *order* of philosophy? He was no expert on philosophy, though he was well aware that everyone lived in varying degrees of *some* philosophy -- as unconscious of that fact as they may be.

Paul agreed totally with Rand's put-down of the ivory tower intellectuals whose works and lectures seemed to obfuscate rather than elucidate. It was no wonder that the highly sophisticated academic's opinions of the masses appeal to the commercial and conspiratorial were considered as so much liberal gibberish. The defrocked former vice president to Richard Nixon, Spiro Agnew, characterized it with his expression: "Those . . . nattering nabobs of negativity." The word '*liberal*' is now despised almost as much as the word atheist, if one is in accordance with the rantings and fabrications of Rush Limbaugh and Ann Coulter. William F. Buckley, Jr., on the other hand, and for good reason, surgically dismembers careless liberals all the time.

But that is not to say that so called *conservatism* is preferable to those known as liberal issues. Without liberals there would not be Social Security, Medicare, repeal of Prohibition, abolishment of slavery, women's rights, these United States, the Scientific Method, or even the Christian religion. Instead, we would still be near the dawn of civilization arguing about how best to maintain our traditions. Who would escape the certain torment after making the claim that the earth was not the center of the universe? Was not John Stuart Mill correct when he said: "*Although it is true that not all conservatives are stupid, it is true that most stupid people are conservative.*" But as disturbing as the Cultural War is, the issues of liberalism versus conservatism offer a necessary balance that keeps human efforts in check. It is a sort of falsifiability: that nothing is sacred in a free society, even though the latter constantly uses piety as a shield -- as well as its base.

Ayn Rand's criticism of the many intellectuals who would reduce philosophy to similar ambient parameters that adorn religion, is valid. *Religion is a philosophy of life,* not the other way around, he thought. Then he realized what was bothering him: it was as if he had been smacked up the side of his head by an old friend – someone who wanted to wake him up to a further consideration of reality. Religionists are always so defensive. Why? Because they function in a large bubble within the universe of ideas. They are an aberration, represented and enabled by minions determined to maintain an *order violating inversion* that grows more precarious as the planet shrinks.

In order to survive, religion must continue to effectively *contain* and subdue – otherwise, the question would become apparent: **who needs religion if its principles are subject to a worldly master?** The worldly master being humanity's derivation and implementation of *Philosophy*! Religion, with all its attraction and power – subtle in charity, but gross in self-preservation – is really a sub-phylum in the *true order* of things. Paul finally realized something he unconsciously suspected all along: that **Religion is, in itself, a product of humanity's fertile mind.** It *had* to be so – one followed the other as surely as a tail follows a lamb. And the proof lay in the negative struggle of the competing sects -- each, like squabbling schoolchildren, claiming different truths!

He had uncovered an intellectual proof that mankind's derived gods -- whoever they may be, whether singular or plural – were, pure and simple, fabrications of wishful entities not unlike the Easter Bunny and the Tooth Fairy.

However, as important as this discovery was to him, he could not go to the head of the class. This was confidential information to be shared with no one until he was safely beyond his military obligation. And then could it be shared with anyone except for a select few, until Philosophy once again ruled supreme? Or would this revelation serve as the catalyst mighty enough to right the unnatural inversion – to set the order of the phylum right?

XXXVI

The Waiting Game

Erin was now in the role of homemaker in their newly acquired abode. For the first time in many years she found she had an abundance of hours in the day, and she capitulated to the temptation of surfing the Net. Especially intriguing were the chat rooms that could be brought up on just about any subject under the sun one wanted to discuss.

She soon found herself involved in defending her freethinking ideals against service veterans who had implored God to preserve and keep them in their pursuit of killing the enemy (who presumably did as much imploring and begging for survival from *their* own personal deity). She rebuked those who could see only a Creator responsible for the existence of everything in the universe, with the question: "How did the Creator come into existence?" It was such great fun to poke holes in the wimpy logic of the unthinking multitudes that tried to push their security blanket onto others: " . . . after all," they would proselytize, "the price of eternal salvation was so cheap – all you had to do was *believe.*"

Belief! Is that not what conscientiousness is all about? Beliefs are manifested in the sum total of one's experiences in learning. It was no mystery to her that the more read and traveled a person was, the more likely they were to be removed from the parochial concerns of those who were tethered to their ancestral homes and heritage. She remembered reading that over 90% of the world's leading scientists did not believe in any supernatural deity, be it a god or a devil. She remembered reading about travelers from Protestant countries who visited the Latin world to be amazed at the squalor and insipid character of many of its populace. It was as if the Church had not only taken over responsibility of their souls, but their meager earnings as well, blessing those who would seek a life of poverty while the priest class luxuriated in prestige and indolence.

But after a few weeks she found, more and more, that she missed her books. She yearned to spend more time at the town's library instead of the meager time allotted to her on her twice weekly forays into town for groceries, etc. At their next weekly Saturday afternoon meeting she decided she would broach her husband and Ted about maybe setting up an hour or two on a daily basis when she could get out to the library.

As usual on Saturday afternoons, Ted stopped by under the auspices of watching the ball game on T.V. Instead, they discussed security and any suspicious developments in the ongoing saga of entrapment.

"It's the librarian in me, guys. I've got cabin fever and need to get out!"

"Surely we can play what appears to be a compromising of security to some advantage." Paul said on her behalf.

Ted rubbed his chin in deep concentration. "Perhaps it can be allowed . . . in some controlled way."

"Controlled way -- what do you mean?"

Ted leaned forward, alternately eyeing each of the couple. "We could have you leave the library at a set time each day . . . a routine of sorts . . . that *Sick Bear* might just pick up on!"

"That's an idea!" Paul agreed. "It might just set a timetable that our mark finds convenient – and we'll have the convenience of looking for him to show up at *that* time."

"True enough. I could be parked in my car on stakeout – say, 4:30 every afternoon watching the library's entrance, ready to move at the instance you appear on the street."

"Whad'ya think, sweetheart?" Paul said taking her hand into his.

She raised her eyebrows and smiled almost naively. "I suppose that will get me my library time. And I'll know for sure where Ted will be at 4:30."

"Then that's what we'll do." Ted announced. "I'll info the town cops and Sergeant Piper on this. I think they'll agree that this may be a better way to set up and control a kidnap attempt!"

"You guys are geniuses." She allowed reluctantly, visibly shaken by the "k" word.

Another week went by and the routine of her leaving the library at 4:30 every weekday afternoon met with no untoward event. In the second week, on a Tuesday, Erin looked up from the table she was sitting at to see a scruffy, bearded man staring at her from the magazine racks. He quickly looked back to the publication he was holding, as she made mental notes of his dress and stature. Erin was sure that he wasn't a regular – that she had never seen him before, and certainly didn't appear to be a bookish type. He struck her as being well over six feet tall, but appearing wiry in his jeans and boots. Muddy -- his boots were muddy -- and he appeared to be in his fifties but the unkempt hair and beard might have disguised a younger age.

Her study of the man was accomplished with discreet glances aside, as if in deep reflection of the novel before her. Within minutes, the man was gone. She agonized over whether to mention him to Paul when they talked that evening, but she sure was going to mention it to Ted when she got home and called him.

The following Saturday, they discussed the strange visitor at length.

"You've never seen him around town?" Ted couched the same question for the third time in hardly subtle variations.

"No, but I've seen men, and some women, dressed similarly, buying cigarettes at the convenience store."

"Probably on Friday nights, when they come down out of the hollows to watch the traffic light change colors, . . . for something to do." Ted remarked rather unprofessionally.

"Hey! Easy with the redneck image – your tramplin' on my feelings, seein' that I come from a hollow not far from Harlan County, Kentucky."

"Sorry! I suppose I've been on this assignment too long . . . but I heard *this one* the other day from a state trooper . . ."

"Yeah?" Paul was all ears.

"What's a young lady in West Virginia say to her lover after having sex?"

"Okay, I'll bite?"

"Git off me , daddy – you're crushin' mah cigarettes."

"That's gross, Ted!" Erin reacted.

"We're not that distant from West Virginia – I've heard some stories about incest being practiced not far from *here*. The mentality of our Sick Bear is really not too far removed from such dysfunctional stereotypes."

"God, Ted! Please keep a *close* eye on me!" she said, with flashbacks from *"Deliverance"* popping into her head.

"I will, Erin. I will!"

The following week, Erin thought she saw the strange guy leaving the super market, but was interrupted by a pin hole puncture in a soda pop can spraying its contents into her eyes. After wiping her face and hearing the apologies of the offending child's mother, she could no longer see the guy or which way he went.

On Thursday of the next week, she noticed a tall man fumbling through the card catalogue. He seemed familiar, but was clean shaven with hair trimmed not too long ago – as a matter of fact, she gathered that the man had just been to the barber because of the tell-tale cologne that permeated the air. When she wasn't looking, she could feel his eyes on her. Either, this is our man or it's someone else who wants to hit on her. She quickly ruled the latter out because her wedding ring was prominently on display. She pressed the sensor on her leg.

Shortly thereafter, he left, and she went to the desk and inquired of the man. The librarian didn't know anything about him.

"We're getting close to the time, I think." Ted offered. "Unfortunately, I haven't seen this guy yet – he leaves before I get into position."

"Can you get into position around 3:30?"

"Sure. I started doing just that on Friday. From now on, when you leave your house give me two presses on each sensor – to test the equipment and put me into motion toward your house. When we pass each other, give me a wave if everything is okay. If there is a problem, don't wave, and I'll be on your tail like a flea on a dog!"

"He knows me from my picture being in the paper."

"Yeah, he's sizing you up – probably seen more of you than you know."

"Ted, you can be so insensitive at times." Paul growled.

"I'm sorry. It's just that . . . I have to assume the worst!"

"It's all right. We're all getting a bit edgy about this whole thing."

"We know you're doing the best you can." Erin reassured.

"So how long do we play this cat and mouse game?"

"Best case scenario is that he comes into the library again,

Erin or I see him, I call for backup, and then proceed to arrest him on the spot."

"And, worst case scenario?"

"He does not come into the library but intercepts Erin on her way to her car."

"You'll be out there, seeing a man fitting his description . . . on the sidewalk, right?"

"Right! When that happens, I'll call for backup from both the town cops and the State Police. From Monday on, the State boys will have a cruiser on the north side of the Pike and another on the south side."

"Can you arrest him for loitering?"

"I can detain him for due cause-- if Erin identifies him as her stalker. The stalking charge should allow us to hold him long enough to run a make on him."

"What if there are two of them – and she can't identify the guy?"

"Boy, Paul, you are a pessimist!" Ted exhaled. "Then the variables increase inordinately. Bastards do have brothers, and *that is* a possibility."

"One other question."

"Shoot'"

"Is the town cop or cops willing to arrest a local boy who has his sights set on knocking off an atheist?"

"Short of subjecting municipality employees to an examination, that is a wild card possibility. It comes under *'shit happens.'* Like, can a rookie cop pull the trigger when the chips are down. It's something we'll have to live with – the cop might lie under examination anyway."

XXXVII

Contact!

They did not have long to wait. Ted had gone over the necessary changes with the local police, and the Turnpike Detail of the State Police. The new defense strategy was set in place and all eyes were on Erin when she left the house at 1:30 to run errands before proceeding to the library on Main Street. Everett Borough's main east – west street was also known as the *Lincoln Highway* -- a segment of the original U.S. Route Thirty, famous for being the first coast to coast highway in America. The town had long been by-passed with a sleek four lane highway, skirting the business district on a northerly route, but there still remained a fair amount of truck traffic on State Route 26, the north – south corridor.

Unfortunately, Route 26 turned east onto Main Street at a traffic light, and progressed two blocks, passing the library before turning south again at the town's only other traffic light.

At 2:30 P.M., Ted was in position facing west at the first parking spot along the curb just west of the intersection where Route 26 turned south. He was four doors east, with a good view of the library's entrance. But his problem was the constantly changing barrier of the trucks that obstructed the view of vehicles parked on the south side of the street. In anticipation of this problem, he had arranged for one of the two town cruisers to periodically patrol Main Street from west to east, as frequently as was possible. They would be in radio check at all times between the two traffic lights.

Mid afternoon was a busy time along the thoroughfare, and this Monday was no exception. There were a few men on the street that fitted Erin's description of the perpetrator, but they passed innocuously by. Just at 4:25, he saw a rather short man cross Main Street and head toward him on the north sidewalk. The description didn't fit the card, and Ted dreamily scanned the panoply of traffic before him wondering when the town's cruiser would start chirping its radio check. It was due anywhere between 4:30 and 4:40 P.M., depending on the traffic.

He looked back to check on the short man, but he was no where in sight! 'Damn,' he muttered, chastising himself for failing to keep a closer check on the man. It was now 4:30 and Erin appeared just outside the library's entrance. She would turn right toward where her blue sedan was parked. Wait! There was the short man directly behind her closing the distance between them as they headed west. He could see a visible reaction from the now erect stature of her frame as the man apparently jabbed her in the lower ribs with something. Now he knew there were *two* of them -- Sick Bear and an accomplice.

The buzzer from her sensor sounded in his car just as he was calling the expected cruiser:

"TOWN ONE, TOWN ONE, WE HAVE CONTACT! . . . I REPEAT, WE HAVE A BOGEY ESCORTING OUR LURE WESTWARD ON NORTH SIDE OF MAIN STREET, -- THIS IS ALPHA AGENT! -- OVER!"

"Roger, copy that ALPHA AGENT. Proceeding to Main Street, post haste! – Over."

'What!' he thought, his mind going numb. 'What do they mean "proceeding to Main Street!" They're supposed *to be* on Main Street!'

Just then, as he was pulling from the curb into traffic, he

saw Erin and the man dodge between parked cars and get into a brown SUV that looked like a late 90's Explorer pointed in the same direction as he was. He could hear the wailing siren of TOWN ONE approaching the controlled intersection in front of them. And he saw the SUV shoot through the light as traffic pulled to the curb. "That's just great!" he muttered aloud, stuck in traffic. "TOWN ONE, TOWN ONE, BOGEY IS PROCEEDING WEST THROUGH YOUR INTERSECTION IN A BROWN FORD EXPLORER. THERE ARE TWO OF THEM!"

"Roger that ALPHA AGENT. We saw him scoot through the light toward Bedford . . . and we are in pursuit! – Over."

'Bully for you!' Ted thought. His mind raced through the difficulties that they now faced.

He was sure the State boys were monitoring communications. "CRUISER NORTH, CRUISER NORTH, THIS IS ALPHA AGENT – DO YOU COPY?"

"ALPHA, THIS IS CRUISER NORTH, CRUISER 43 proceeding east on Thirty from Lutzville Road. Monitoring your situation and will attempt interception. TOWN ONE, TOWN ONE, What is your status? –Over."

"Roger 43, THIS IS TOWN ONE in direct pursuit, nearing Borough limits . . . Advise! – Over."

"TOWN ONE, stay in pursuit 'til we make visual contact. Have you hit any tires? –And do you have a plate number? -- Over."

"NEGATIVE your first, 43. Plate number is Bravo, Tango, X-ray 4977. Will stay in pursuit – ALPHA AGENT is on our tail!. – Over."

"ALL UNITS, ALL UNITS! THIS IS BASE! All Cruisers north of turnpike Proceed to Hospital Hill area and set up road block at bottom of Penn Knoll ramp! All Cruisers south of turnpike proceed to intersection of SR 2023 and SR 1004 and set up roadblock. I repeat: THIS IS BASE! All Cruisers north of turnpike Proceed to Hospital Hill area and set up road block at bottom of Penn Knoll EAST ramp! All Cruisers south of turnpike proceed to intersection of SR 2023 and SR 1004and set up roadblock. TAKE ALL PRECAUTION AS BOGEY IS PROBABLY TWO ARMED MEN WITH KIDNAPPED WOMAN! CRUISERS ON THE PIKE SHOULD PROCEED TO NEAREST TOLL BOOTH AND LOOK OUT FOR 1997 BROWN FORD EXPLORER . . . Plate number Bravo, Tango, X-ray 4977 – that may attempt entry to Turnpike! Most logical point of entry is BEDFORD! -- BASE STATION CLEAR! – OVER!"

Ted's head was spinning with the possibilities now that the trap was ineffectively sprung. Would the APB control Sick Bear? This country bumpkin probably knows every shortcut and back road for sixty miles along the Allegheny Front. If he makes it to the mountains . . .

He shuddered violently at the thought, remembering the older trooper's stories he had heard about the Shade Gap standoff and the Cooper family's protection of Gary, their escaped convict son.

XXXVIII

Pursuit!

Erin learned the names of her kidnappers not in any sense of a formal way. She assumed their names were what they called each other in the confusion of the chase. They were a visibly shaken twosome that reacted as if they had walked nose first into a hanging hornets nest.

"How the devil did them cops know what we were up to?" the short man asked of Nolan, who was driving.

"The Devil's workin' overtime today. Shows the sorry state this nation is in . . . The police and courts protectin' queers and atheists!"

"We got some fancy drivin' to do to make it back to the ridge!" the short man said whose name she gathered to be Furrell.

"Don't worry, Furrell – God is on our side! He'll show the way!"

With Nolan's statement, Erin thought of Hitler's troops in World War II whose belt buckles were stamped 'GOTT MIT UNS.'

" . . . And then this atheist bitch will git her due!"

"Ain't we goin' to take her to Preacher Dunn . . . like you said?"

Dammit Furrell, Dunn's New Testament . . . too much New Testament – turnin' the other cheek an' all! The Old Testament metes out the punishment these heretics deserve here an' now! 'Thou shalt not suffer a witch to live' is clear direction for me . . . as it should be for you!"

Just then the Penn Knoll roadblock came into view. "Hold on, we're takin' the scenic route!" And he steered the SUV left into a one-eighty. "That dirt road'll take us to the Upper Valley, and up over Snake Spring."

"Yikes man, ya just about turned us over!"

"Shut up Furrell and get a shot off at that fuckin' cop!"

"Right! But I gotta tell ya . . . it don't look good for the home team!"

"God an' me'll get us up over Snake Spring . . .don'tchu worry none!" and then he added in quick succession. "Nice shot, I think you hit 'im!"

Ted slowed as he saw the Explorer turn back toward him, watching the town's cruiser veer into the ditch. Before he realized what was happening the SUV was cutting across his path into a farm lane. "Shit!" he exclaimed as he overshot the back road. "ALL UNITS, ALL UNITS AND BASE, THIS IS ALPHA AGENT. TOWN ONE HAS BEEN HIT! BOGEY DID A ONE-EIGHTY AND TURNED NORTH ON FARM LANE. REPEAT, TOWN ONE IS IN DITCH AND BOGEY CUTTING NORTHWARD ACROSS FARM TO MAYBE UPPER VALLEY ROAD . . . REQUEST CHOPPER TO UPPER SNAKE SPRING VALLEY, A.S.A.P.! – OVER."

Erin could hardly keep her balance in the back seat as provisions spilled from grocery bags and rolled around on the seat and floor as Nolan forced the vehicle left, then right on the rutted, dusty road.

"See what ya caused, atheist bitch! Uppity wimin forcin' their ideas on innocent people when they *should* be home makin' babies That's what witches do – git in the minds of the innocent! Well, yur days of corruptin' minds are over . . . bitch!"

She long suspected that zealots like her two abductors

248

existed in America, as they do in Islamic countries – now her worst suspicions were confirmed and she was the bait that coaxed them out from under their rocks. "You what they call Phineas Priests?" she heard herself yell. Somehow, she wasn't as frightened by the turn of events as she thought she would be, though she had been separated from her purse – and the Kel-Tec P-32 – when she was shoved into the vehicle.

"What d'ya need ta know fer, atheist bitch . . . you're dead meat! Put a round through her lef' tit, Furrell -- if ya can't hit that sonufabitch behind us with the red light!"

"But Preacher Dunn said . . . "

"Fuck Dunn, dammit. You lissen ta me!"

"But . . . she's a good hostage as long as she's alive. Besides, she'll be a better fuck if she's still hot!"

"Furrell, yur startin' ta think . . . and it's scarin' me!"

Ted was doing all he could to keep his government sedan within sight of the cloud of dust before him. The red blinking portable magnet light had helped him around traffic but now offered a pin-point target for the bogey to aim at. He thought of switching it off, but then the helicopter—when it comes—might consider him a target, too. He got on his radio: "ALPHA AGENT CALLING ALL UNITS NORTH OF THE PIKE – LISTEN UP! BOGEY IS APPROACHING UPPER VALLEY ROAD AND WILL PROBABLY HEAD FOR THE PASS OVER SNAKE SPRING . . . ADVISE!"

"ALPHA AGENT, THIS IS BASE. THREE CRUISERS ENROUTE NORTH ON LOWER VALLEY ROAD TO . . . MOUNTAIN INTERSECTION. CRUISER 27 HEADING NORTH ON UPPER VALLEY ROAD -- AT YOUR DISPOSAL! ACKNOWLEDGE!"

"ROGER THAT, BASE! THIS IS ALPHA AGENT -- OVER AND OUT!" The cloud of dust dissipated as the Explorer burst onto the paved Upper Valley Road, and Ted thought of that winding road leading to the top of Snake Spring Mountain. Not knowing how far up the cruisers were on the Lower Valley Road, he feared that he and the bogey would cross the "T" intersection before their arrival, since the Upper Valley Road was a bit shorter. Both roads were rife with dangerous, unmarked hairpin curves and the lower road was steeper. He cursed himself for not reconning the road north of the mountain pass -- he had planned to do that some morning this week.

Snake Spring Valley was a twelve mile long limestone cleft in the surrounding mountains, shaped like a triangle with its northern apex being the peak of Snake Spring Mountain. The secondary state road crossed over, at that point, into a broad farming cove to the north. All entrapment plans centered on the perpetrators using the Turnpike to advantage, with his (now, their) lair being west of Bedford in the higher mountains of the Allegheny Front. Ted couldn't help thinking that the route of the chase was forced to the north by circumstances that were difficult to control. Of all escape routes there were only two to the north as opposed to four crossing the Turnpike to the south.

His worst fears were realized as they crossed the "T" with no sign of the State Police in sight. He reached for the mike: "BASE, BASE – THIS IS ALPHA AGENT. I'M STILL IN PURSUIT OF BOGEY, CROSSING THE SNAKE SPRING "T" INTERSECTION. I'M NOT FAMILIAR OF ROADS OTHER SIDE OF MOUNTAIN BUT WILL ATTEMPT TO KEEP BOGEY IN SIGHT 'TIL YOU GUYS CATCH UP. ANY THOUGHTS OF A CHOPPER AT THIS TIME? -- OVER!"

"ROGER, ALPHA AGENT – CHOPPER ENROUTE FROM SOMERSET. ETA OF BACKUP CRUISERS TO "T" INTERSECTION IS TWO MINUTES. –BASE OUT."

"Where the hell are we goin', Nolan?"

" . . . Used to work on a farm over in the Cove . . . we could go there, or double back over the mountain into Dutch Corner – I know they'll never follow us on *that* road in them cruisers!"

"Wut if the road is blocked by down'd trees?"

"Jeeze, Furrell . . . yur such a wet blanket. Four wheelers'll have that track cleared – clean as a whistle, this time of year.

"We goin' campin', boys?" Erin taunted, knowing her prospects weren't looking good. She couldn't believe her cavalier attitude.

"You shut yur fuckin' sass up, atheist bitch! Pump one into her NOW, Furrell!"

Furrell leveled his 38 Special at her and she ducked forward, lunging for her purse as he fired. He pulled the trigger again but heard only a click as she reached into the handbag. With her head between them, Furrell, with a vicious swipe downward, struck her with the broad side of his piece, knocking her out. "So wut do we have here?" pulling the handbag from her clutch. And he pulled out her Kel-Tec P-32. "Nice automatic, Nolan." He said, showing the slim handgun to the driver. "We should've searched her!"

"Yeah, like we had the time. These fuckin' cops were on us like my hound dog comes onto 'is bitch friend." They swerved to round the next turn where the road straightened out somewhat. "Tie 'er up an' gag her. If'n ya want to feel 'er some, be my guest."

"Gotcha, Nolan! I'm glad we didn't have to kill 'er – the Ten Commandments an' all."

"The Ten Commandments are fer God fearin' people – She's not one of us! She's a disciple of the Devil – a devil worshipper that must be destroyed, like any witch! You need to join in Dunn's Bible study, more—'specially, when he talks of the Old Testament. This bitch ain't human . . . she's an *evil spirit* an' you can do wut you like with her 'cause she's dead meat when we have no need of 'er anymore – capisc ?"

"Yeah." Furrell answered, wondering what *capisc* meant.

Ted maintained sight of the SUV but could not see anything coming in his rear view mirrors. "Damn, where's that chopper?" he continually asked aloud. Then he saw the Explorer veer to the left on what appeared to be another road. "ALL UNITS, ALL UNITS, THIS IS ALPHA AGENT! BOGEY HAS TURNED LEFT AT BOTTOM OF MOUNTAIN . . . ON ROAD TO SALEMVILLE." He hesitated until the green sign could be read, indicating destination. "I REPEAT: THIS IS AGENT! BOGEY HAS TURNED LEFT AT BOTTOM OF MOUNTAIN, ON ROAD TO SALEMVILLE – I BELIEVE THAT TO BE SR 1026. NO SIGN OF AERIAL SUPPORT! --OVER" Pennsylvania's lesser secondary state roads were marked with small metal plates, which were difficult to read, even under normal circumstances.

"THIS IS UNIT 27, I COPY THAT, AGENT. THREE UNITS BEHIND ME . . . WILL MAKE LEFT TURN ONTO SR 1026. –DO YOU COPY?"

"I COPY THAT, 27. –BRING A HELICOPTER WITH YOU! --THIS IS ALPHA AGENT, OUT!" Ted surprised himself with his unprofessional outburst of frustration. 'So fire me!' He thought, thinking of Erin's non-improving predicament. He slammed his fist down hard, loathing himself for letting conditions get so far out of control.

He then heard the condescending voice of Base's dispatcher: "ALPHA AGENT, THIS IS BASE! CHOPPER ABOVE SNAKE SPRING VALLEY, NOW! WILL BE IN

YOUR VICINITY, FIVE MINUTES. –OVER."

"ROGER THAT, BASE. – THIS IS AGENT –OUT!"
Seeing is believing he thought to himself.

Just then, the SUV turned left again, in a built up area of
several houses. 'This must be Salemville.' He muttered as he
looked for a road marking sign. 'MOUNTAIN ROAD T-
561' marked the intersection – 'a township road,' he muttered
again. 'Looks like rough riding time, boys.' "ALL CARS,
ALL CARS! THIS IS ALPHA AGENT, BOGEY HAS
TURNED LEFT ONTO MOUNTAIN ROAD, T-561.
REPEAT, SICK BEAR HAS TURNED SOUTH ON T-561
AND IS HEADING FOR HIGH GROUND!" –OVER!"

"HEELO ONE, HEELO ONE! DID YOU COPY
ALPHA AGENT?"

"THIS IS HEELO ONE – AFFIRMATIVE! COMING
UP ON RIDGE TOP NOW, WILL APPROACH AREA
FROM THE EAST, --OVER!"

"Nolan, this road's from Hell; when's the last time you
been over it?"

"It's a bit washed out – but them State boys aren't going
to follow very far in their fancy cruisers!"

"Yeah, but they got them Jeeps. They might try comin'
up the other side."

"Yur thinkin' agin, Furrell – and that's good. That
thought had crossed my mind, too.

We may have to make a stand of it . . . at the top o' the
mountain!"

"Ya mean . . . stand off the whole State Police?" Furrell
gasped.

"We got this atheist bitch as a hostage! We're okay as
long we got 'er!"

"Good thing I missed her and clunked her on the head
instead!"

"Jesus is lookin' out fer us, Furrell. We'll suffer no witches an' Jesus will be just fine about all this."

"You mean . . . we'll kill her anyway?"

"If they don't let us go an' we run out of provisions . . . we got to, Furrell!"

"But then they'll kill us!" Furrell looked glummly at the dark, enclosing forest canopy. "I ain't ready to die!"

"We got some time. We'll see wut develops."

Just then they heard a thundering noise as the police helicopter passed directly over them.

"Shit! I think they spotted us!"

Ted pulled over when the road got too rough, and waited for the trailing cruisers. The last one stopped to pick him up before proceeding into the forest. "The chopper has them in sight, Ted. They'll not get away, now!"

He wasn't worrying about them getting away so much as he was about the inevitable standoff. These zealots – like their lunatic counterparts in the Middle East – feel they are following the dictates of their God, and will gladly die for that privilege. He had nothing but foreboding of Erin's chances on this mountain – three days standoff, then, bang! -- murder and suicide. Tears welled to his eyes as he saw the units before them crawl to a stop because of not having enough under-carriage clearance.

The jarring of the Explorer brought Erin conscious again, and she heard Furrell's cry of fear. Because her head ached and she was gagged and tied, she knew the picture looked bleak for her survival and her thoughts went to Paul back in Carlisle, who probably did not yet know this was happening. She thought of their moments of love and how they had experienced a happiness that very few experience in a lifetime. Somehow, this absolutely chaotic situation made perfect sense to her. It explained all the sadness there was in the world. And she would die a martyr to the world of reason! This might be the crossing that would turn the hearts of the world . . .to question non-provable, non-fullfillable religious agendas that always came up short.

She had nothing to lose, and she was surprised at being unafraid of her inevitable death. The sorry state of affairs would be lost in a field of pain and then she would return peacefully to the non-existence of eternity that she had come into this life from – it was as simple as that! She remembered Paul laying in bed, remarking that if confronted with being burned at the stake, he might go into a laughing fit at the stupidity and seriousness of his executors. Somehow, she felt that detachment now, even in the teeth of her luckless position.

Momentarily, the SUV crested the ridge, and was stopped by a downed red oak. Nolan and Furrell knew better than to get out of the vehicle until they got off a couple of rounds at the buzzing helicopter.

"We'll wait in here for dark, and then scoot out toward Brumbaugh – I know a path that just might get us down out'ta here."

She feigned unconsciousness as Furrell retrieved the provisions into manageable sacks, stealing a feel of her breast and thigh in his efforts. Nolan kidded him about his sophomoric touching of the victim and said: "How often does your wife let ya into her drawers?"

"Prob'ly more than I should – I reckon."

"C'mon, Furrell, you can tell me – how many times a month?"

"Hell, Nolan, wut does it matter?"

"Just curious, watchin' how you touch this atheist bitch."

"You know . . . sex is just fer procreatin'."

"Yeah, I know . . . but we're all sinners – so wut's a little

255

extra nookie now and then?

Christ already paid for *that* on the cross!" Nolan rubbed his whiskers. "So how off'n you git it?"

"Twiced, maybe three times if I do somethin' that tickles her fancy."

"You *know* . . . you're the boss – she *must* submit to you, accordin' to *Ephesians 5:22*."

"Wut if I only feel like procreatin' twiced, -- three times a month. Anyway, I git so confused why we can an' can't do the *act*."

"Let *me* back there! I'll show you how to sin, *good* -- boy."

Just then the helicopter passed overhead with a megaphone blaring: "LEAVE THE VEHICLE NOW – WITH YOUR HANDS OVER YOUR HEAD!"

"How can you think of sex at a time like this, Nolan?"

"Yur right. I got turned on watchin' you feelin' 'er. We better collect ourselves a bit. I reckon we'll have company after supper."

"Yeah, here's a can of beans and some chips."

"BASE, BASE, THIS IS UNIT 27, ME AND UNITS 16 AND 40 ALPHA AGENT ARE BOGGED DOWN, QUARTER OF THE WAY UP MOUNTAIN ROAD TO DUTCH CORNER. SOME OF US PROCEEDING ON FOOT! –OVER."

"ROGER YOUR LAST, UNIT 27. SICK BEAR SEEMS STUCK AT TOP OF YOUR RIDGE, BUT HEELO ONE CAN'T FIND A LANDING SPOT. HE'LL CIRCLE FOR ANOTHER HOUR OR SO 'TIL FOUR WHEEL DRIVE UNITS CHOP THEIR WAY THROUGH FROM DUTCH CORNER! DO YOU COPY? –OVER."

"AFFIRMATIVE, BASE. SOME OF US TAKING RATIONS NOW, AND THEN WE"LL RELIEVE

TROOPERS CLIMBING TRAIL! –THIS IS UNIT 27, OUT."

Ted was in the vanguard with the troopers assaulting the steep grade. He had promised Erin and Paul, nothing was going to happen to her, but now he realized that had been too much to expect. Shit happens, and so it did this day – a Monday, a day many find it difficult to even get out of bed. He hardly noticed the cloud of mosquitoes coming out and buzzing him in the twilight of the ridge's north face. At their location, the sun was casting long shadows, but darkness was two hours away and the sun's rays still danced on the metal top of Sick Bear's SUV.

"Wut are we goin' to do?" Furrell continued to defer to his leader's ideas.

"Depends on where the State boys are, come dark. I reckon we'll be surrounded afore then – somewhat, anyway."

"Is that the trail to Brumbaugh?" Furrell pointed out his side of the vehicle.

"You thinkin' what I'm thinkin . . . that we should head out that way while they're still climbin'?"

"Just a thought."

"Sometimes I like it when you think, Furrell. Finish eatin' an' let the atheist bitch have some a them beans –she's gonna need her strength."

"Fuckin' A!" Furrell agreed, and he pulled the rag out of her mouth.

She shook her head free.

"Eat somethin' bitch. We're goin' on a hike."

Her voice calmly chirped: "You boys go on without me – I think I'll just stay here."

"Whoa," Nolan exclaimed. "a funny girl we have here!"

"I just thought I'd cramp your style, hangin' up on the briars and all."

"YOU *are* our protection, atheist bitch!"

"I thought Jee-sus was all the protection you needed." She taunted them.

"Well, now . . . sometimes he needs a little help." Nolan answered sarcastically and remarkably low key.

Dialogue – theistic dialogue might buy some time she thought. "It don't look like your Jee-sus has been much help to you today!"

"Neither has your Devil been much help to you! 'Cause yur gonna die, soon!"

"I don't believe there is a Devil, Nolan. He's *also* part of the pack of lies we were *all* forced fed since we were young pups."

Furrell's jaw dropped an inch in awe of her announcement. "Wut's she sayin', Nolan?"

"Never you mind – she's lyin'. She's in cahoots big time with that rascal from Hell!"

"But she needs him more than ever . . . to save her skin!"

"I'll tell you what this atheist bitch needs, Furrell, . . a good fuckin'. Hold 'er down while I undo 'er drawers."

"I don't remember such an act bein' approved in the Bible."

"Shut up an' do as I say, Furrell . . . she's not one of us! *Numbers 31:18* gives me this right over the vanquished enemy."

"You sure?"

"Sure, I'm sure . . . dammit! Now hold her down while I rub my willy 'ginst her!"

"All right, git it over quick 'cause we're startin' to lose the light."

"I bet he comes quicker than when he's with his old lady, Furrell!" Erin teased.

"SHUT UP BITCH!" Nolan cried and he slapped her face

back and forth.

Half crying, she continued "You . . . your such a little man for the big talker you are." She said, staring at his waning penis. "I don't think he can penetrate in his sorry condition."

"Gag 'er, and blindfold her. I'm goin' to have a piece of her ass!"

"Nolan, we best be hittin' the trail afore it's too late. I'll hold 'er down fer ya, later"

The sound of the helicopter masked the noise of Ted and the troopers as they neared the top of the ridge. The SUV was now in full view -- parked on the narrow peak, and they witnessed activity of the occupants inside the banged up vehicle.

"Wait." Ted held up his hand to the four troopers. "Call off the copter for now – have him set down and standby as near as possible . . . for now. We need quiet, to see what their next step is!" The order was passed by walkie-talkie to the bogged down reserve force, and shortly later, with only another hour of daylight left the copter swung wide and headed north toward Salemville.

"He must be low on fuel." Furrell observed, as the chopper left the scene.

"Low on fuel, my ass . . . that means the cops are nearby - - on foot. We gotta stay here, now."

"Why don't you boys surrender now . . . and then God will spring you from the lockup?"

"And you get to live! Fat chance, devil woman."

"Why am I such a threat to you and your Jesus . . . if he is so powerful, and ready to take you to his Heaven?" She stopped mocking him, trying to draw him into a rational conversation. She sensed that Furrell was amenable to a more reasonable venue.

"'Cause Earth is his kingdom and must be cleansed in preparation for his return. Evil must be fought and the Devil denied his craving!"

"Isn't it enough just to accept Jesus as your savior without bothering others. I always thought that if you have faith – you were a shoe-in for salvation, right?"

"The end times are near an' yur a witch . . . '*Thou shalt not suffer a witch to live*' it says in *Exodus 22:18*."

"But the Bible also says '*Thou shalt not kill.*' And '*Judge not lest ye be judged.*'"

"The Commandments are for our own – the Godless enemy is fair game!"

"You're sure of that, 'cause if you're not, you might just be blazing a path to Hell, for yourself and for Furrell."

"Sure, I'm sure, or I wouldn't be pointing your nice little automatic at you ready to pull the damn trigger." And he pointed to Furrell to move further away. "Where do you get the audacity to quote from *mah* holy book, anyway?"

"Where do *you* get the audacity to kidnap and do bodily harm to me when I haven't done anything to you?" She wondered to herself how long she could continue to hold him in conversation.

"You're history, lady!" and he pulled the trigger, only to find that the unfamiliar piece was double action only.

"She gulped, and said: "But this is America! Don't you believe in your country?"

"There's no one more loyal to the US of A than Furrell and me." He cocked the hammer. "This country was founded by God fearin' folk . . . and by God, only God fearin' folk should live in it!"

"If that's true, then why don't you operate by the laws of the country you love?"

"'Cause the judges are corrupted! They're only fat-assed

lawyers on the take that purchased their way to the top o' the heap . . . and they're out of hearin' range of people like me."

"So that's why you're my judge, jury and executioner!"

"You finally got it, baby!"

"You can't wait for heaven on Jesus's terms . . ."

"Ssch! Furrell, are you keepin' a look out? I thought I heard somethin'"

". . . you got to force God's judgement and make your heaven right here on Earth." She surprised herself finishing the sentence before he pistol-whipped her. "you're just like those al-Qeada Arabs, forcing their religion on others – no difference!"

"SHUTUP!"

"NO DIFFERENCE!" she screamed, knowing she was talking to a blind, deaf troglodyte.

"NO DIFFERENT . . ." and the shot rang out.

At the start of the yelling the troopers, unnerved, intuitively moved toward the vehicle. After they heard the sound of the gun shot, it was quiet.

Ted yelled: "ERIN?"

The only answer was the splintering of glass and a shot that nicked him in the forearm as it whizzed by.

Gaining his senses, he lunged behind a tree. Everyone sought out better cover. "ERIN, ARE YOU OKAY!" He yelled again, his voice cracking in despair.

The other troopers looked toward him for direction, and his eyes filled with tears.

Suddenly, they heard the anguished shout: "NOLAN, NO . . ." and two more shots in quick succession reverberated on the mountain top.

XXXIX

Religionists always say that men and women must have 'faith' – faith in a Creator or God. They say that unbelievers like atheists, agnostics, secular humanists and other freethinkers have little to no faith. But that is not true. There are many things the so-called heretics have faith in: science, history, reality and objective education rank high on that list the latter finds stimulating.

And, perhaps, even more striking was Paul's faith in the existence of intimate love. He had tasted it early on with his association with Carrolyn. His loss of her never extinguished the hope of experiencing that wonderful station in life again, though he recognized the odds of his finding another soul mate were not too likely. Carrolyn's appeal to him appeared during the unfolding and awakening of his psyche. The driving impetus was biological, though he soon became cognizant of her intellect and like-minded feelings that confirmed his developing interpretations of life.

Erin's wonderful intervention in his life commenced with that same biological arousal that stimulated his experience with Carrolyn. Yet, more significantly, he had found Erin after his psyche had fully awakened – at least to his *weltanschauung*. Both were *complete* in their affirmations of life – consumed by its myriad and delectable offerings. They had a faith in an *optimism* that allowed them to find each other among all the sad mongers who failed to appreciate the opportunity to live. Faith in reality and its complement, hope – when fulfilled -- is an all-inclusive reward earned *in this* lifetime without the begging and kowtowing to some nebulous notion of eternal reward – for *what*?

* * *

Several months later, Paul, again, woke up sobbing. He rose from bed and washed his face, and looked at his crimson eyes in the mirror. Then, looking out his apartment window, he viewed the ever changing panorama of autumn colors in the trees.

The dream was always the same, he considered. He was seated in his favorite armchair in Hypatia's library, trying to understand Plato's *'Republic,'* when Erin would come into view.

He would watch her approach him, and he basked warmly in her knowing soft smile.

The words she said to him were *always* the same. "Let's go and have some fun." And he would rise, laying the book down, and they would stroll -- fingers entwined -- toward the sun.

The End

Printed in the United States
23076LVS00001B/1-51

9 781932 672206